FROM THE 'WE ARE
SERIES OF PUBLIC
THE KAZAKH PI

KAZAKH
PEN CLUB

КАЗАҚ
ПЕН КЛУБЫ

MADI AIYMBETOV

Bopai-Khanum

Published by The Kazakh Pen Club, © 2024

Translation copyright © Simon Hollingsworth, 2024

Bopai-Khanum
© **Madi Aiymbetov, 2023**

All rights reserved. No part of this book may be reprinted, reproduced or utilised in any form or by any electronic, mechanical or other means, known or hereafter invented, including photocopying and recording, or in any information storage or retrieval system, without the prior written permission of the publishers.

KAZAKH
PEN CLUB

КАЗАК
ПЕН КЛУБЫ

MADI AIYMBETOV

Bopai-Khanum

Translated into English by Simon Hollingsworth

Published under the supervision of
President of the Kazakh PEN Club
Bigeldy Gabdullin

Cover design by Madina Niyazbayeva

Printed in the United Kingdom

ACKNOWLEDGEMENTS

The publishers would like to thank the Kazakh PEN Club for their continual support on this project. The project was initiated by Kazakh PEN Club President **Bigeldy Gabdullin**, designed to expose the best works of classic Kazakh writers to the global literary stage through their translation into the English language. Through the tireless efforts of Mr Gabdullin, the project gained the financial and logistical support needed from influential Kazakh state organisations and private companies.

BI-BATIMA — BATIMA
PROLOGUE

One early spring, once the snow had all melted away and the meltwater was in full flow, the Tabyn, one of the two clans of the Tobysh-Adai people, headed upstream towards the Zhem[1], following the course of the River Elek, where they usually camped over the long summer season until the autumnal frosts set in. Only Syuindyk's aul lagged behind the others — that year, they were in no hurry to reach their summer pastures, the *zhailyau*. Syuindyk's eldest wife was heavy with child and, worried she might not survive the long journey, decided to delay the move, at least for a little while. After dispatching ahead many herds of horses and several shepherds, their flocks and light yurts, he held back about ten families at the wintering ground.

On the eve of the first April New Moon, Askyrga's waters broke. Syuindyk left his restless wife with his daughter-in-law and a young woman helper, specially invited from the nearest Adai aul, relatives from Shonai, and departed. The cold wind that spring morning found its way right under his clothes. Cranes were soaring high up in the blue sky and their clanging sound, barely audible, made Syuindyk anxious. He fastened his homespun camel-hair robe right to the very top.

This time of year offers no sunshine at all and I don't sense it's going to get warm any time soon! he thought to himself but he was soon distracted by cries of *Suyunshi!*[2] *Oh, what joy!*

'We now have a beauty to wear beads and necklaces!' the young helper's voice heralded cheerfully.

The birth of a daughter made the new father Syuindyk's heart leap and he prayed, thanked and praised Allah, 'Oh,

---

[1] Also known as the Emba River.
[2] A Kazakh tradition whereby the bringer of good news is rewarded with a gift.

Almighty God, grant a long and happy life to my baby girl! Oh, holy mother Bi-Batima, protect my child and be her support!'

Performing the rite of naming the child, Syuindyk proclaimed the adhan and said the name into the infant's ear three times, saying, 'Oh, light of my life, my beloved child, be like the daughter of our Mohammad, Bi-Batima, the virtuous keeper of the hearth, worthy representative, the rod and staff, and the hope of all your family. Let your name be Batima, Batima, Batima!' It seemed that at that moment, the name of the newborn Batima–Bopai echoed beneath the vast vault of the heavens.

CHAPTER 1

As the evening drew in, Syuindyk's aul descended from the white, rocky plateau that stretched away to the boundless pasture lands across an entire band running from south to north and came to a stop by a hill on a plain to the west of the Ustyurt Plateau. The camels were lowered to their knees. Batima, tired and bored from the week-long journey, overtook the camp and rode a reasonable distance further on. Her young dark-bay horse with its star marking on its forelock had been tamed the autumn before and broken in at the very start of the summer, but it was still extremely lively and could often buck its rider, so, under the pretext of training the horse, Myrzatai kept close to his little sister, but always kept back just a little, right until they returned to camp.

Unrestrained by the reins, the two-year-old colt felt the firm, grassy surface of the vast plain beneath its feet and galloped off at full pelt. The wind whistled in Batima's ears and blew right into her young face as she sped away over the endless steppe, its sides rolling away into the distance. An impetuous feeling swept over the young girl and she rushed ahead without a thought of stopping, as if she wished to rid herself of a vague sense of unease that had been lingering deep inside for a number of days. The boundless plain stretched out before her and only when the round disk of the sun had begun to turn scarlet and the evening silence had gradually begun to spread its invisible wings over the steppe did she pull on the reins. Only now did she understand how far she had gone from the aul that remained in the foothills below, about a lambs' herding stage from where she stood. She swung the colt, who was champing at the bit, flaring its nostrils and snorting, and galloped off at full speed, like a whirlwind, back home.

Everyone, young and old, had gathered for early evening tea at the central yurt of Syuindyk and Askyrga, which had only just been erected, and Myrzatai met Batima with an admiring, approving look, by the ridge where the aul had set up camp.

Batima was dressed for riding — a white silk shawl covered her forehead and ears, and she wore a light, tailored *chapan* gown with a short hem, which was girded with a thin leather belt decorated with green velvet and silver details. Seeing Batima's glistening eyes, Myrzatai realised that she gained great pleasure from riding the bay horse, its flanks now a darker shade from the perspiration.

'That's really something, Batima! You've really driven that favourite horse of yours this time! I'll throw a blanket on his back and leave him to stand until morning, and you get off home!'

On that first night at the new summer camping ground, Batima lay in bed and could not get to sleep. The moment she closed her eyes, it was as if she were in a world she had never seen before, in that limbo between sleep and consciousness. The countless lights in this fathomless world shone from all sides, blinding her with their colours. At one moment, her entire being trembled from a wave of colour and her soul surged and soared from the emotion up into a vast, boundless space. Enveloped in bright light, Batima barely touched the ground; her arms were now wings and she took off and soared for a long time before returning to earth. Finally, she woke up, quite exhausted from her recurring visions, and shuddered from the cold sweat running down her back. She wasn't unwell but felt herself completely worn out. It was only nearing morning when Batima finally dropped off to sleep.

In that pre-dawn hour, she had the most wonderful dream. A strange woman of venerable age, wearing a large white shawl, wiped a warm hand over the girl's brow. Her eyes glowed with an all-encompassing, kindly light, enough to make Batima's heart ache in sweet languor. She half-opened her eyes and raised a hand to hold onto those caring, comforting hands for just a moment, but all she sensed was a gentle waft as if she had been touched by a tiny, fluffy cloud. 'Dear child of mine! This is a special gift to you — cherish it and be sure not to lose it! Henceforth, those suffering and seeking solace will find healing in your hands. I have come to you from the sacred world of your noble ancestor Tabynai with this message. By running my sacred palm over your brow, I have bestowed this special gift upon you. Now, sleep peacefully, my child! My hand will lift the weight on your shoulders and all your fatigue. At first light, you will rise fit and healthy!' Saying these words, the woman suddenly vanished.

It seemed to Batima that she had lifted herself carefully on tiptoe, afraid to disperse the white cloud by her feet, and she suddenly took off. She didn't know how long she had been soaring, but eventually, her feet touched the ground and she woke up. She awoke feeling invigorated and the moment she opened her eyes, she cast them down to her hands. The spot on her hands where she had dreamed of touching a delicate cloud now ached and burned. This mysterious vision, a sign of healing powers, had come to the very young Batima in a dream on her first night at the new camping ground. From that moment and throughout her youth, not a day, night, early morning or evening went by without her feeling that special burning excitement. She had only to place her hands, that burned with her inner heat, on the head of her sister-in-law, tormented by a migraine, or a long-ailing shepherd from the aul, for their pain to subside and for Batima to sense her heart beating faster.

Batima's mother put this peculiarity down to her daughter growing up and attached no importance to it. Her father, Syuindyk, only occasionally witnessing this unique gift, saw it in his fatherly way as nothing more than the inappropriate manifestation of his spoiled daughter's capricious nature.

That summer, Syuindyk's aul moved several times from place to place in search of the richest pasture lands, moving upstream along the River Zhem. The lush grassy foothills of the Munalzhar, the land of his ancestors, finally proved to be the best pasture for the numerous herds of Syuindyk's horses, and he decided to stop there.

At that time, the Kalmyks would regularly raid the lands along the course of the Zhem, crossing over to the other side of the Edil[3] and stealing entire herds of horses. The main objective of these daring raids was to get their hands on the hardy Adai racers for their endless military campaigns.

The batyr-warriors, Altai from the Ak-Kete clan and Karak from the Mangyt clan, came together to protect against the Kalmyk incursions into the lands along the Zhem, and they brought their thousand-strong army to the place where Syuindyk's aul had settled.

Myrzatai, who had only managed to cultivate a few wisps on his top lip instead of a full moustache, had gathered a detachment of young, armed *dzhigit* horsemen like himself from the nearby Adai auls and intended to unite them with the warriors of Altai and Karak. At this time, while Myrzatai was training horses and selecting bows and spears for the campaign a short distance from the aul, his sister would be by his side. She was dressed in the lightweight field clothes that the young men normally wore. Her brother never prevented her from getting involved not only because she was a decent shot with a bow and arrow. He knew his sister's nature well — she was uncompromising and strong-willed, and she would always get her way.

Her father Syuindyk, who loved her dearly, could likewise do nothing about her obstinacy. However, he did warn her that if the Torgauts were to threaten their borders,

---

[3] The Volga

he would not let her out to fight them. He repeated this paternal order, but inside he could not help admiring her courage, thinking it was a shame that it was that she had been born a girl, for she would have become a glorious warrior like her bold ancestors.

No sooner had the penetrating damp of the autumn frosts set in and the waters of the Zhem acquired a thin crust of ice than the days grew overcast and cold, and Syuindyk's aul and his herds of horses set off to the east, to the foothills of the Ustyurt Plateau.

As before, the Kalmyk detachments were continuing their occasional raids. The united detachments led by Adai Shotan, Altai from the Ak-Teke and Karak from the Karakalpak Mangyt finally repelled the enemy, and the Kalmyks, unable to fight back, took to scattering in small groups. However, failing to make it across to their side of the Zhem, they ravaged the Adai auls as they went.

It wasn't that Myrzatai's warrior stood aside, but the battle-bled, embittered predators were intent on meting their vengeance on the peace-loving civilians. On one such day, the echoes of violence and confusion reach the outskirts of Syuindyk's aul. The desperate cry of a guard from Myrzatai's detachment sowed panic throughout the aul, where the people had been peacefully busying themselves for the migration to the wintering ground. Syuindyk quickly rode out to face the enemy with ten of his trusted dzhigits, and Batima followed on her bay horse.

The Torgaut Kalmyks were descending the slope of a long ridge. The group of about thirty or forty men surged forward with so much as a cursory glance to left or right. Realising that their forces were no match for the enemy, Syuindyk held his horses on the hill and waited for Myrzatai and his detachment, who were rushing to meet them in a cloud of dust. At that moment, a lone rider appeared, riding out of the aul in the distance.

'Who on earth is that? Hey, take a closer look! Could it be that someone from the village has sent a messenger with news?'

Syuindyk tightened the reins on his roan stallion, which was restlessly beating its front hood and chomping at the bit. His face turned pale in an instant and he was seriously worried.

'Just look how they're hurrying!'

'But that's our Bopai; I recognise her horse!' one of the dzhigits cried out.

'Bopai!'

'Bopai, you say? Oh, just look at her go!' Dressed like a young man, with a bow over her shoulder and a short, four-edged spear with edging beneath her right knee, Bopai circled them and stopped immediately in front of her father.

'Father! Don't scold me!' Bopai said, her fair skin now blushing crimson. 'Forgive me and don't be angry! You might not approve of what I have done, but I am here now to fight against the enemy who dares to trespass on our land. I will not turn back!'

'If that is the case, then join the ranks!' Syuindyk said, giving her a fearsome look. He pointed his bent whip at his men and said, 'They are fearless, every last one of them! And when battling the enemy, don't you dare hide behind them!'

'I am not here to hide, father! I give you my word!'

From the way she held her proud head high, standing just ahead of the line of warriors, her father could not mistake her unwavering determination and courage.

'Oh, Allah! This lass really is from the Tabyn clan, for she is courage itself!'

'Oh, that girl is what you'd call gutsy!'

'I'll say! She is raring to rush into battle!'

The aul's dzhigits were both amazed and full of admiration for this strong, single-minded young woman, who was not the least bit timid of her father.

Without delaying any longer, the detachments of Syuindyk and his son Myrzatai, who had now joined him, rushed to where they were to meet the Kalmyks head-on. The Torgaut Kalmyks, who were still running amok in search of easy pickings, must have heard the relentless stampede of countless horsemen drawing ever nearer, for they divided into two groups to circle around and split their pursuers. Father and son advanced side by side, and they quickly realised this cunning strategy and their detachments maintained their current course. The archers were sent out to the flanks while a group assembled in the centre, making room for a surprise attack from right and left. Bopai, who had spent the entire summer training with Myrzatai's warriors, joined the archers' ranks. With lightning speed, a continuous wave of arrows brought the Torgauts to their senses and got them seriously worried for their lives. The archers fired incessantly until the enemy was well within range and their quivers were half empty. Excited by the chase and the shooting, Bopai forgot all fear and fired arrow after arrow. The sharp four-edged arrows, capable of tearing through protective chest armour, either killed or seriously wounded, either way rendering the enemy out of action.

Myrzatai ensured he never lost sight of his sister on the battlefield. Unbeknownst to her, he had made sure his finest bodyguards were lined up around her. Perhaps it was for this reason, or perhaps it was the spirit of her ancestor Tabynai, but not a single arrow ever reached Bopai, who continued fighting, raining her arrows down tirelessly upon the Torgauts. At one point, in the very heat of the battle, Bopai caught sight of one Kalmyk in a fox-fur cap, breaking away from his detachment and fleeing. She reached immediately for her quiver, steadied the soles of her soft, curved-toe boots in the stirrups, drew back the tight string on her bow, its ends curved like the horns of a ram, and took aim at the back of the fugitive's head. The whistling arrow missed the deserter's head but did strike him in the back. The galloping Kalmyk fell from his horse, his fur cap flying from his head and rolling away.

Seeing she had hit her target, Bopai was about to reach for another arrow but quickly pulled her hand away. Her entire body was violently shaking. Looking around, frightened, she looked down at her trembling hand. It seemed as if dark crimson blood was oozing from her fingertips. The realization of her involvement in the death of another person and the full horror of what she had done truly darkened her soul. However, not allowing a moment of weakness to break her resolve, she clenched her teeth, stealthily wiped a tear with the edge of her sleeve and returned to the battle. The young girl was shaken by this first encounter with the harsh reality of a desperate battle and from witnessing the inevitable horrors of a bloody struggle. Bopai could not rid herself of the awful, frightening image of the Kalmyk warrior, struck by her arrow and falling to the ground. It seemed to her right then that the very slopes of Munalzhar were moaning and weeping.

Syuindyk's detachment emerged victorious from the battle, with only minor losses, where more than half the Kalmyks had been killed. Ten or so of the enemy were taken prisoner.

* * *

The shackled Kalmyk prisoners were locked up behind a high willow hedge at the edge of the aul. The moans of those among them, injured or crippled in battle, gave Bopai no peace throughout the day. Unable to sit and listen to the suffering, she went over to the warriors who were guarding them, determined at least to alleviate the pain of the injured men.

'You think these villains will appreciate your sympathy and accept your help?' one of the guards said, trying to reason with Bopai. 'They are merciless Kalmyks, who will spare no one if they get their hands on them.'

'However cruel these enemies might be, they are now helpless, and what kind of people are we if we don't aid these unfortunate souls?'

First, Bopai went over to a young Kalmyk, who had injured his hip after falling from his horse and was now unable to move. She sat down beside him and ran her hot hands over his wound before using her right hand deftly to reset his bone. The young man was about to wail as if his soul had been ripped from him, but sensing the relief, he calmed down and fell silent.

The prisoners were startled at Bopai's sudden appearance, her healing abilities and her unexpected desire to care for them. They didn't know if they should believe what they were witnessing and watched her with bated breath.

She reset another prisoner's broken shin bone, then took some clean bandages from her sister-in-law, Myrzatai's wife, dressed head wounds on others, and soothed their pain by applying her hands on foreheads, temples and backs of heads.

Helping the exhausted captives, Bopai herself felt a sense of relief, as if a heavy burden had been lifted from her shoulders. For a moment, it seemed she had rid herself of the awful feeling of horror that had seized her during the battle with the Kalmyks.

Syuindyk was not best pleased to hear about Bopai's kindness, but he said nothing of it, seeing his daughter's mercy and care for the helpless enemies as her fulfilling the will of Allah.

* * *

In the first warm days of March, the plain that led across to the Sands of Sam, in the northern part of the Ustyurt Plateau, the aromatic, verdant grass made the head spin.

The bright days of spring were growing longer, cheering the aul dwellers who were tired of the winter cold. The livestock out on the spring pastures filled the land with their bleating and neighing, and the foaling and lambing were in full swing. The harsh winter had given way to warm sunshine. Mountain goats had gathered in the foothills with their kids.

A small group of amateur falconers headed by Zhanibek, a dzhigit from the prosperous *Tore*[4] aul, was out hunting on the slopes of the Ustyurt Plateau. One of them, a young sultan[5], broke away from the others and steered his dapple-grey stallion to the western slope, where he stumbled across a flock of grazing wild goats and rams with their offspring. Catching sight of him, a mountain goat with huge, incredibly beautiful horns, who had been standing alert at a small distance from the main flock, turned and scampered away. The sultan had no weapons but a bow and a whip, so he grasped his bow and pulled an arrow from the quiver, but the goat proved faster. The hunter loosened the reins and the chase began.

The goat, well experienced in evading pursuit, began to dart and weave from side to side, continually changing direction. The sultan's steed, now hot from the chase, kept up the chase and when its master took up the reins once more to turn him, it jumped sharply, throwing him from the saddle. The horse appeared not to sense it had lost its rider and continued galloping until it was a good distance away. The mountain goat nonchalantly continued on its way.

Myrzatai, who was out inspecting sites for summer pastures, spotted the young sultan, who was smashed up on the rocks of the Ustyurt Plateau, quite by chance.

---

[4] A lineage of Genghis Khan's descendants, who made up the upper aristocratic class that ruled in the Kazakh Khanate.
[5] A non-hereditary rank of nobility in the Kazakh Khanate. Sultans were elected from among the *Tore* and the khan was elected from among the sultans.

The hunter's horse, which had caught the dangling reins with its front left leg, had returned to its prostrate master and was standing over him, snorting and twitching its ears. The dzhigit, barely able to move his pale lips, was able to say that his name was Abulkhair and he hailed from the *Tore* aul on the eastern side of the Ustyurt Plateau.

Myrzatai had to take the poor man to his aul as soon as he could. First, he gave him a few sips of cool, fresh koumis from his leather flask that was tied to his saddle. Then he carefully lifted the man, his equal in physique, sat him in front of him in the saddle and headed home, leading the sultan's faithful horse behind them.

That evening, settling Abulkhair in his home, Myrzatai sent his wife to his father's house to fetch a 'certain someone'. The patient felt pain in every part of his body and barely noticed any of this. Evidently, this is how fateful encounters come to pass for, a short while later, he saw the wonderful eyes of that 'certain someone' and, from that moment, he was utterly bewitched. Myrzatai's sister, who had a delicate and delightful beauty, ran her warm hands over the wounds and set the crippled hunter's broken bones and dislocated joints, one after the other.

Despite the intense pain, with muscular fists clenched and teeth chomping, the dzhigit did not take his eyes off the young healer, thus making her blush crimson. Although the young beauty felt great compassion for the wounded hunter, a smile involuntarily broke out in her eyes.

That sparkle in her eyes and the tenderness of her fair countenance quite thrilled the sultan, who had been displaying incredible patience and resilience. Something pinched at his heart and he shivered. The warmth of her soft hands spread calm over his body and he sank into a blissful reverie. Abulkhair half closed his eyes and it seemed to him that wafts of a fresh spring breeze were caressing his face.

The entrance opened and a fair-faced young woman entered the yurt. It was Myrzatai's wife.

'Bopai! Bopai!' she spoke softly. 'It looks like they're looking for you in the central yurt.'

Aktorgyn called her sister-in-law Batima *Bopai*, for that is the affectionate name her grandmother had given her in her early years when the chubby little thing would run about the place so adoringly.

The sultan heard that his saviour, this young enchantress, was called Bopai. *Bopai! Is that truly her real name?* he thought wearily. The suffering from the accidental wounds gradually subsided and the pain faded, and soon the dzhigit fell into a deep sleep. He did not hear Bopai carefully rise to her feet and leave.

It was now a month that Abulkhair had lived in Myrzatai's home in Syuindyk's aul, gradually recovering from the injuries he had sustained from his fall. With each passing day and each passing minute, the ray of light that had shone into his heart and filled him with passionate thoughts burned ever brighter inside, giving him no respite.

During this time, Bopai — the favourite of the family with her fervent nature — became particularly close to him. Whether it was sympathy or compassion that attracted the young woman was unknown, but Abulkhair looked forward more and more to her visits and enquiries about his well-being, and her presence had an astonishing effect on him. He did not notice how this new feeling had completely overcome him.

Aktorgyn watched Bopai's every step and could see clearly, with her ever more frequent visits to Myrzatai's yurt, that her husband's little sister was very much in love, and it was this that had changed her behaviour. The sister-in-law also knew that the central yurt did not approve of these visits to a young man from another aul, even if they were under the pretext of needing to treat his wounds. However, Aktorgyn of course would not dare stop everyone's darling Bopai from seeing him. All she did was make sure that the young couple were next left alone. Bopai continued to visit Abulkhair until he had completely recovered. Originally born of compassion and later growing into a deeper feeling, the young healer's pure and sincere excitement was seemingly conveyed by the silent movement of her healing hands. Aktorgyn only had to conceal her knowledge of these wonderful, secret feelings that the pair expressed to one another without words, yet so passionately and so reverently.

You are like a ray of life-giving sunshine and I look forward to seeing you every minute of every day, my bright-eyed healer! Abulkhair thought excitedly to himself. He was overwhelmed with feelings, but he didn't know how to express them. Eventually, however, when one day they were finally alone, he plucked up the courage and confessed to her. Having barely heard him out, Bopai flushed with embarrassment, sending the sultan into confusion.

'Oh, Bopai, the healing warmth of your hands has truly bewitched me! Do you know that by ridding me of the torment and wounds to my body, you have kindled an unquenchable fire of an altogether different torment?! Now that I am well again, I must say farewell and if only you knew how heavily that thought weighs upon me. Over this time, you have become the most precious to me and so close to my heart. Perhaps the power of the Almighty has played a part in my ailments that brought me to you.'

Bopai's strict sister-in-law watched their every movement and saw every glance and every silent word they exchanged, but when the moment came and the two of them were all alone, Abulkhair found the words to speak of his pure feelings. The young Bopai listened to him, blushing slightly and responding with a radiant smile. However, her touching silence spoke more eloquently than any words about the secret of her heart, and the dzhigit's passion was rekindled. He immersed himself in Bopai's fathomless eyes and he surrendered his heart to this exhilarating feeling. On the day of his departure from Syuindyk's aul, managing to find just a single moment alone, Abulkhair merely touched Bopai's trembling, hot hand.

'Fate itself has brought our paths together! I will wait for the moment when I can return to you, Bopai!' were the only words the loving sultan managed to say. It seemed to the blushing Bopai that her heart was about to jump from her chest. *And I thank fate that I have met you, my dearest! I cannot forget your words. I healed you but invested a little more into the warmth of my hands than comfort to your wounds, drawing you closer. Now I am sure that our meeting was Allah's will. Now I know that I was born for you, I am ready to wait for as long as it takes. Know this and be on your way. I will await your return and miss every moment of your absence.*

Bopai could not express these feelings out loud and made them known only by a look, the secret language of her heart. They understood each other without words and heard each other with their hearts — they wanted nothing more. Just as silently, they embraced and just as silently said their farewells.

The dzhigits who came for Abulkhair had already prepared his dapple-grey horse, which had put on a fair amount of weight over the month it had been with Myrzatai. Emerging from the yurt, the sultan jumped swiftly into the saddle and headed away without turning back; he was superstitious and thought that if he were to look back at the home that had become his own in that time and where his beloved Bopai was living, he might never return.

Abulkhair set his horse to a trot without his whip, and the further he rode from Syuindyk's aul, the more he yearned for the one and only, whose pure image had possessed him, mind and soul. The further he got from the Adai aul, the home of his darling Bopai, the stronger the pullback became, like a lasso around a horse's neck. The faith that he would soon return there gave him strength.

* * *

That summer, the rain fell little and seldom, and the steppe could grant the nomads no lush greenery. The spring reserves had maintained the vegetation until June, but now the thin grey-green wormwood and heather, the wheatgrass and the sagebrush had withered and yellowed. In midsummer, when the Seven Sisters lit up the night sky, Syuindyk, the aul elder, moved all his people to more abundant waters in the lower reaches of the Zhem. Here, too, however, the once lush green hills were now dry, and the herds of horses, emaciated from the lack of grass, were forced to graze among ravines and along water courses. Concerned for the welfare of his horses, Syuindyk spent the entire summer changing the direction of the migration.

During these days, Myrzatai barely ever climbed down from his horse and would tend the herds for weeks at a time with his dzhigits and would seldom see his family at the aul. Bopai sometimes helped her father by heading out on scouting missions around the surrounding area. She spent more time, however, at her brother's yurt so as not to leave Aktorgyn, who was now heavily pregnant.

Continually migrating and driving the grim-looking herds of horses, Syuindyk personally sought out the best grazing areas. He also had to keep watch over the horses day and night. If the droughts were not enough to contend with, there were also the Torgauts with their daring raids on the Adai auls and frequent episodes of *barymta*[6] honour rustling from certain neighbouring clans.

Three or four dzhigits would travel with Syuindyk and occasionally he would involve Bopai in the common cause as well. She needed to be always prepared to ride out into the steppe at a moment's notice, so she kept her three-year-

---

[6] A means of resolving clan disputes, involving the rustling of livestock.

old colt near the house. It had been broken in the autumn before and had decent stamina, a calm temperament and an attractive fetlock.

Dawn had only just broken and Bopai awoke to the chirping of a lark. No matter how hard she tried, she was quite unable to get back to sleep. A dog barked incessantly on the outskirts of the aul and somewhere, a young camel was bellowing. She could smell the aroma of smouldering dung cake in the hearth. Every living thing was slowly waking up and a new day was beginning. Aktorgyn, who had swollen considerably with her pregnancy, was slowly making her way to the exit, holding a long *beshmet* tunic of thin fabric in front of her with both hands.

A young servant woman of Myrzatai's approached her master's dwelling, walking quickly from the direction of a small, dark-grey, inconspicuous yurt. As always, she untied the binding that held the night cover that topped the yurt.

The soft blue sky shone through the yurt's half-open *shanyrak*[7] element. White clouds floated slowly by, one after the other. Bopai admired the beauty of these weightless celestial nomads as they drifted by on the gentle breeze and warmed by the sun's rays. Suddenly remembering she needed to head out to the pasture, she quickly jumped from her bed and ran from the yurt. Not far from the house, she heard the snorting of a stallion, which was standing in a hollow, densely overgrown with cheegrass. It seemed at that moment that the aul was enveloped in the translucent ether of the morning silence.

At about midday, three riders, with Bopai at their head, set off to the south from Syuindyk's aul. After a short distance, they separated and remained in line of sight from one another as they closely studied the local area.

---

[7] The central structural element of a yurt.

There was a ringing silence all around. In the distance, the smoky-blue hills appeared through the misty haze like a river flowing on one side of the vast steppe. Bopai set her colt to a trot and climbed to the top of a small elevated plateau, where she stopped. The sultry sky and the yellowed, dusty steppe had been equally tormented by the long drought and both thirsted for just a droplet of water. Bopai scanned the land around her, seeing nothing but the rippling waves of a clear river on the horizon. *I wonder where in this boundless steppe the one who has captured my heart now walks,* Bopai thought to herself. She remembered the young sultan's warm words in parting: *I will wait for the moment when I can return to you, Bopai!* Her heart ached with sadness and longing. Her melancholy at that moment appeared in unison with the weary steppe, forming mirages in the distance.

For many days since that time, whenever she was on her own, Bopai had succumbed to sweet longing and secret dreams of love, carefully concealing these stirrings of the soul from prying eyes.

After scanning an extensive area during the hours of daylight, covering every hillock, ravine and hollow, the scouts met up again before sunset and headed back to the aul. When the sun had almost sunk beyond the horizon, a black cloud appeared as if from nowhere and cast a shadow over the crimson twilight glow. Gradually, the evening sky filled with rain clouds, and bright flashes of lightning, one after the other, struck from all sides. The thunderclaps seemed to render the sky in two and the lightning continued to flash every second, casting its steel strokes to the ground and illuminating every corner of the dark sky in the process.

The first large drops of rain fell tentatively at first, then transformed into a downpour and then a wall of rain and the entire world seemed to be at the mercy of the raging elements.

Wet through and shivering from the cold, Bopai finally made it home.

'Oh, Almighty Allah! Water our tormented steppes with an abundant flow, fulfil the people's every desire, and be merciful and bounteous!' Syuindyk prayed with tears in his eyes. 'Inshallah, alhamdulillah!'[8]

Aktorgyn spent the entire evening caring for her sister-in-law, who had become chilled to the bone in the torrential rain. She wrapped her in a warm blanket and gave her hot tea with camel's milk, but this did not prevent her from developing a fever. Bopai's entire body shivered and by the middle of the night, she found it hard to breathe. Askyrga sat the entire night by her daughter's side, praying to Allah for her good health and tirelessly changing cold-water towels on her forehead. It was only nearer morning when her exhausted daughter fell asleep, much calmer judging by her expression.

Bopai found herself caught in a state of limbo, not awake and not asleep, and she dreamed that Abulkhair had come to her, placed his warm hands on her head and then stroked her whole body to her toes, thrilling her with every touch. *You came back to me, my darling!* she muttered in her sleep.

Askyrga was getting hard of hearing and did not hear the words, but she did notice her daughter's lips were moving. She looked over at her daughter-in-law and gestured to ask her what Bopai was saying. Aktorgyn understood about whom her husband's sister was thinking and to whom her half-delirious words were directed, but she could not give her mother-in-law an honest answer.

'She is probably just delirious,' Aktorgyn said as indifferently as possible.

'Almighty Creator! Keep my darling safe from harm!'

The torrential rain fell throughout the night and it was only at dawn that it stopped after completely soaking the

---

[8] Glory be to God.

arid steppe, and the fuzzy clouds dispersed.

Bopai felt better and the shivering subsided thanks to Aktorgyn's caring hands. Her sister-in-law gave her thick camel's milk with melted broadtail fat and millet, and with each spoonful, she perspired more and more, which helped her recover from her cold. Bopai awoke in good spirits, no sooner had the sun's rays burst through the open shanyrak above her.

The bounteous early-August rain had watered the eviscerated steppe and transformed everything. That morning, Syuindyk's aul breathed in the clear air, fresh from the rain.

* * *

Abulkhair's return to Syuindyk's Adai aul, where his beloved Bopai was waiting, did not come soon. A campaign to the north awaited him.

The Bashkir Tarkhan Aldar Isyangildin had revolted, no longer able to tolerate the yoke of Russian autocracy, and the news, brought by the tarkhan's messenger, mobilised all Kazakh batyr warriors and sultans roaming the summer pastures between Munalzhar and the Ustyurt Plateau, and in the southeastern part of the Urals. The native people asked their own for help in defending their ancestral lands, and the Kazakhs sent a three-thousand-strong army of their best warriors to the northwest. At their head rode the pride of the *Tore* aul — the young sultan Abulkhair.

Only occasionally giving the horses a chance to rest, Abulkhair reached Ufa without delay, where Aldar himself came out to greet him.

After repulsing the latest attack by the Russian regiments of General Khokhlov from Ufa and Sidor Aristov and Colonel Ridar from Kazan, sent to suppress the rebellion, the remnants of Aldar Tarkhan's army were resting at an encampment in a large pine clearing at the foot of a mountain. A Bashkir scout, catching sight of the considerable army of Kazakhs advancing towards them, turned his horse sharply back to the camp and galloped to impart the good news.

'The Kazakhs are coming!' he cried and the echo of his voice reverberated through the forest. 'Brothers, Abulkhair is coming with his warriors!' The news clearly cheered the Bashkirs. Aldar himself, a large and agile man, greeted the stately and energetic young Sultan warmly

and embraced him tightly.

'Most honoured Aldar-aga[9], the moment we received your news, we gathered together without delay to support you. And here we are,' Abulkhair replied sincerely and respectfully.

'Just recently, I headed a large Bashkir army and won fame for myself in the campaigns of the Russian tsar against the Crimea and the Turkish Azov. Now, I am forced to defend my people from the reckless autocratic rule, oppression and humiliation meted out by the Russian authorities. I am immensely grateful to you, sir, for not abandoning us in our moment of need!' Aldar Tarkhan said, tilting his head in a show of appreciation to the young sultan.

Soon, the Ufa and then the Kazan detachments were defeated. The Bashkir morale was high and they were determined to continue the battle. The representatives of the Russian authorities and the Bashkir governors who supported them appeared to have been taken by surprise by this resistance, believing the Bashkirs to be fully subordinate to the tsar. What they expected even less was that Aldar Tarkhan would seek help from his neighbouring Kaisaks; now, they had no option but to loosen their grip to prevent the clashes leading to uncontrolled bloodshed.

Fighting side by side with the Tarkhan, and sometimes

---

[9] A respectful form of address to an older relative, literally meaning 'uncle'.

independently, Abulkhair acted decisively and commendably repelled the bloody, ruthless attacks by the Russian soldiers sent to punish the rebels. It was not long before he was heralded as a true Bashkir hero.

By this time, Aldar Tarkhan had reached a venerable age and was particularly well-disposed toward the young sultan, a descendant of the Chingizids who had an innate ability to lead his people. *Now, here is a true descendant of his noble ancestors and someone worthy of the Khan's throne. Not a year has passed since he has been among us and already the Russians have been forced to stop,* he thought and one day even began a conversation with Abulkhair about his hopes in this regard. Much to his regret, however, Abulkhair did not give him the answer he was hoping for. The young sultan was preoccupied with the fate of his people, who were being threatened by the Torgauts from the Edil and Zhaiyk[10].

'Aldar-Aga, I understand your aspirations and I see your good intentions, and I am truly grateful to you. However, it appears we, too, need to fear our neighbour to the north, who has you in a vice-like grip. The Dzungars are pushing in from the east and the south. I simply cannot abandon my native land and people to their fate. However, if you suddenly find yourself in a difficult situation because of the pressure of the Russian authorities, always remember that the Kazakhs are your kith and kin and we will always be ready to lend you a helping hand. You need only send us word when the time is right.' Aldar Tarkhan was truly grateful to Abulkhair for being so frank with him.

'Abulkhair, you speak the words of a real man and a true patriot! You have pleased me greatly. You are a worthy son of your people, someone who always thinks and worries about their well-being. May Allah help you! If ever you need our support, the Bashkir people will not stand idly by, for the fates of our people are similar and our lands border

---
[10] The Ural River

each other. May your path in life be a happy one, Abulkhair, my snow leopard!'

No honour on the lands of the Bashkir Esteks, not the tempting life under Aldar Tarkhan, with all its prosperity and reverence could make Abulkhair forget his Batima, his dear Bopai, whom he had left so far away. The memories of her warmed his heart and evoked a lingering longing. The closer came the time for him to return to his homeland, the more eager he was to return to his one and only. For two years now, Abulkhair had heard nothing of Bopai and he was troubled by anxious thoughts. When he had been in Myrzatai's home, wounded and weak, cared-for and tended, Aktorgyn had never let her sister-in-law Bopai out of her sight and had looked at him cautiously and even coldly. Remembering this made him feel even more anxious.

Plagued by yearning and worry, Abulkhair was still on Bashkir land when he received word from Turkestan that the Kazakhs' sworn enemies, the Dzungars, were threatening to attack from the east once again. With Aldar Tarkhan's blessing, the sultan led his army to his homeland.

* * *

Even after returning home from the land of the Bashkirs, the sultan could not go straight to see his Bopai. The heads of the three zhuzes, the batyrs, biys[11] and elders all gathered for a kurultai[12] in the Karakum, to the north of the Aral Sea, and Abulkhair, too, was in attendance.

The nobles came from all corners of the steppe and held council on how, once united, they could repel the looming threat of a Dzungar invasion. Their hopes lay with

---

[11] A judge or sage who the people of the steppe would go to for advice and adjudication.
[12] Imperial and tribal assemblies convened to determine, strategize and analyse military campaigns and assign individuals to leadership positions and titles

Abulkhair, about whom word had already spread about a worthy sultan of the Chingizids, an experienced commander who had fought several times against the Russian troops and Edil Kalmyks, invading the Junior Zhuz along the Zaiyk and who had supported the Esteks in their hour of need when faced with the tsar's wrath.

The young sultan hailed from a branch of the descendants of Jochi Khan and his family was of modest wealth. It was at this kurultai that the clan elders proclaimed Abulkhair Khan of the Junior Zhuz. The elders also resolved to name Bokenbai commander-in-chief of the entire army, comprised of several detachments from each clan. Bokenbai hailed from a Tabyn clan and was famed for his exploits in battles of the Junior Zhuz with the Kalmyks. This splendid warrior, in assuming this considerable responsibility, proudly declared, 'We will fight to the last drop of our blood and will never lay down arms. It would be better to die in battle than to be crushed and humiliated by our enemies.' Thus, the Karakum kurultai brought Abulkhair and Bokenbai together, and they became faithful companions and brothers in arms.

Soon, the news that Abulkhair had been proclaimed Khan and was returning home reached Syuindyk's aul. Myrzatai's wife Aktorgyn came to the central yurt and, once alone with Bopai, told her with a smile,

'I hear, my dear, that the young sultan who was injured while out hunting and whom you brought back to health is returning to us as Khan. Our people, headed by your brother Myrzatai, have left for the *Tore* aul to welcome their new Khan.

Hearing Abulkhair's name, Bopai suddenly flushed red but tried her best not to reveal her emotion to her sister-in-law.

'Well, he is Khan, and good for him!' she said.

Knowing how Bopai could be single-minded, Aktorgyn replied light-heartedly,

'Oh, Bopai, I was simply sharing the news, my dear!' However, her sister-in-law's blushing face revealed her true feelings.

That obstinate lass is trying to keep a secret from me. I only had to mention the sultan's name and her cheeks flushed scarlet... She was overcome with excitement and thought I was blind and couldn't see! We'll see what will become of you when your sultan one day comes to call! Now, he holds a high title and if he so desires, he can show up just like that, with no reason. Back then, it was obvious he had taken a liking for our Bopai; he could barely get himself to say goodbye. I cannot see that he will abandon her because he has become Khan. I could see in his eyes how much he desired her. It was obvious that he had seriously fallen for our favourite. Aktorgyn looked over at Bopai and smiled, seeing her so excited. However, she had not told a soul about Bopai and Abulkhair's secret.

Finally, two years after falling from his horse and being healed, a time that had passed in a maelstrom of events, the long-awaited moment came for Abulkhair-Sultan to return from Karakum as Khan. Learning about the situation from Myrzatai, with whom Abulkhair had grown close over the time of his stay there, the new Khan informed him of his intentions and by the middle of that same winter, a group of matchmakers had been sent from the *Tore* aul to the Adai wintering ground beyond the Ustyurt Plateau.

The deserted steppe had recovered from the winter cold and with the arrival of April, the Adai people had migrated to a summer pasture to the southwest of the Zhaiyk, in the lower reaches of the Zhem. One sunny spring day, Syuindyk's aul saw off its bride-to-be — Bopai-Batima. The matchmakers from the Tabyn auls were invited to a grand feast along with many distant relatives from the Alim family. Delighted with the warm sun after the winter, leaving their worries behind them, the people gathered for the festivities at the Adai aul to rejoice for the young couple.

That said, on the eve of the wedding and on the days prior to that, Syuindyk had been very anxious about not being able to give his daughter away, according to the paternal traditions, to the party that had made plans for Batima's marriage earlier, before, Abulkhair. He afforded a reception as was fitting to Abulkhair Khan and his faithful companions, the batyrs Zhanibek and Bokenbai, the matchmakers, and the representatives of the Khan's aul, in line with every custom, and yet a certain tension still prevailed inside. This did not escape the attention of the matchmakers, but they did their best not to show their concern. Before the matchmakers left the main dwelling, Bokenbai, who was sitting in the seat of honour, looked over everyone to either side of him and spoke in a ceremonial tone:

'Syuindyk, you are a respected elder brother of a noble clan and you know well and honour the long-standing traditions, and so we await your approval and your consent. Your Bopai will not be falling into the hands of strangers but into the *Tore* aul. She is following her path with the young Abulkhair, who has become the worthy leader of his people. We are the true companions of the Khan, as chosen by the people and raised on a white rug. How many times have we set off on campaigns together and hardened our resolve in battle with the enemy who eyes our lands and encroaches from all sides? As we move to the future, we will not change this righteous cause. You are the leader of the Adai people and we all know you will spare nothing, yourself included, in order not to bring shame on your people, your homeland and your ancestors. And we await your blessing for your daughter, too!' When finishing his speech, Bokenbai gave a slight nod and looked questioningly at Syuindyk's pensive face.

Syuindyk did not miss a single word of Bokenbai, who had spoken in a balanced manner and to the point. He realised that the batyr was addressing him in this way, having registered his mood, and it was clear that Bokenbai wished to learn the true reason for the coolness in their reception. However, he was in no hurry to answer.

Finally, having looked over all the guests and pausing for a moment, Syuindyk turned to Bokenbai and said,

'Oh, Bokenbai, you too are well versed in the order of things, I see. If I had not approved all this, would I have really received you all like this? Would we really have shown this respect and honoured you, who came for the bride?'

Probably because of his agitation, Syuindyk's fair face had turned pink and the furrowed lines on his broad brow first bunched together, then smoothed out, in alternation.

In a sign of his acceptance of these words, Bokenbai placed his right hand on his chest and bowed his head.

'How can I possibly oppose the wishes of my daughter, whom I love and whom I have raised like a son? And if she wishes to live hand in hand with this man, who bears the burden of looking after his native land and is prepared to fight for the hope of his people, then that is her choice and her decision. I release her from her family home, where she grew up free, and I grant her my paternal blessing! If you wished to learn my thoughts, then there they are!'

'Now, that is a speech! Beautifully said. Thank you so much, Syuindyk, for your words.'

Bokenbai felt relieved and did not conceal his gratitude to Syuindyk. Syuindyk, too, relaxed and proceeded to display considerably more warmth and friendliness to the matchmakers.

Bopai departed for the *Tore* aul at dawn the following morning. The Adai people saw her off with songs and lamentations, as was the custom on this important day.

The warm rays of the April sun swept over the tender springtime green shoots that gave off a delightfully fresh aroma. Abulkhair and Bopai, seated on two grey-white horses decorated with feathers, headed to the east to the River Irgiz, accompanied by their ceremonial entourage.

* * *

In those first months at the Khan's seat, a specially prepared large yurt, Bopai felt unusually awkward. The people of the *Tore* aul also seemed to follow her every step with attentive, evaluating glances. That was perhaps why the Khan's young wife was reluctant to let Abulkhair go when he was there. When he departed on important business that required his involvement as the Khan, we very much looked forward to his return. Not only that, but Bopai had to get used to managing the servants assigned to her home to perform daily chores.

On one languid day of an agonising wait and painful loneliness, Bopai suddenly felt changes inside. By the evening, she felt a slight shiver and trembling sensation, both near her heart and just below. Her eyes blurred over and she felt nauseous.

From that moment on, she would now and then come over wholly apathetic to everything. Her fair face turned pale; she lost her appetite and felt sick over even the slightest smell of food. She refused the dishes that were offered her, she could not eat her usual food and, more and more often, she hankered after something in particular. Bopai was in a state of half-consciousness, it seemed, and she tried to hide this from Abulkhair.

This unusual state was accompanied by the strangest dreams, which took on a very dark turn at times. Bopai began to sleep long hours at night and even during the day, she would have these dreams. One early morning, she dreamed that she was walking alone on the deserted steppe under a completely calm blue sky. There was not a soul around. She did not know where this narrow path would lead, but she continued without stopping or lingering for even a minute as if an invisible force was pushing her forward. She had no idea how long she had been walking, but suddenly, a river appeared before her, its waters splashing in noisy waves. She had no idea what this large river was into which her path had led. Where was she to go now that there was nothing but deep water in front of her? She looked back. A wolf was walking right behind her, huge, ferocious and with its fur bristling on its neck. Meeting her eyes, the seasoned hunter suddenly took a step back and froze. At this same instant, her fear subsided and extending her arm to the animal. She called to it like people usually call to a dog: *Come, come, my little wolf cub. Come to me!*

The wolf understood her words perfectly and, drawing closer, extended its muzzle and stepped right up. When he was nuzzling up and licking her neck and face with his hot tongue, the waters of the turbulent river parted and a wide road appeared to the other side. On the opposite side was heaven on earth. Lush green trees rustled their leaves, orchards were laden with ripe fruit and a vibrant spring of purest water was tinkling by. Bopai was enchanted and could not quite believe her eyes — her heart was filled with joy, not of this earth. She even forgot that she was completely alone here. This most beautiful of worlds took her into its embrace; the sun's rays caressed her with their gentle warmth, a gentle breeze kissed her face and she sank into a magical sense of tranquillity. The melody of this wondrous place lulled Bopai into a state of utter bliss. Time here passed slowly and imperceptibly. Suddenly, though, she recalled the wolf who had led her here along the road that had opened in the middle of the river. Vexed by her forgetfulness, she looked around, but the wolf had disappeared without a trace. She ran all over, quite beside herself with worry in her search for the grey wolf and, eventually, she burst into tears, saddened beyond measure. She knew not how long she had spent crying, but weary from the worry and now a little calmer, Bopai heard a wolf cub squealing. The tiny creature shuffled over to her, barely able to place one paw before the next. Bopai took it in her arms. At that moment, the wolf appeared in the distance but instantly disappeared from view, leaving the wolf cub behind with its little eyes barely open.

Bopai woke up, panting slightly from the joy that had overwhelmed her and, still affected by that dream, she closed her eyes again, sinking into her featherbed. She thought that the river in her dream was a good sign — the prophet and patron saint of water, Suleiman, must be protecting and supporting her. The wolf that showed her the way and the wolf cub that sat in the palm of her hand, she believed, were good omens of positive events to come. A warm smile broke out on the charming face of the Khan's young wife, like the rays of the morning sun.

Abulkhair was accustomed to going out hunting in early winter and that year was no exception. It was mid-October when a thin sheet of ice covered all bodies of water in the early morning. The Khan and the hunters in his party had been camped for some ten days on the northern side of the Ustyurt Plateau and they returned to the aul that day before dusk. The carcass of an enormous wolf was lashed to Abulkhair's saddle, its teeth frozen in an eternal grimace, its fur on end and its tail hanging to the ground. The Khan's servant untied the catch and threw it down before the storehouse by the yurt.

With a light, warm camel-hair gown over her shoulders, Bopai was standing on the threshold of the yurt to meet Abulkhair. Seeing the wolf's carcass, she suddenly imagined the taste of the stewed dish made from the wolf's heart, and she felt incredible pleasure from the simple anticipation of the meal to come.

'Abeke[13], believe it or not, but I could eat a stew of wolf's

---

[13] Diminutive form of 'Abulkhair'.

heart this very minute! Honest to God, I would love some stewed offal and all the rest! I don't know why, but I would really like some wolf meat fried in its fat!'

Hearing the excited Bopai express her desire so frankly would have normally surprised Abulkhair, but he quickly realised what was going on.

'Break open the breast there and bring me the heart first,' he ordered a servant. 'And gather all the fat from inside, too, down to the last drop!'

Bopai devoured the wolf's heart dish with such gusto, savouring every bite, that she finished the meal with beads of sweat on her forehead. Having not eaten in recent days, Bopai was tired of her poor health and finally had her fill. She now felt a sense of inner contentment and relief.

That night, she fell asleep in her warm bed, at peace and replete with a blissful sense of the changes that were taking place in her womanhood. Nine months and nine days after she had eaten the wolf's heart, having completed all the stages of nurturing a new life, Bopai gave birth. The labour was difficult, but the pain and the suffering were forgotten in an instant when she heard her baby's first cry. All the young mother's feelings were reflected in that moment in her gentle smile.

The painful contractions had begun one early morning in a sultry July and it was well past noon when Bopai held her first child in her arms — Nuraly. Holding her newborn son to her breast, she felt a profound happiness that only a mother could feel.

Abulkhair, taking the throne in his twenties, had become the happy father of an heir whose vitality had been given him by a wolf's heart.

A lot of water had flowed since that time. Time had followed its course. Nuraly grew up and became a young sultan at the Khan's seat, an aide to his father, who trusted him with serious affairs.

CHAPTER 2

The water level of the Irgiz, which had burst its banks in mid-April, had fallen back and now the river had returned to its normal course. The spring days were warm and clear. The Khan's seat was a hive of activity, all linked with preparations for meeting a special envoy from Saint-Petersburg, diplomat and interpreter of the College of Foreign Affairs Alexei Ivanovich Tevkelev, and Bashkir leader, the *voivode* Aldar-Tarkhan, who had left Ufa about a month before.

On the day before his arrival, Aldar-Tarkhan sent a messenger from his overnight lodgings with news of his imminent arrival and as soon as Abulkhair learned of this, he sent Nuraly with a small entourage to meet him.

Crossing the rivers Kabyrga and Ulkeyek, the young sultan rushed to his guests of honour as soon as he saw them, bowing most courteously.

'Who is this young man?' Tevkelev asked, nodding with an air of importance to Nuraly while looking at him questioningly.

'Most honoured sir, I am Nuraly-Sultan, son of Abulkhair, and I have come to meet you and I am at your disposal. You are most welcome here!' Nuraly replied.

Well, this young man, the Khan's firstborn, is indeed worthy of his title. He has fine manners. This must mean that Abulkhair is already preparing for his future khan's status. We come to him on an important mission and he doesn't send just any close advisor or a clan governor but his own son. We will view this as a true and positive step by the Khan. Indeed, such upbringing and tribute to tradition have been in the blood of the steppe leaders since the time of Genghis Khan. This thought flashed through Tevkelev's mind as he observed Nuraly, who had met them with true aristocratic courtesy — as befitted a khan's family — and now showed them the way.

Recently, due to the provocative conduct of the Russian

authorities, the raids of the Esteks, Edil Kalmyks and Zhaiyk Cossacks on the Kazakh auls had become more frequent, and the Oirats were now threatening them from the east. The current situation was complex and needed a resolution. The attempts made four years before to establish friendly relations with Saint-Petersburg had been unsuccessful: the Russian Tsar had never responded to a dispatch sent by Abulkhair to the northern capital together with his old friend, the reliable ambassador Koibagar Kobekuly. Since then, the Khan had relied solely on his forces and was prepared for any eventuality.

Russian autocratic rule not only refused to enter a military alliance with the Khan of the nomads but also concluded that it needed a treaty of unconditional submission, which, in turn, would open free access to all roads to Asia. This mission had been entrusted to Alexei Ivanovich Tevkelev, a baptised Bashkir who knew well the language of his nomadic brethren and how they thought. Tsar Peter the First had once given him a verbal instruction that stated, *By any means possible, even if considerable monies need to be spent, you must bring me a document with the seal of Abulkhair that specifies that the Kaisaks voluntarily become part of the Russian Empire and its subjects.*

Of course, it could not be assumed that this instruction could be implemented immediately. Kutmukhambet Tauyekela, who had changed his name to its Russian equivalent, found his mission was greatly complicated by military conflicts between the Khan's horde, defending its lands on the shores of the Edil and the Zhaiyk, and Russian subjects, and the confrontation with Orenburg. As for Abulkhair Khan, no matter how powerful he was, the decisions, as a rule, were made by the heads of the clans, the biys, who spoke for their people and defended its interests, and the elders — and Tevkelev had known this from the very beginning. And, knowing this, he devised all sorts of tricks to gain the trust of the Khan's inner circle, creating the impression he was a sincerely sympathetic and understanding person.

Engaging Aldar-Tarkhan in this particular mission, who enjoyed friendly relations with Abulkhair, was one such trick. Tarkhan could significantly influence the decision to send a letter to Saint-Petersburg or elsewhere in Russia, which would have reduced the tension between the Bashkirs and the Kazakhs. This was the main objective of Tevkelev's spring visit to the Khan. Abulkhair took the presence of Aldar-Tarkhan at Tevkelev's side as a good sign. On the eve of the meeting, while discussing the pending arrival of their distinguished guests with Abulkhair, Bopai had remarked,

'My Khan, it would be appropriate to send not just any clan leader to meet Tauyekela and Aldar-Tarkhan, who are visiting the horde for the first time, but Nuraly. Your son might be young, but these high-ranking guests will appreciate his involvement in this affair as a sign of your high degree of respect for them.'

'We'll see,' the Khan responded and fell into thought.

The Khan had already begun to involve his eldest son Nuraly in occasional important matters, but his wife was clearly talking sense. Yes, his son should pass another serious test. The Khan thus decided to instruct the young sultan to meet his guests who had travelled so far and to keep an eye on him. Having listened attentively to his father's instructions, Nuraly-Sultan fulfilled everything that had been asked of him, welcoming the guests with full honours and escorting them to the Khan's seat.

After the traditional welcome addresses and enquiries about certain affairs, seated on the place of honour on a white felt cushion in the centre of the tall, spacious yurt to the right and left of Abulkhair, Tevkelev and Aldar exchanged courtesies with the leaders of the clans and elders headed by Azhibai and Bokenbai.

The Kazakh elite also respectfully welcomed the envoys: 'Welcome, most venerable guests! May your visit be for

the good!'
'We are delighted to have arrived in good health!'
'May all your good intentions be fulfilled!'

During the ceremonial reception in the central yurt, the young serving women did not miss a single one of Bopai's gestures and continually refreshed the guests' wooden bowls with fresh koumis.

Afterwards, in the guest yurt, tea was served with a fine spread, which was followed after a short interval by a special treat. In observance of all customs, wooden dishes were brought to the table, laden with boiled young horse meat mixed with cured horse-meat sausage from the winter reserves. Having enjoyed this delicious meal and finally full, everyone switched to the main topic of their meeting.

Aldar took the floor.

'Abeke Khan, I have known and respected you since the time you were a sultan and I hold your friendship dear. The reason for our special visit to you with Mister Kutmukhambet is this...' Aldar furrowed his brow a little and cast reflective eyes over the hushed listeners. 'Since the best representatives of the clans elected and proclaimed you Khan, your people have known no peace or respite from the constant battles to preserve the integrity of your land. You stop at nothing to ensure peace on your land, and you apply every effort. No one understands you better than me. I am well aware that you know what is needed to put an end to his endless struggle. I know that you do not want to be like us, your neighbours the Bashkirs, who occupy a small area of the Urals and who have trapped their people into allegiance and dependence on others. Naturally, this makes me respect you for your courage and resolve. But is there not another way to reach agreement and somehow negotiate an alliance without the need to bow your head, Abulkhair? What do you think?'

'Saint-Petersburg rejected our proposal, or were you not notified of this?' Abulkhair turned to Tevkelev with a stony expression. 'After all, Kutmukhambet knows about this, and yet...'

Weighing up and thinking over everything that was being said around him, Tevkelev nodded in agreement but did not utter a single word.

'Back then, we realised that our alliance would be possible only if we accepted subjugation and acknowledged the dominant authority over the khanate. We communicated our thoughts that we were unable to come to a peaceful agreement with Tsarist Russia with the establishment of trade relations with the East and other things if denials continued about attempts to seize our lands and if nothing was done to put a stop to raids by Torgauts and Russian Cossacks. However, Saint-Petersburg took our proposals on an agreement as a call for a military alliance. How else, then, could we conclude an alliance agreement?'

Having heard Abulkhair's firm response, Aldar-Tarkhan then expressed his own opinion.

'Abeke, dear Khan, I am aware of all this, but these talks were held during the time of Peter. Now you need to send a letter about the agreement you expect to achieve to Empress Anna Ioannovna. This time, you can only raise the issue of the Russians hindering your interactions with us, the Bashkirs, in the western part of your lands. A peaceful resolution of this issue could put a stop to the despicable antics of the Cossacks, from which the Bashkir people are also suffering. They attempt to shift the responsibility for their bloody actions against the Bashkirs onto the Kazakhs from Munalzhar and, as a result, the conflict is only exacerbated between related peoples. I have come here as an envoy to conclude a peace agreement with Saint-Petersburg.'

Abulkhair did not doubt Aldar's sincerity. However, he was plagued by doubts as to what else could be behind the signing of such a letter of petition as the first step to concluding a treaty with the authorities in Saint-Petersburg.

Bopai was observing the events from a distance and, at that moment, she read the question that was on Abulkhair's face:
But why is Tevkelev saying nothing? Why is he remaining silent? Perhaps he wants to speak at the end. And what do the elders and clan leaders think about a letter to the Russian Empress about entering into such an alliance as Aldar has spoken about?

Bokenbai seemed to have heard Bopai's thoughts, for he pulled his whip from his boot and threw it before himself as a sign he wanted to speak.

'Many words have been spoken in this time, but they all boil down to the same thing: what will the future relations between the Khanate and Saint-Petersburg look like? I believe that the arrival here of such an important ambassador as Kutmukhambet Tauekeluly indicates this to us. Of course, the respected Kutmukhambet will speak his weighty word and something tells me that he will speak about finding a compromise by any means possible.

'If this agreement will make it possible to bring our old enemies, the Russian Cossacks, to reason, who are currently driving a wedge between our peaceful neighbourly relations with the Esteks, who among us could object?'

The clan leaders and the biys supported Bokenbai. Finally, Tevkelev voiced his key thought.

'Most respected Khan, it is currently extremely important for Saint-Petersburg to achieve a letter on a bilateral agreement, written by your hand and bearing your seal. This letter will be drawn up in two languages. Mustafa, the interpreter from the diplomatic mission who has accompanied us here, will translate the letter you write into Russian, unaltered and unabridged. He is a Turk by nationality and a most literate chap, for he knows Chagatai, Turkish and Arabic. He will not omit a single word, a single comma or a full stop; he will translate everything scrupulously. After this, Her Majesty will need some time to consider and approve the paper. After that, both our sides will conduct our affairs in the requisite order, in accordance with the requirements therein.'

This important meeting, which ran until midnight, culminated in the text of a letter written under Abulkhair's dictation. The letter, written on a single page on Chinese paper, was carefully transcribed by Koibagar Kobekuly, who knew Chagatai.

We extend our deepest respect to you, great and all-merciful benefactress of her people, ruler of your great power and fair-faced queen. May your fortune increase and your reign enjoy health and prosperity every day and every year. We express our most humble request to Your Majesty, which involves the following. We are quite unable to establish amicable agreements with Your Majesty's subjects, the Ural Bashkirs.

In order to obtain Your Imperial Majesty's support in defending our lands and finding peace, we are sending our ambassador to you together with Aldar, the voivode of Your Majesty's subjects, the Ural Bashkirs. The reason for this is that Aldar asked that we send to Your Majesty an envoy and so we, Abulkhair Khan and my multiple subjects of the Middle and Junior Zhuzes, send our compliments and deepest respects.

To conclude my letter, I express our will: we wish to enter into a peace agreement with your loyal slaves, the Ural Bashkirs. According to your degree, we are prepared to live with them in peace and harmony.

I am sending my envoys to deliver this letter and I request that you receive Kutmukhambet, whom I have appointed my senior envoy, and also Seitkul.

Upon his arrival in Orenburg, Tevkelev realised that the letter Mustafa had translated contained not a single hint about accepting the Kazakhs as subjects, and this upset him unspeakably. The cunning Abulkhair Khan had neatly signed and beautifully sealed the paper, which expressed merely a desire to support the Russian authorities in their peace accord with the Bashkirs. It was obvious that the

Empress would never approve such a letter. Tevkelev took his quill and entered changes to the concluding sentence of the Khan's letter, as follows:

...and so we, Abulkhair Khan and my multiple subjects of the Middle and Junior Zhuzes, send our compliments and deepest respects, and as your faithful servants, as a people, ask for your protection and wait for patronage and assistance in facilitating a peace agreement with your loyal slaves, the Ural Bashkirs. We wish you every prosperity and will be your true subjects.

Tevkelev, who had mastered all kinds of tricks in political and ambassadorial affairs during his service at the royal court, a hardened official and a cunning diplomat, thus 'successfully' completed the case with Abulkhair's Khanate, achieving a positive result and also considerable kudos. Now, he could look forward to the Tsarina's total approval in Saint-Petersburg.

On 19 February 1731, Anna Ioannovna signed a charter accepting the Khanate of Abulkhair Khan into the Russian Empire. The ceremony where the Kazakhs would be familiarised with the charter and would sign it was entrusted to the same Alexei Ivanovich Tevkelev.

In early October of that same year, a large number of people gathered at Abulkhair's seat on the bank of the River Irgiz near Mantobe. Over two or three days, the entire area was filled with the clan heads and biys, with their messengers and assistants, from all corners of the Middle and Junior zhuzes. There was a buzz of voices.

'If it is true what they say, the Khan plans to swear allegiance to the Russians in front of all his people.'

'Why would he suddenly decide to do that? To bow and subjugate himself?'

'If the Khan subjugates us to them, does that mean we will be handing over our land?!'

'If he wants, then he can become their subject and hand his sons as an *amanat*[14]! What has that got to do with any of us?! We have no pledge of allegiance or land to spare for the Russians!'

'Right, then let him take his court and migrate to a place under their wing!'

'So, what, we will hand over our land to the Russians after having fought the Dzungars for it?!'

Conversations like these were rife among the elite and common people alike, and they finally reached the ears of Abulkhair and Bopai.

'My Khan, I fear that all these rumours might start a fire! If all these people at the foot of Mantobe suddenly decide to revolt...'

However, Abulkhair paid little attention to what Bopai was saying.

'Stop it; there is no need to worry over some idle chit-chat. The clan heads and the biys have gathered here not to agree to become slaves of the Russian Empire but to confirm the conclusion of an agreement with the Russian authorities on peace with the Esteks, who are being incited to attack us. We are embroiled in endless battles with the Edil Kalmyks and Zhaiyk Cossacks, so it is important at least to render the northern side from the Russians. This is something these people will probably support.'

Bopai realised that the Khan used the expression *these people* to refer to the clans of the Junior Zhuz that bordered the Karakalpaks in the south and some leaders of the Argyn clan from the Middle Zhuz, who would never welcome any agreements with the Russian Empire.

However, understanding that extra precaution would never be out of place, Abulkhair summoned Nuraly and instructed him to form a guard of decent warriors around the seat.

---

[14] A pledge of allegiance to confirm one's faith.

Sirius was shining over Mantobe on the early morning of 5 October, having appeared at midnight in the southeastern part of the sky. Work had been frantic at the Khan's seat since dawn. Abulkhair emerged from the main quarters, followed by the Russian ambassador Tevkelev, the advisers and elders, and the entire group headed for a semi-circular, grassy clearing, where they were awaited by a considerable number of people, some sitting in a circle, others standing.

Abulkhair stood before them all in his smart *chekmen* tunic of dark-red cloth, trimmed with a beaver collar. He raised his right hand, immediately drawing the attention of the noisy crowd.

'My people, the most-respected Mister Kutmukhambet has arrived here with the royal charter, bearing the seal of Her Majesty the Russian Empress! I, please, ask you all to show patience and calm down. This document is very important for us because it grants guarantees to us of peaceful relations with our neighbours to the west, the Esteks, who are loyal subjects of the Russian Empire, with whom we have recently seen an escalation of conflicts. The text of the document will be read to you by the Secretary of the Koibagar Kobekuly. We should all express our approval of this agreement. If you do approve it, we will secure our northern borders and make an important step to ensure the integrity of our land!'

'Let him read it! We are listening!' came the rasping voice of Barak-Sultan, who had arrived in Mantobe the evening before with the Argyn, Konyrat and Nayman elite of the Middle Zhuz and a group of batyrs headed by the undefeated military commander Kanzhygaly Bogenbai. Barak's pale face and prominent features expressed a strict nature and even severity.

Tevkelev's young Tatar aide and adjutant took the charter from a small box and handed it to his boss.

Koibagar took the paper from Tevkelev and read the document loudly and expressively. After a second's pause, outcries of indignation began to sound from all sides.

'Tell me this: with which of the elder Argyns or Kereys other than from the Junior Zhuz did Abulkhair Khan agree and write all of that?'

'What was Abulkhair-Khan thinking?! What is this, without the Empress in Saint-Petersburg, we would never have settled our affairs with the Esteks?'

'The agreement must have been dictated by that quick-witted baptised ambassador!'

'He's no ordinary fellow, this general, it turns out!'

'He's a general for his own kind, for the Russians, he is, and has adopted their faith! I say he should be gone from here while he's still in one piece! Failing that...'

Hearing his name and the clearly angry words addressed at him and noticing the rumble of discontented voices growing on all sides, Tevkelev became very worried. An unpleasant chill ran down his spine, and he felt a tight lump of fear in his stomach. The crowd seemed to be shouting louder and more angrily, ready to pounce on him at any moment. He looked over at Abulkhair, who was standing next to him. The Khan's stony face remained impenetrable. Only from the acute gaze in his burning eyes and the movement of his cheekbones could he guess that the Khan was struggling to contain himself.

At that moment, the authoritative voice of an Eset from the Tam clan was heard:

'Hey, brothers! Why are you muttering to yourselves like old women, hiding your faces in the crowd, eh?'

Eset-Batyr strode forward through the crowd and stood to his full mighty height.

'Listen, Barak, you can boast both intelligence and valour. If you value the peace and prosperity of your people, don't stir up the crowd for no reason! Think and understand why Abulkhair Khan did this. Not a single Dzungar dares show his face on our land, be it from over there or from the east! Was it not only yesterday that

Abulkhair led all of you to defend our land, stopping the onslaught of the enemy? Now, our neighbours from the north and the west continue to threaten us. If you want to fight, then throw all your forces there and smash them all to pieces! The people are tired of all the wars and, what, you wish to exterminate them?!'

Not daring to contradict the passionate words of the Eset, whose speech was full of righteous anger, the biys and elders present all thought it best to say nothing.

'Ah, nothing to say?! The Khan undertakes obligations before the Russians and pledges his allegiance not for his own salvation. Rather, he is making a compromise and has faith in this treaty, thinking of the prosperity of his people to ensure our lands are not seized by others. And his people, thinking only about their personal interests, have split down the middle! All of you think only about your interests and you are happy to go your separate ways and fight among yourselves! No one is being forced or compelled to do anything. If you don't agree, then you know where the road out of here is! I support the Saint-Petersburg document that approves the Khan's decision and I will not step back from the need to swear allegiance to conclude a peace agreement with the Russians. I give my word and my bond!'

The Eset's decisive and confident words made many others stop and think. Bopai was particularly affected by the words that said the Khan would give over his sons as a pledge. This reverberated in her maternal heart with unspeakable sadness. She wanted to speak about this agreement herself, but who knew how the people would have taken the news of this *amanat* pledge from her or Abulkhair. They might have thought that this was their way of justifying their actions before everyone else. However, the main thing was that, at that large meeting that day, both Abulkhair and Eset were able to convey to everyone the true meaning of the Khanate's policy and, for that, Bopai quietly thanked God.

The October meeting at Mantobe ended with twenty-six elders headed by Bokenbai, Eset and Kudaimendi approving the royal charter. The Bashkir Tevkelev, who had concealed his insidious, dark deed, hurriedly left for Orenburg.

CHAPTER 3

The ring of the *dangyra*[15] broke the silence over the river and startled a lone wild goose. The goose slapped its wings on the water's surface and the noise alerted a white hawk on its perch. It jerked its head and turned its sharp yellow eyes.

'Bismillahir Rahmanir Raheem! God be with you!'

Nuraly said, releasing the reins of his young stallion that was chomping at the bit and his hawk with its wings at the ready, impatient for the hunt. The bird shot straight up into the sky.

On that cool June afternoon, Abulkhair was riding with the warriors of his guard and hunters along the deep Shet-Irgiz river, overgrown with a jungle of reeds, its banks covered with thick, lush grass. Reaching the top of a hill, the Khan came to a stop. His eldest wife, Bopai, both braids of hair tucked into her light gilet and with a scarlet headscarf tied round her forehead, also pulled up the reins on her grey-white mare, leaning her light and short boots with comfortable, rounded toes on the iron stirrups. The hawk shooting up towards its prey flapped its wings so fast that their movement was barely visible. Abulkhair delighted in the flight of this trained hunter. 'What speed! Just look at him flying, true as an arrow!' the Khan said, raising his voice. On this occasion, the hunting party included John Castle, a half-German, half-British artist, sent by Ambassador Tevkelev from Orenburg to the Khan's seat on a special visit. The Khan had decided to show the foreigner how they hunted with hawks and had included him in the party.

Leading the game beaters and then following behind the main group, the men carefully observed Nuraly, who, up ahead of everyone else, had launched his hawk to catch the

---

[15] A traditional Kazakh musical instrument, similar to an Irish *bodhran* with tambourine-like bells attached.

wild goose.

Abulkhair turned to Kalben, the Tatar interpreter who had accompanied them, and said,

'Ask through the German interpreter if our guest is not tired and whether he would like some water.' He glanced at John, who was watching the powerful flight of the diving hawk with his mouth literally open in amazement and admiration.

Noticing the Khan's gesture in his direction and addressing the Tatar interpreter, Castle placed his right hand on his chest, tilted his head slightly and spoke courteously. The interpreter immediately translated his words:

'Most respected Khan, Mr Castle expresses his particular gratitude to you and says that falconry is a wonder, the likes of which he has never seen before and that he greatly admires this show of skill.'

At the same time, Castle began to speak very quickly and without stopping to his German interpreter.

'He also conveys his deepest respect and admiration for the courage and agility of Nuraly-Sultan, a worthy son for his father, the Khan.'

With a warm smile, Abulkhair turned his entire body slightly to Castle as a sign of acceptance of his courteous words. At that moment, the hawk flashed its white plumage, turned sharply to circle the goose and then regained altitude before shooting down upon its prey, who was trying in vain to evade pursuit. The powerful blow sent the goose tumbling, its wings flapping clumsily, and it began to drop to the ground.

'He's got the goose! There, look!'

A young falconer spurred his bay colt forward and, in a matter of moments, pulled up next to Nuraly, who was closely watching the flight of his hawk.

The Sultan turned to the falconer, with eyes aflame and nostrils flared with excitement.

'Well done, my man! The white hawk has worked well today — you have prepared him wonderfully!' the Sultan said, his fair face breaking into a smile of obvious satisfaction.

'It went so well, Nuraly-aga!' the young man gushed, almost choking with delight. 'Take a look at that white-haired Russian Castle! Just see how those blue eyes of his are sparkling. He is so amazed, his jaw dropped! You see, the Russians have nothing like this, hunting with hawks.'

'Hey, why do you call him Russian?!' He might look a little bit like one, but he is no Russian! Not an Englishman, not a German, from some obscure nation, it seems.'

'Well, I never! I could have sworn he was a white-haired Russian for sure...' the falconer said, his eyes wide in amazement.

'Anyway, that's enough wasting time marvelling at foreigners. Go and find that fallen goose in that overgrown pond!' Nuraly said to the falconer, his tone now commanding, as he rolled up his whip, its handle beautifully decorated with silver ornamentation. The falconer spurred his horse and galloped off.

At the end of the hunt, the day continued back at the Khan's seat, located on the now blooming slope of the Mani mountain in the middle of the Irgiz Plain. The honoured guest from afar was afforded every possible honour.

The Khan's white yurt with a full sixteen anchor ropes was particularly stately and grand that day. A throne stood in the place of honour. Almost immediately next to the Khan, only behind a veil of fine silk, sat his wife, whose beautiful face seemed to radiate light. Next to her sat her little son, with a tuft of hair sticking from the top of his head and falling to his back. He was playing with his bag of *assyk* bones.

The artist's attention was immediately drawn to how picturesque the Khan's family were.

Abulkhair sat back on his throne with a free, relaxed air

while Castle sketched away with pencils on his dense white paper secured to a board. He continually looked up at the Khan from his paper, which made his dishevelled red hair bounce about on his head. Doing his best to sketch an accurate likeness of Abulkhair, Castle also tried not to miss out the slightest change in the facial expressions of the Khan and his beautiful wife when they spoke with each other; he also noted the habits and antics of the five-year-old Adil, whose childlike, delicate nature made him appear more like his mother than his father.

Bopai noticed that, although Abulkhair appeared not to have a care in the world, he was preoccupied with something. Even during the earlier hunt, he suddenly frowned or seemed to seethe at something for some reason, and Bopai sensed that the Khan was troubled by thoughts of which he could not rid himself. However, no opportunity presented itself to find out what the matter was.

'Abeke, you seem worried about something today. What is it that troubles you?

Bopai turned slightly towards Abulkhair, not wanting others to notice her question, and she delicately hid her worries behind a soft smile. Instead of answering, the Khan raised his eyebrows for a moment and, glancing at Bopai, turned affectionately to his son and said,

'Son, how about a game of *khantalapai*[16]? We'll call that smaller throwing stick over there the *khan*.'

A shadow was cast over Bopai's fair face and she fell into thought. At what could the Khan be hinting by offering a game of khantalapai with his son and not giving her a direct answer to her question? Many people were unhappy with the just actions of the Khan, whose objective was invariably to preserve the unity of his people and the integrity of their land on the vast plain that stretched from the Edil to the Zhaiyk, both among his fellow Kazakhs and those from

---

[16] A game played with knucklebones of sheep.

other clans, who placed their interests above all else. There was also displeasure among the representatives of the Russian authorities, who concealed their hostility behind a veil of sweet promises while advancing ever closer to the borders with the land of the Kazakhs. Of course, the Khan's heart was torn over their intentions to split apart the people subordinate to him... So, who would win the *Khan* stick in that game of *khantalapai*? What did he need to do to stop himself from being beaten and to protect and safeguard his land from the enemy? *This is my greatest worry*, was what he probably meant, Bopai concluded to herself.

To the right of Abulkhair at the feast spread, which was bursting with food, sat Bokenbai, Myrzatai and other nobles, while a little further on sat Nuraly, who had also sensed his father's anxiety, which was well hidden from everyone.

At one point during the ceremonial meal, Bokenbai addressed the Khan, saying,

'Abeke, here's the thing: we don't yet understand with what message and what intention this guest has been sent from Mister Tauyekela, the Ambassador,' he said, smoothing the tips of his moustache with the long fingers of his right hand. 'We should surely hear at least one useful word from him through his interpreter. He just sits there, looking about and then rummaging about in his papers! What is this man from a foreign clan or tribe actually hiding? Is he an envoy, ready to listen and heed the will of the Khan, or is he an agent hiding his true intentions?'

Although no one asked for a translation of Bokenbai's words, the Tatar interpreter Kalben hurried to deliver them in Russian to the honoured guest's German interpreter, a fair-haired young man called Dietrich.

All the while, John Castle was trying to capture the fair and restrained beauty of the Khan's wife, Bopai, who was sitting to the left of Abulkhair and so full of dignity. The artist was completely immersed in his world, but he instantly straightened up and turned to Bokenbai, a stout man sitting solemnly beside the khan, his neat black beard emphasising the prominent features of his pleasant face. Castle placed his right hand to his chest as a sign of respect and, with an amiable smile, nodded to the words as translated by Dietrich.

'Why does he nod like a horse trying to shake off a fly?' Myrzatai spluttered. 'Hey, interpreter, lad, you don't need to translate every single word that's spoken, you know!'

'As you say, sir!' Kalben replied with a slight bow of the head to Myrzatai. 'However, the guest seems not to want to miss a single word that is spoken...'

'Right, hold on a minute!' Abulkhair said, stopping the interpreter short in a curt tone. 'I wonder what he has to say himself in response to Bokenbai's words.'

Coughing incessantly and pronouncing each word separately, Castle spoke at length, but Kalben conveyed only the essence of what he said.

'Judging by the words of this man, the purpose of his visit is to view these lands, get to know the people and familiarise himself with the way of life of the Kazakh people he knows so little about. He sees himself as being far from an official position and the politics of Orenburg when it comes to the nomadic Asians... And, yes, when he says *nomadic Asians*, he means us... And our respected guest assures you that you, most respected Khan, are aware of his mission.'

Bokenbai did not like what the Tatar interpreter had relayed and he did not utter another word. Silence reigned at the Khan's seat.

The Khan, too, did not continue the conversation. He turned slightly to his son Adil, who was taking out the knucklebones from their bag and then putting them back again.

'Papa! Papa-a, but you promised to play *khantalapai*,' Adil said, pouting.

The Khan looked at his aggrieved and impatient son and smiled.

'Then let's play. Throw the bones you're holding, son, and try to toss the *khan* stick so that it stands on the bones!' The Khan stroked Adil's head.

'If the stick lands to rest on the smaller side, then that's *khantalapai*!'

Bopai looked with a smile at Abulkhair, who had so abruptly interrupted the council to speak with his son.

'Son, don't interrupt your father from his conversation. Come here and we'll play *khantalapai* together,' she said, extending a hand to the child. 'It is embarrassing in front of our guests...' But Adil had no wish to heed his mother's gentle request and shuffled closer to his father, threw the bones down and with a cry of, '*Khantalapai! Khantalapai!*' used two hands to pick up the bone that had fallen onto its smaller side, the only one of all the bones he had scattered.

'Well done! This time, you have won at *khantalapai*!' Abulkhair said and embraced his son, saying, 'So, son, you make sure you always win and never give in!'

Castle was again drawn to the attentive gaze of the Khan's wife. A profound intelligence shone deep in Bopai's incredibly beautiful eyes, making her appear even more attractive. The artist found her pensive gaze a mirror of her whole being. The image of this incredible woman encouraged him to seek particular colours to convey her unique beauty.

Bopai watched a little anxiously as her husband allowed himself to be distracted by his playing son during this ceremonial occasion in honour of a foreign guest, and her expressive eyes and delicate facial expression so inspired Castle that he tried to capture Bopai in his memory in different ways and from different angles.

The Khan's wife was the most memorable thing for John Castle from the long reception at the Khan's seat; his only concern was to make his sketches.

***

The people had departed from the Khan's seat in the undulating Mantobe Valley in the Irgiz floodplain, rich in meadows and forests. Bokenbai and Myrzatai were the only ones remaining with Abulkhair. Just the three of them had gathered at the elder wife Bopai's home. To keep the number of servants in the yurt to a minimum, the hostess left only a personal assistant called Mandi and took it upon herself to prepare the dinner.

'See to it that fresh morning koumis is brought her in a small vessel,' she said to her servant, lowering her voice slightly. 'And keep an eye to make sure that those outside don't kick up a fuss.'

Abulkhair had been seriously troubled about something over the last few days, only occasionally distracted from his thoughts, and it was at this council of three that he finally decided to start talking.

'There is unrest on the borders of our land and our enemies will not rest, even though we have repelled them several times. You already know that the Russian authorities know all this, but pretend not to know anything of this feuding that is going on right under their noses. How can this possibly be seen as right? Now, the Orenburg Governor appears to have forgotten about the peace treaty that Tauyekela, sent by the white tsar in Saint-Petersburg, took away with him. They were supposed to prevent the bloodshed. So, what are their true intentions? Exert pressure? Or set their accomplices — the Kalmyks and detachments of Cossacks, the henchmen who roam either one side of the Edil or the other — to break the unity of our people? And if that is the case, what are we supposed to do about it?'

Bopai now understood clearly the reason for Abulkhair's anxiety and worry. She cast a glance at the men speaking with the Khan. Bokenbai was listening to the emotional and somewhat incoherent Abulkhair, taking in his every word and thinking deeply; his thick brows had formed into a dark frown. Myrzatai's face had turned stern scarlet in an instant.

Waiting for an answer, Abulkhair first turned to his faithful and knowledgeable adviser, his right-hand man and leader of his army, Bokenbai. Before speaking, Bokenbai cleared his throat hesitantly, but he only had to look at the Khan and his face reflected a fiery determination.

'My Khan, tell me what needs to be done! It appears to me that the January reprisals against the Esteks, who rose in protest against subjugation to the Russian Tsarist authorities, is a warning of sorts to us Kazakhs from the Russian powers that be, who seem rather lenient when it comes to us. They will say that if we get arrogant about relations, then we get the same treatment! If our attempts at resistance end that way, where will it all lead?

'The Adai people who live on the slopes of the Ustyurt Plateau and in the floodplain of the Elek and the Zhem are being overpowered by enemies from all sides!' Myrzatai added in an agitated voice. 'The Turkmens launch their frequent raids too! Hmm, so what are we to do? Should we avoid responding to our enemies in kind, should we seek to negotiate, or...'

'...or what?' Abulkhair interrupted him, voicing the thoughts that were troubling him. 'So, what is this "or"? Sitting around and wondering how our "or" will end is not an option either! You know full well that from the very beginning, our plans were not to bow before the Russian Tsar or subjugate ourselves to Russian authority, as the Edil Kalmyks have done. Were we not thinking of a mutual peace when we sent that letter? And of the inviolability of borders? Were we not dreaming of a quiet life for our people and the strengthening of our khanate without dividing it all up among our brothers?! And if, as if they have forgotten about all this, instead of stopping their subjects from violating agreements, they encourage them into acts of provocation, can we possibly agree to this, Bokenbai?!'

'That is the case, yes... And it was not for nothing that the nobles, the biys and batyrs, with Azhibai at their head, distrusted the ambassadors that the Russian Empress sent here. And then, there is that artist with his strange appearance and the way he speaks in a foreign language — he comes here from Orenburg across the Or, with his prompts from Tauyekela, he comes to the Khan's seat... No, my Khan, we are not a fan of this chap visiting us here. This Castle says he is here to study our land and get to know the people, but, in fact, perhaps he'll learn what he can about the state of affairs in the Khanate and pry out our intentions as regards the Russian authorities.'

'And quite right! I agree with you!' said Myrzatai, hurrying to back Bokenbai up and, glancing at the Khan, could see he was deep in thought.

That council of three at the heart of the Khan's seat revealed to Bopai-Khanum the true depth of Abulkhair's anxiety over those days. Their neighbours to the northwest who had now clearly displayed their toxic intentions, were set on plundering not only the lands between the Edil and the Zhaiyk. The Khan understood all too well that the policy of the Russian authorities since the reign of Tsar Peter was aimed at expanding trade relations and enriching the treasury by seizing power and exerting pressure on the countries of Asia. This could be achieved by subjugating vast territories from the great Volga (the Edil) and the Ural (the Zhaiyk) in the west to the lands of Turkestan in the east. That was why their main aim now was to force the Khan and his people first to bow and then become fully subjugated. So, how would they gather all their forces and protect the people from this? Bopai realised that it was about this that Abulkhair was thinking.

In the cool of the next morning, Bokenbai and Myrzatai left the Khan's seat early. Having said his goodbyes to them,

Abulkhair took several warriors and his bodyguard, Bektore, and went to the hill in the upper reaches of the Irgiz to unwind a little. Tired from the exertions of the last few days at the Khan's seat, he missed the vast expanses of the summer steppe. Bektore knew that the Khan was usually in the habit of hunting on such journeys and he had taken with them a pair of hounds and one black borzoi, a tazy with tattered ears and a white spot on the chest.

The pleasant June breeze, with the fragrance of wormwood and the boundless, blooming steppe, stretched out before him, took Abulkhair's breath away. The companions rode leisurely among the hills, where the herds of the Shomekei clan were grazing on the summer pastures, and shepherds' dwellings were dotted here and there. From time to time, the hounds, sniffing out the ravines and hollows, picked up the trail of a hare or a fox. Bektore tried to keep them away from the burrows of small field animals, which had just had their litters. In any event, the dogs themselves were not particularly interested in such game. Only the borzoi tirelessly shot off and chased hares, but even she seemed to have had her fill after catching one or two, stopping her incessant chasing and trotting along behind the hounds.

Towards evening, at the turn by a large hollow overgrown with tamarisk, the dogs, following at their masters' heels, smelled the odour of a wolf's lair and set off in that direction at quite a pace. At the entrance to the lair, the cubs had only just finished their meal — the she-wolf had regurgitated the swallowed meat and the little ones were greedily devouring the bloody pieces. The plump pups, full and contented, were now frolicking about by the entrance. Suddenly, catching the strange scent, they darted into the lair and concealed themselves deep inside.

The wolf and she-wolf, who were not far from their cubs, surveying the surrounding area from their elevated position, spotted the hounds and rushed to the foot of the ravine. No sooner had the dogs made it to the entrance to the lair, at the base of a large clump of tamarisk bushes, than they were faced by a mighty wolf with teeth bared and fur on end, blocking their way. At the same time, the she-wolf rushed to the whimpering cubs, disappearing into the deep lair in the blink of an eye.

The hounds, with their ears pressed back, approached the wolf from both sides and launched a lightning-fast attack.

Abulkhair's small party caught up with the hounds to witness a fierce struggle between a calf-sized wolf and the dogs, all trying to force it down. The wolf would not allow the dogs to get a hold of its chest or throat, and it frantically defended itself, with all its animal ferocity to the fore.

'Oh, wow, it is standing its ground even against two!'

Bektore was about to rush forwards but brought his horse to an abrupt halt when he heard Abulkhair's warning.

'Don't distract the dogs, Bektore. Stay back!' Abulkhair could not take his eyes off the battle between the monster-like wolf and his hounds. 'Distract one of the dogs and the wolf will have its throat.' The seasoned *arlan* wolf resisted for a long while, not allowing the dogs to grasp him by the scruff of the neck with their bloody fangs, the vulnerable part of the hind legs or the throat. The wolf, who was fighting for the life of his offspring to the very death, was an inspiration to Abulkhair. *It is too late for anything to try and separate these hardened predators. Whichever of them stops will perish in an instant. That is a true fight for life, a desperate struggle to stay alive.*

At one point, the now exhausted wolf tried to slip between the dogs and rush to the slope of the ravine, but one of them managed a death grip to the ear and the other one sank its fangs into the animal's throat. Squirming and then falling to its side, the wolf flinched its hind legs only once and fell dead.

The she-wolf did not emerge from the lair, only roared

angrily, protecting her cubs, all huddled beneath her.

Abulkhair ordered Bektore to pull the dogs off; they had abandoned the dead wolf and had turned to dive into the lair.

'Don't touch them! Let the cubs remain alive with their mother. There is no need to embitter the wolves. Besides, this *arlan* here wanted to save his offspring... Let them live. Don't touch them.

Bektore silently consented, as if to say, *as you wish*, only looking at the Khan incomprehensibly.

Abulkhair turned his horse and went on his way.

The desperate battle of this steppe predator, not for life, but for death and, in the end, his death from the fangs of the dogs unexpectedly stirred Abulkhair's soul. The brief calm and sense of freedom across the peaceful steppe had melted away without a trace. The passion that had possessed him during that intriguing hunt that day had gone, and the Khan hurried to return home.

* * *

Myriads of twinkling stars peered into the eight-panel white yurt through the shanyrak, which was only half covered. The whitish belt of the Milky Way seemed to engulf the entire world, spread out beneath a heavenly dome.

Through the shanyrak of the yurt that had been erected especially for him, John Castle gazed at the bright stars that dotted the black velvet of the sky as he pondered every moment of the ten days he had spent at the Khan's seat.

Indeed, the world of the Asians who live in this vast, boundless and naked steppe is mysterious. It is no easy matter for a person who has never known or heard of such a world to understand and get a sense of these people who live in such a remote wilderness. Their clothes, manners, behaviour, and even their conversations are so attuned to their exceptional being and nature!

Take the Khan... In an elusive moment, he enters a maelstrom of thoughts and then suddenly flashes with a fiery determination and energy. His moods are so different... Every unique moment conjures up a new trait, a new touch for a portrait. Of all the women at the Khan's seat, it is the Khan's wife who appears the most unique. She is simply marvellous! How can one not admire the radiant eyes of this young woman, whose beauty shines so bright?! Or her face at moments when she speaks with a smile or the beautiful, tremulous movement of her snow-white neck?! She is the very embodiment of a steppe Madonna!

Fortunately, both my daily diary entries and my sketches will help me preserve the memory of all the incredible impressions of the inhabitants of this boundless land. The Kazakh Khan and his Khanum, their little prince, playing with his knucklebones, and the courtiers — their sketched images will be the most valuable thing I take away from this trip. Indeed, this will be a gift for Her Majesty, who awaits information from me on the affairs at the Khan's seat.

And I must complete a portrait of the Kazakh Khan and his Khanum, whatever it takes, not least because I have now gathered more than enough sketches! I think I will get the opportunity to see certain details in their faces for the final missing brushstrokes.

Castle rose from his bed and, opening his diary that lay on the round bedside table, he began writing down the thoughts and images that had just come to him.

At yesterday's ceremonial gathering at the Khan's seat, Abulkhair's three wives sat in a row behind a four-panel silk curtain to his left. The most charming of them was the beautiful Khanum, the Khan's first wife, who sat at their head, nearest her husband. She wore a red silk dress decorated with golden flowers. On her head was a high headband, akin to a Turkish turban, decorated with gold braid and embroidery. The Khan's other two wives were dressed in red Bukhara velvet with white chintz headscarves.

The artist also recorded in his notebook that a particular example of Asian elegance could be seen in the way the Khanum chose to dress. Then he went back to bed, threw back his head and trained his gaze back into the abyss of the night sky. He could clearly see one star through the shanyrak, shimmering somehow differently in the centre of the patch of black velvet. *There it is! That star is called Bopai-Khanum!* Castle fell asleep with a smile on his face from that sudden, beautiful thought.

* * *

The twenty days that John Castle spent at the Khan's seat flew by. On the morning of his departure, the artist came to the Khan's central quarters to say his farewell. Through his interpreter, he expressed his gratitude to Abulkhair and Bopai for their hospitality.

'During this time, you have been very kind and very attentive. Most honourable Khan, I leave your seat with a unique feeling that I have discovered a unique new world. I have too many impressions to count! Your sincerity, without a shadow of guile, and your genuinely human nature have greatly impressed me. I have learned a great deal about steppe democracy and the traditions and customs of your aristocracy. I have recorded your unique images on paper, too. I consider myself most fortunate in all this!'

Abulkhair reservedly accepted the words of gratitude from his guest envoy, Castle. Glancing at Bopai, who nodded slightly and smiled courteously, the artist noted her white shawl and pointed headdress and noticed her long, snow-white fingers. He felt the warmth of her heart reflected in her eyes and once more, he admired the beauty of the Khan's wife.

'I wish you a pleasant journey home, Mister Castle. May your wishes be fulfilled and good luck befall you! My son Nuraly-Sultan will escort you from our lands and set you on the right road.'

* * *

It was now passed the middle of the summer. The heat

had begun gradually to subside in the final days of July when Castle and his companions, exhausted from their long journey, reached the outskirts of the fortress town, standing at the point where the River Or flows into the Ural. This was the compact town of Or, the location of the official office of the Orenburg Expedition, which had been formed in Saint-Petersburg.

The expedition commissar Ivan Kirilov met Castle as he had been accustomed to do over the years of his service to the royal court, according to the traditions of the upper echelons of Russian aristocracy. He greeted him in his office on the third floor of the building, with statues of reclining lions with flowing manes on both sides of the broad entrance stairs. Kirilov extended his hand to Castle, who greeted him by placing his right hand on the left side of his chest and bowing his head as a sign of respect.

'Welcome back from the Khan's seat, Mister Castle. It is good to see you in good health. You might not be a real nomad, but it appears you have become much like one!'

Kirilov led the artist to a large round table with a globe in its centre. Castle's usually pale face had indeed grown darker and visibly more weathered in the dry wind and heat, and now his tanned skin was the colour of the sun-dried steppe itself.

'I hear you have a great many impressions from what you have seen and heard. All the things you have recorded in your diary — the everyday life, the views of the world, the notions of steppe life that were hitherto unknown to you, the customs and traditions, habits, Asian morals and views of those wild people under the Khan's leadership — are most commendable and evidence of wonderful diligence on your part.'

Kirilov spoke like a scholarly geographer and researcher, which Castle immediately found attractive and disposed him positively for a frank and informative discussion.

John Castle officially reported that he would prepare a

personal account of his trip and after that, he began laying out pictures from a neat pile, one after the other, onto the broad table to show them to Kirilov.

'This is wonderful! These are all so valuable! They are very important, incredible pictorial documents about the Kazakh Khan! If only you knew how important it is, from the standpoint of history, that Her Majesty Anna Ioannovna sees with her own eyes what the main Kaisak in the Horde actually looks like! Congratulations!

You have portrayed the Khan wonderfully and accurately conveyed not only his appearance but also his inner world! This picture will go down in history! Wonderful, what a stroke of luck! It is your trophy if you like!'

'Mister Kirilov, please would you now take a moment to look at this portrait.'

Castle took his portrait of Bopai-Khanum and placed it in the centre of the vast table.

'This the main khanum. Bopai-Khanum! The nomadic beauty! She is not only beautiful but intelligent and wise as well.'

'So, you say this wonderful woman is Bopai, Bopai-Khanum? I have heard this name. I had no idea that she was so attractive and graceful. My, she is a genuine nomadic Madonna! Just look at her eyes! What eyes! Such a flame burns in there! You say she is about forty years old?! We say that our second youth begins at forty and this woman is indeed now blossoming. It transpires that it is not only European and Slavic women who are especially beautiful at this age; the same applies to Asian women, too, does it not? What flawless beauty this is when a woman is beautiful both on the outside and the inside!'

'You are right — beauty and common sense go together most harmoniously in this woman. She is not only the Khan's true love, but, according to her status, honoured Mister Kirilov, she is considered the second leader at the

Khan's seat! She is a wise and judicious mother and a reliable support for the Khan in leading his people, both in word and deed. This woman is worthy of the title *Khanum*! Speaking in European terms, she is a true queen! I would say that her prudent authority carries weight in the Khan's seat. After Abulkhair-Khan himself, of course.'

Kirilov listened to Castle speaking about Bopai with great interest and he did not hide his admiration.

'It is nothing new for Asians that a woman takes up the reins and leads the people. It is in their blood! Take Tomyris, Queen of the Saka, who inhabited much of this vast land. She lived in the sixth century before the common era! Perhaps you have read the story by the ancient Greek historian, Herodotus, the father of history, about the life of Tomyris... Even earlier, the Saka were ruled on the banks of the Syr Darya River by Zarina, who was famous for her beauty and courage. There were many such brave and, at the same time, feminine warrior queens among the Saka people, and, as you know, the Saka are one of the ancestors of the present-day Kaisaks! And this Bopai-Khanum is undoubtedly living proof of this!'

'And you know what else, Mister Castle,' Kirilov went on enthusiastically, 'you must have heard of the name of the Arabic geographer and traveller Al-Idrisi? Oh, you haven't? Then forgive me... Anyway, this audacious wandering scholar, who lived about seven centuries ago, studied the lives of the Kipchak nomads in great detail in his time. In his famous historical and geographical work *Entertainment for the Weary Wanderer Through the Regions*, he writes that the Kipchak women can be very beautiful, strong and proud. I remembered those words... And there is more! The Ancient Roman Emperor Julian ever wrote the following about them: *Their women are all warriors on a par with the men — they are exemplary equestrians and archers, and they never flinch and always fight fiercely in battle.* So, you see, and we just call them savage nomads! What a paradox!'

Castle marvelled at Kirilov, who shared his knowledge with no little grandstanding, and he thought, *He recalls so much historical information just like that as if he has learned it all by heart!*

'Yes, you are absolutely right, Mister Kirilov, sir! I think that Bopai-Khanum is certainly not a weak person! She hails from aristocratic blood, too, as far as I have heard and understood. She is the daughter of a valiant *bahadur*, a warrior called Syuindyk from an Adai tribe of people inhabiting those parts. It is said that, from an early age, she was trained to ride a horse and fire a bow and arrow. She grew up a single-minded woman.'

'Right, information about her origins merely confirms the truth! Be sure to point this out in your official report of your expedition to the Kyrgyz-Kaisak Horde, Mister Castle! When you return to Saint-Petersburg, the first thing you must do is seek an audience with Anna Ioannovna. Her Majesty must learn first-hand from you, and not from third parties, about the things you saw and heard at the seat of the Kyrgyzes. Not only that, Mister Castle, but you were sent there as the official representative of the royal court! Be sure to remember this at all times! The Empress should, therefore, grant an audience without delay. After that...'

Kirilov was an educated aristocrat and a high-ranking official, and he behaved accordingly. Looking intently at Castle, who was listening attentively, he paused and then continued,

'Hm... After that, you should embellish these pictures more to make them a real work of art for a gallery. Naturally, you would have done that without me saying so, I know. And yet, please don't be cross for reminding you of this. After that, you can bring the official information about your diplomatic mission into order.'

John Castle gave Kirilov's detailed advice considerable thought. Of course, presenting a report to the Tsarina would be no easy task. However, sooner or later, he would have to fulfil this important duty. And so, Mister Kirilov, who had seen a lot in his time, had reminded him of this in advance.

Sitting in the office of the head of the Orenburg Expedition, John Castle again vividly recalled the days spent at the Khan's seat on the banks of the Irgiz... The now distant Irgiz... The luxury of the Khan's summer camp. The banks of the River Kabyrga... That shimmering star in the centre of the sky that appeared like a piece of black velvet through the shanyrak. That star really should be called *Bopai-Khanum*! Once more, he recalled that night he had spent in his yurt, gazing up through the shanyrak.

At that moment in the conversation, Kirilov looked at Castle and noticed his state of rapture and delight. Naturally, any modern European of the time would see the land of the Kaisak people in the heart of Asia — considered the ancestral home of the ancient Turks — as something genuinely exotic. However, the day was not far off when the Kaisak people would finally become a part of Russia, accepting their subjugation to the great empire. This would represent a colossal victory in Russian history. The Kaisak Khanate, the holder of the legacy of the Golden Horde and which once subjugated the Russian princes, would now fade away into nothing, one way or another. And this ridiculous history with it! Indeed, it had to disappear, Abulkhair, his Bopai and all! And everything that you've seen, Mister Castle, will remain only on yellowed paper, to be but a myth for future generations, a vague shadow of a distant past.

Seeing himself as an undoubtedly enlightened individual, Kirilov grimaced squeamishly inside from such arrogant thoughts. He was a scholar of geography and understood quite clearly that every nation, regardless of race and origin, has its place in the history of humankind as a whole, and such considerations were wholly inappropriate here.

Swept away by his dreaming, Castle did not suspect for

a minute what Kirilov was thinking and what his true intentions were, as a representative of the tsarist authorities, towards the nomadic people. He was silent, awaiting questions from the head of the expedition.

'Ah, yes, Mister Castle, another thing I wanted to say in closing: I am confident that your truly valuable and important work in studying the lives and customs of the nomads during your time among them will be given its due appreciation! I wish you every success!'

With those words, Kirilov gently made it obvious that their meeting was at an end. He nodded and shook Castle's hand.

***

It was early October. The incessant Saint-Petersburg rain was oppressive and the perpetually grey sky seemed to push down to the ground. The Empress's new Winter Palace stood facing the Admiralty. Everything was quiet. There were very few people walking the paved streets leading to the palace and the bridges over the Neva.

John Castle arrived at the Empress's winter residence with his customary punctuality at precisely noon, as appointed by the head of the Imperial Chancellery. He went up the large, curved, blue-granite staircase from the entrance and stopped in front of a pair of wide-open tall doors leading to the opulent throne room. A mid-ranking Imperial Guard officer escorted him further and pointed him in the right direction. Walking over the light-grey marble floor of the throne room, Castle heard the quiet sound of his fashionable, fancy, thin-soled boots, but it was the echo that reverberated from the tall dome above him that rang in his ears. On the floor of the next room, where the audience was to take place, there was a carpet, and the sound of his footsteps became quieter; Castle was finally able to catch his breath.

Overcoming his nervous excitement, Castle cast his eye

over his paintings, which were arranged in a row in a prominent position. As required according to the rules of the Imperial Chancellery, his paintings had been requested from him in advance. The first picture of a portrait of Abulkhair, completed in oils on canvas, followed by a watercolour portrait of Bopai-Khanum, then sketches of the Khanum and the little prince, as well as pictures of the reception at the Khan's seat. Castle once again made a mental note that he would present the paintings to the Empress in that order after his detailed report on his visit to the horde.

It was probably an unwritten rule for receiving ordinary visitors, but Castle had to wait some time for the Empress. Finally, the door at the far end of the stateroom, with all its pompous furnishings, slowly swung open. The Tsarina slowly entered, wearing a light-green silk dress tailored to her stately, full figure, with its long, wide hem rustling softly with every step. A brooch with a precious jewel glistened on her breast. The Tsarina smiled warmly in response to Castle's bow and allowed his lips almost to touch the long fingers on her hand. He then spoke courteously and with expressed formality,

'Your Majesty, please accept my deepest gratitude for devoting your precious time to receive me, your humble servant John Castle!'

It seemed that Anna Ioannovna was not particularly interested in the artist's detailed and thorough account of what he had learned at the Khan's seat, his report on the people, the way of life and the features of the nomads' social structure. Quite quickly noticing this indifference, John Castle concluded that the Tsarina was not ready at that moment to gain an insight into the intricacies of nomadic life, and so he hurriedly turned the conversation to the paintings.

'I ask you to consider the other details that I have set out in my detailed written report that I prepared for Your

Majesty and which has been officially presented. For now, though, Your Majesty, if you have no objection, I would like to present to you these paintings as the artist. They relate the things that I saw in the land of the Kaisak nomads.'

It seemed that the Tsarina had been waiting solely for this moment, for, from the very beginning of the audience, she had been looking at Castle's paintings. Now she turned with undisguised interest to the pictures on which the artist had depicted the nomads, conveying his attitude to them in the language of painting.

'Of course, Mister Castle, of course! I was drawn to your paintings from the outset. All right, let's take a look, and you can tell me who is depicted.'

As soon as the conversation turned to the paintings, based on his personal impressions, Castle began speaking in a completely different way. He spoke passionately and in great detail about each character, their nature and behaviour, relationships with other people and ways of expressing their feelings.

'Oh, I think you have shown accurately and truthfully in your painting what this man Abulkhair is like. Two years ago, we received a Kaisak delegation sent officially to Saint-Petersburg by Abulkhair-Khan. It was then that it became clear to me that he enjoys considerable authority among the Kaisaks. Judging by the words of his envoys, as the head of his horde, the Khan is diligent and places the interests of his people above his own; in diplomatic affairs, I believe he is direct and not prone to flattery. In your depiction, he appears just as I imagined him. Indeed, you have depicted the Kaisak Khan Abulkhair most correctly on this canvas.'

The Empress looked long and hard at the portrait of Bopai, painted in light colours and warm tones. Returning to this painting, she gazed intently at the image of the Khan's wife.

'A steppe Madonna, you say? A nomadic beauty? Whatever you might say, Mister Castle, surely this means just one thing, that the Kaisaks are indeed an eternally nomadic steppe people, does it not? You have most accurately captured both the delicate beauty and the bold determination of this Khanum Madonna. You have managed most wonderfully to convey the image of a beautiful, intelligent and courageous woman! My dear artist, what can I say — you have truly proven this!'

'Your Majesty, I am extremely grateful for your high appreciation and generous praise for my humble work. I noticed that, compared with other Asian women, the Kaisak women are particularly beautiful. It is this that makes them unique.'

'You say that this Bopai-Khanum is so intelligent that she even advises her husband, Abulkhair-Khan. But how true is that? As far as I know, the nomads live and are brought up under strict patriarchal rules. Am I right? Such rules mean that, in such a situation, a man and a high-ranking khan will not resort to the advice of a woman under any circumstances.'

'You are aware of the origins of these people, Your Majesty. Their closest ancestors are the Turks, followed by the Saka and the Huns. And, according to historical records, the matriarchal freedom-loving consciousness in the blood of their girls...'

'So, you really believe that?! You want to say that their courage, wisdom and beauty were inherited from those distant ancestors... Well, perhaps you are right; it is quite possible...'

What thought came to Her Imperial Majesty by the end of that audience was not something that John Castle was thinking about right then. For now, he was simply happy to be able to talk about his impressions about the Khan's seat and, in so doing, he achieved his main goal of coming to the Winter Palace of Empress Anna Ioannovna.

The northern capital on the banks of the Neva was still shivering from the incessant rain under the afternoon sun on yet another gloomy autumn day.

CHAPTER 4

In the summer of 1738, Donduk-Ombo-Khan, Ayuke's grandson, crossed over to the eastern bank of the Edil with twenty thousand troops. The son of Donduk-Ombo, Galdan-Norbo, the commander-in-chief of the Kalmyk Army, was to march along the course of the rivers Zhaiyk and Zhem, crush anyone who got in their way and then defeat Abulkhair.

As soon as the alarming news about the Kalmyks reached the Khan's seat, Abulkhair urgently sent an army, with Nuraly at its head, to the upper reaches of the River Zhem, where detachments of Bokenbai and Eset stood, forming a human shield. Having sent the troops, the Khan set about preparing for a difficult venture of another kind.

Seeing off her son, Bopai gave him her blessing,

'Nuraly, your father is sending you on a difficult and dangerous campaign against the Volga Kalmyks — this is a huge test for you. Your father has survived many a battle with the Torgauts, and now he has entrusted you with the protection of your people. I think you understand that the time has come to prove yourself. Try to pass this test with dignity and justify the hopes of your father, the Khan. You be careful and protect your father, my dear! May Allah help you!' She then repeated the prayer several times to herself. The Kalmyk troops, heading to the Zhaiyk from the southwest, emerged onto the shifting sands of Naryn. The Torgauts slowed their advance a little as they crossed the sands. They fed their horses with fresh water from shallow wells and let them eat their fill of the juicy fire bush, sea lyme and kumarshyk. The dense thickets of tamarisk and aspen in the lowlands between the hills saved them from the scalding summer heat. Galdan-Norbo did not wish to overwork his men before the difficult battle that awaited them when they left those sands, and he gave them a brief period of respite.

Later, after leaving Naryn behind, but before reaching the banks of the Zhen, Galdan-Norbo's army encountered the three groups of warriors of Bokenbai, Eset and the newly arrived Nuraly. The combination of the desperate whooping of the enemy combatants rushing to meet each other, the galloping hooves of the warhorses, their wild neighing, and the tense shrieking was ear-splitting.

Abulkhair stood dark and tense on a nearby hill with a small detachment of warriors, watching the battle unfold below.

As soon as the vanguard of Kalmyks rushed into the attack, they were met with a shower of arrows, whistling one after the other. Those who had time to protect themselves from the barrage of arrows with their shields surged forward and fought with wild rage, wielding spears. The horses of wounded warriors floundered and galloped chaotically away into the steppe. Some of them caught in dangling reins, writhed about fearfully, unable to escape.

The warriors from both sides, accustomed to fighting on horseback, were now fighting a life-or-death battle. It seemed that in this desperate battle, they had forgotten the meaning of fear, for they continued to swing their blades and spears without mercy. For as long as they could remember, they had been engaged in bloody battles and the destruction of others like themselves.

Abulkhair suddenly thought that he had lived through many such battles when the steppe was stained in blood and the outlines of distant mountains were lost in clouds of dust. These battles took place in all corners of the vast steppe, an area that not even an eagle or the hardiest onager could traverse. Was this to be his destiny? Were these dzhigit warriors fated to fight in the wild steppe for months and years without ever descending from their horses, abandoning all thought of a normal, peaceful life? And if this were the case, that there was no escape from fate, then none of them would ever see an end to these continuous battles! This was the greatest sadness of his people. With these dark images in his mind, borne of his anxious thoughts, Abulkhair steered his horse down the hill. The outcome of that day's battle was already predetermined — the Kalmyks had suffered a crushing defeat.

The battlefield, crimson from the bloodshed, seemed to groan in pain.

No matter how desperately the Torgauts might have fought in that bloody struggle of several days, they could not break the resolve of the Khan's warriors. The broken detachments staggered back over the Naryn sands and retreated to the banks of the Volga. The Torgauts failed to put up defences in time; the Kazakh detachments tracked them down and pushed home their advantage before they could fight back. As a result, hundreds of Kalmyk warriors were taken captive. Those who avoided capture fled in all directions and perished in obscurity.

Donduk-Ombo was seriously angered by his son's failed campaign and although he tried not to surrender entirely, he was forced to admit that his army had been completely defeated. In his turn, Galdan-Norbo harboured his rage and planned to depose his father from the throne — because he had no wish to follow what he saw as Donduk-Ombo's senseless and reckless intention to destroy Abulkhair's seat — cross the Irgiz and the Chu, reach Balkhash and join the Dzungar Khanate. He never managed any of that, however, and soon, the Russian authorities captured the Kalmyk Khan's dishonourable son and sent him into exile.

After a gruelling military campaign, which culminated at least in victory, Abulkhair was unable to return to his seat until the autumn cold spell had set in. Having brought Nuraly back from the opposite side of the Zhaiyk and sending him to the aul on the Irgiz, the Khan headed urgently for Orenburg. His reason for this was the unexpected news that, by order of Vasily Tatishchev, head of the Orenburg Commission, an eight-thousand-strong and heavily armed Kalmyk army had set up camp near the city. Since this news had been delivered by a reliable man who had fought alongside Bokenbai, the Khan had no reason to doubt its veracity.

Abulkhair set up camp in a place from where he could see Orenburg, stationing the numerous detachments of Bokenbai, Eset, Shotan and Myrzatai, who had travelled with him, side by side. The Khan remained diligent, for he was prepared for highly likely intimidation or some other hostile action on the part of the Orenburg authorities.

Vasily Tatishchev, who learned of the Khan's sudden manoeuvres that same day, was seriously alarmed and not a little frightened. Tatishchev had heard many times of Abulkhair's uncompromising nature and that he never backed down from a plan. It had been mentioned by ambassadors and envoys who had visited the Khan's seat and even Saint-Petersburg courtiers. Recent proof of this nature was Abulkhair's crushing victory over Donduk-Ombo, a Russian subject. If he was not afraid of storming Orenburg, then what? After all, it was likely not without reason that he had approached the city at arm's length and with a host of warriors!

Before the matter went too far, Tatishchev began looking for ways to engage with Abulkhair. There was no time to wait for Tevkelev, who had left for Ufa on a special errand. Perhaps he should send Abulkhair an invitation and receive him in his residence? Or would it be better if he went to see the Khan himself? The head of the Orenburg Commission nervously dithered from one idea to the next before finally deciding to lay on a ceremonial reception for the Khan. He sent an escort in his name to greet Abulkhair, headed by the garrison commander, with an invitation to come to Orenburg with his military commanders.

Abulkhair was surprised to receive such an invitation, which was delivered through the Tatar interpreter, and had not expected such compliments from the authorities in Orenburg. Moreover, Abulkhair found it suspicious that he was being invited as a guest of honour at that moment when he had stationed large numbers of troops on the outskirts of the city. However, he could not turn down the invitation and so, at noon on that day, he arrived at Tatishchev's residence with Bokenbai, Eset and ten reliable warriors.

Vasily Tatishchev, a true example of the Russian aristocracy, a scholar and engineer, welcomed Abulkhair courteously and with special care and attention. His light brown hair, parted in the middle and falling to his shoulders on both sides, and his blue cloth jacket with a slightly elongated hem gave Tatishchev more the sheen of an intelligent scientist than the gloss of a high-ranking official. His open, high forehead glistened and his lean, fair face bore the most obliging smile. After a ceremony of warm greetings, the guests were invited to take seats around a large table in the centre of the room.

'Most honoured Mister Abulkhair and valiant military commanders, please accept my deepest respect and honour!' Tatishchev paused for the interpreter to translate his words and, looking over each of his guests seated opposite him in their seats of honour, he continued in a measured tone, 'I would like to inform you that the Orenburg Expeditionary Commission is keen to avoid any further misunderstandings in the existing relations and agreements reached on seeking peaceful solutions to political matters between our people.' Abulkhair, Bokenbai and Eset understood perfectly well what this governor was hinting so delicately and tactfully. On the one hand, the defeat of the Volga Kalmyks was to the advantage of the

Tsarist authorities, to whom they had long been subjugated. It was clear that Russia did not support the intentions of the Kalmyks to leave the banks of the Edil, seize the Kazakh lands and join the Dzungar state, for it was the Torgaut-Kalmyks that they had set against the Khan's seat at the given time and used in battles against the Kazakhs.

On the other hand, there was no doubt that the victory of the Khan had been a matter of extreme irritation, for only recently, the Khan's seat had acknowledged the patronage of the Russian authorities and its subjugation by royal charter. It was to this that Tatishchev had been referring in his flamboyant manner. After Tatishchev's formal opening remarks, which had begun tactfully and politely and ended with restraint and deliberation, both sides hesitated and remained silent for a while. Abulkhair realised that the time had come for his official response. He paused for a short while and then spoke, staring not at Tatishchev but at the interpreter, who was fidgeting, waiting impatiently for words to translate.

'We are grateful to the highly esteemed Mister Tatishchev for the boundless courtesy he has afforded us today, which we were not expecting. Please tell him that we have listened to him attentively and we support him. For our part, as his Excellency has said, we will make every effort to prevent misunderstanding in our relations and arrangements. We expect the very same from the Russian authorities and Her Majesty the Empress, too. However, your loyal Kalmyks from the Edil display no such peaceful intent in our regard, and the esteemed Mister Tatishchev is well aware of this. We also believe that it is in his power to answer such questions as, for example, for what purpose has a large group of Kalmyk warriors gathered by the fortress in Orenburg. If we are mistaken, we will bow our heads and duly apologise. In order not to add a further misunderstanding between us, we would like to clarify all sides of this situation.'

Tatishchev was accustomed to judging people's intelligence by the manner in which they spoke and deep inside, he admired the Khan's diplomatic skill and the way in which he conveyed his demands most accurately and concisely. And yet, in an effort to conceal his admiration, he responded sternly and to the point.

'Most esteemed Mister Abulkhair, first of all, I would like you to consider that the Kalmyk troops have not been assembled to send them out against your seat! Speaking truthfully about the Kalmyk troops, their billeting at the Orenburg garrison is temporary and was arranged at the request of Donduk-Ombo, given the political crisis in his khanate because of a power struggle.'

'We shall, of course, take this into account. However, I also wish to inform you that I will not move from my place and shall personally monitor to ensure the Kalmyk troops do not remain in the Orenburg fortress. Naturally, this does not mean that we question the information you have provided; quite the contrary, please take this as our sincere desire to verify the truth because we cannot say for sure what steps might be taken by the Torgauts at the critical moment, for they are not known for turning their backs on deceitful conduct.'

Abulkhair's direct and swift response turned the Orenburg governor's face a shade of crimson, but there was nothing he could say in response to such logic. Therefore, he simply nodded in silence, thus displaying his consent.

Thus, the formal part of the ceremonial reception was completed and the time came for lunch at the heavily laden table. The various dishes with herbs that the Russians ate with knives and forks did not particularly impress Abulkhair and his companions, who were already missing their sweet summer koumis and juicy horsemeat. After the meeting, which had been an outwardly formal affair and which had concluded on a calm note, the head of the Orenburg garrison, with this mounted escort, accompanied

Abulkhair and his men from the city.

* * *

The cold, damp, dreary November days cast a grey haze over the Khan's winter encampment in the lower reaches of the Syr Darya.

During this time, based on agreement with the Orenburg governor-general, about a hundred Cossack prisoners, taken captive over the previous year, were being handed over to the commander of a military detachment that had come specially from Orenburg. Abulkhair had instructed Nuraly to handle this and the sultan did everything required of him precisely and with the minimum of fuss.

Now thirty years old, an age when he could rule his people and lead warriors, the energetic Nuraly-Sultan went on military campaigns on an equal footing with his father, taking on important affairs for the Khan's seat, both on the Khan's instructions and under his own initiative. Bopai genuinely rejoiced at what her son, the heir to the Khan's throne, was achieving. Just as an eagle trains its offspring to soar in the sky once its wings have grown, so Abulkhair gave Nuraly various assignments, knowing that the future Khan must possess the skills for ruling his people, and it was in instances such as these that he could learn a great deal.

Before he departed from the Khan's seat, Nuraly visited the home of his mother, Bopai.

'My son, from now on, it is you who will become the support for your father. You know this without me having to tell you, of course. There are many batyrs and warriors no longer among us — over many years, they stood by our Khan's side and supported him in great battles with our enemies, attacking from the south, the north and from the east. You know for yourself that the Governor in Orenburg and the Russians in Saint-Petersburg share the same goal — to settle once and for all on our land. That is why the tsar sends their dishonourable lackeys here to divide our people. Indeed, our Khan, your father, has had a difficult fate. For so many years, he has been throwing forces to fight off the Dzungars, he has been strengthening our north-western borders in endless battles. And so many times, he has repelled the attacks of Kalmyks, Cossacks and even Esteks, attacking from the Edil and the Zhaiyk! I think you know what your father meant when he said,

The Kazakhs will not allow their enemies to trample over their native land until the waters of the Zhaiyk run dry or the end of the world is upon us. This was a cry from the heart and not simply hot air. These words, without doubt, reached royal Russian ears. Hearing them, Saint-Petersburg realised that your father Abulkhair would never bow his head. My darling Nuraly, you must be careful and remember that nothing good will come from the all-powerful and treacherous Russian authorities. Oh, what times we live in! Even our brothers nearby entertain wicked thoughts. Taking advantage of the constant clashes with the Russians for the land, they hope to get their hands on the Khan's power — you know who they are, for your father has told you. You must always remember that.'

Nuraly listened in silence and although he said nothing in reply, his face displayed a deep understanding and acceptance of his mother's words.

On Nuraly's orders, the Cossacks, pale and shivering in their tattered clothes, were brought from the underground dungeon, lined up and counted, the name of each of them recorded.

A short second lieutenant, hunched and with a red moustache, shouted in a shrill voice,

'At the wish of the all-merciful Governor-General of Orenburg, the Kaisak Khan Abulkhair today releases you from captivity and graciously grants you his pardon!'

Nuraly tightened his grip on the reins to his dapple stallion that was shifting from foot to foot and chomping at the bit, and turned to the messenger Seitmurat:

'Tell our warriors to keep a permanent eye on these men from the moment they begin to leave our borders and until they have crossed the Ustyurt Plateau! Make sure they have provisions and water for the journey. It is important to us that they all make it there without casualties. Such is the command of the Khan!' With these words, he pointed his folded whip at the released prisoners.

The messenger Seitmurat nodded his understanding of Nuraly-Sultan's orders.

'It will be done, sire, just as you have said!'

Several months before this, in the latter half of May that same year, a heavily armed Cossack detachment had crossed the upper reaches of the Zhaiyk, climbed the Munalzhar mountains and, before reaching the River Zhem, had come face to face with Abulkhair's army. The mountain slopes, fragrant with blossoming young wormwood, and the steppe, lulled in the rays of the springtime sun, shuddered to the thunderous sound of battle.

Nuraly fought at the head of the Kazakh army alongside the batyrs Myrzatai and Shotan. The Cossacks, intent on reaching the Zhem, attacked day and night. The auls along the banks of the river, which had just made it through the winter and moved to the spring pastures, had not managed to embark on their usual steppe routine when they found themselves engulfed by endless battles.

The entire steppe was filled with mournful lamentation when Abulkhair and his army reached the site of the battle from his summer base at the point where the River Kabyrga flowed close to the deep Torgai. Abulkhair turned pale and his broad brow was furrowed with the deepest lines. It looked as if he had stopped breathing and with each passing moment, his facial expression became sterner from the rising wave of anger from inside. Nuraly needed no words to realise they were facing a life-or-death battle with an insidious enemy.

Abulkhair clearly felt in his gut that after the Russians attacked from the north, multiple detachments of their Kalmyk henchmen would follow suit from the opposite side. The Orenburg governor-general intended to send armed Cossack Russians to the lands lying along the Zhaiyk and the Zhem and crush the Khan's seat there, thus forcing the Khan to yield to Saint-Petersburg's wishes. In order to break the Khan once and for all, Governor-General Neplyuev had also hoped to provoke an attack by the Bashkirs.

The Khan's army planned to deceive the enemy detachments by allowing them to cross the Zhem and, pretending to retreat, lure them further away, lie in wait, having split into three groups, meet them first head-on and then squeeze them from both sides.

The Cossack detachment fell for this strategy, reached the river and crossed to the other side without meeting any resistance. Failing to place any importance on the fact that, for some reason, the Khan's army was not engaging in battle, the Cossacks believed they had won. Myrzatai and Shotan, too, had not realised Abulkhair's move straight away. However, they felt that there had to be a trap involved because the Khan, who had been through so many battles, would not risk allowing heavily armed enemies to penetrate deep into their lands in order to meet in open battle.

Abulkhair himself remained with the central detachment while the main forces were spread to the flanks: Shotan to the right and Myrzatai to the left, both in full readiness to launch their attack. Once the enemy troops had been drawn as close as possible, the keen-eyed archers released a shower of arrows on the front lines. Many enemy soldiers were killed instantly, unable to defend themselves in time. The Cossacks had barely begun to regain their senses when an avalanche of men with spears bore down on them from both sides, leaving them no opportunity to escape.

Shotan, an experienced horseback warrior from his youth, shone in this battle. Myrzatai, too, was equally fearsome in battle with spears. Even Abulkhair could not hide his admiration for the archers with their pinpoint accuracy from the saddle. The Cossacks, accustomed to fighting with guns and cannons, did not expect such a response from the Khan's horsemen, who were armed with nothing but bows, arrows and spears. The enemies panicked, scattered and, despite fierce resistance, could do nothing, so they were forced to spread out across the wormwood steppe like moss over a stone.

During this battle, when the Khan's troops crushed the Russian Cossack detachments, hitting them from three sides, Nuraly had fought alongside his father. Abulkhair's wisdom and courage in confidently commanding his troops allowed Nuraly to see for himself the mighty warrior who had fought off the large Kalmyk army and emerged victorious at the battles of Bulantin and Anyraqai. Nuraly felt immense pride for his father, but he was worried for him standing at the heart of the battle.

The release of the prisoners who had been seized in that battle not only showed the Khan's desire to ensure peaceful relations with the Russian authorities, who were prone to guile and deceit, but also acted as a deterrent against armed incursions that sought to violate the integrity of their land. Nuraly clearly sensed his father's frame of mind and understood his intentions: they needed time to unite their kinsmen who had been scattered all over the vast steppe and who were tired of the never-ending wars with enemies attacking from all sides.

The Orenburg Governor Neplyuev, a cunning and experienced courtier, understood the essence of Abulkhair's strategy but he had no intention of showing any reciprocal friendliness. Realising that he could not subjugate the Khan's seat while Abulkhair remained at the helm, the governor decided to set Barak-Sultan against him, sowing confusion and further inflaming the enmity they already felt for one another. He knew that neither Abulkhair nor Barak would yield and that their confrontation could prove to be brutal. Neplyuev refused to see the return of prisoners-of-war after the crushing defeat on the banks of the Ural and Emba as a peace-making gesture and, instead, he was greatly angered and harboured a serious grudge.

* * *

In the middle of June, when the Seven Sisters were still concealed beyond the horizon, a string of horses and camels headed southwest from the Khan's summer camp on the banks of the Irgiz. The caravan was on its way to the distant camping grounds of Syuindyk's Tabyn clan.

Out in front, under a red-green silk canopy, rode Bopai in a wide wagon, seemingly floating across the steppe. During the journey, she barely ever left her comfortable wagon, except for the occasional ride on her magnificent bay stallion in the cool of the morning or at sunset. Abulkhair followed alongside the wagon with five or six of his nökers and several warriors.

This large caravan also included a small retinue of servants, who followed after a dozen dromedaries, all laden with gifts that Bopai had prepared for her family. There were ornamented chests, boxes of food, leather wineskins and wooden tubs, in which koumis and camel's milk *shubat* were replenished on the way.

Young singers and musicians, *Palauan* wrestlers and falconers kept the travellers entertained on their journey. From time to time, Bopai happily joined the other singers in performing her favourite songs in her delightful voice. Abulkhair amused himself by hunting with falconers without straying far from the main party.

The luxurious caravan moved on without stopping. Having set off at first light from the Karakia Hollow, the party reached the foot of the mountain ridge by noon. Bopai, dressed lightly and comfortably for riding, rode on her bay horse, looking out over the vast plain where she had spent her carefree youth, and a warm feeling came over her that she had returned for a moment to that delightful time so long ago. Standing on the border of her native land, Bopai felt as if she were experiencing the same excitement from when her fate had first been entwined with Abulkhair.

Abulkhair looked over at Bopai and noticing her excitement and how unusually pensive she seemed, he too indulged in fond memories of his distant youth, lost in the labyrinth of all the years that had passed since then.

No sooner had word reached the Adai elite that Abulkhair was travelling to visit his wife's family in their homeland than guests came hurrying from all over to Syuindyk's aul. It was not simply a gathering of the representatives of different auls but rather a special occasion to greet a respected son-in-law — the Khan himself. The batyrs who had once fought side-by-side with Abulkhair, the distinguished biys and the wealthy bais of the Alim, Tama and Tabyn clans were all eager to make it to the ceremony.

The rich bai Sakinbai, whose numerous herds grazed in the valley along the banks of the rivers Zhem, Sagyz and Kenzhaly, was particularly keen to meet with Abulkhair-Khan. This respected biy and batyr had been a trusted companion of the Khan in his youth.

Soon, like the crests of waves from a vast sea, white yurts of the large aul of the Tabyn Adai clan appeared on the back of the Elek. The village daughters-in-law greeted the guests wearing light *kimeshek* headdresses and snow-white headscarves, long dresses to the ankles with frills, and velvet doublets decorated with gold embroidery. The women generously showered the guests with sweet confetti of *kurt* cheese, Samarkand sugar *nabat* and dried fruits.

Bopai emerged from the wagon, to which two ginger

horses were harnessed. With a bright smile on her lean face, she went over to the women throwing the confetti. Abulkhair pulled the reins on his grey-white steed and, leaping easily to the ground, hurried over to join Bopai. The new arrivals, who had arrived with the son-in-law Khan, were tired after their ten-day journey, but the heartfelt reception somehow gave them new energy and they headed to the sixteen-panel white yurt of Tegisbai-Batyr from the Tabyn clan. Tegisbai was in his mid-fifties yet held himself proud and upright, defying the passage of time. This tall, broad-shouldered batyr, with a powerful neck, prominent features and sharp eyes, met his guests in person.

Abulkhair greeted Tegisbai, looking him in the eye, and then, as befitting the younger man, bowed his head and extended both arms, saying,

'Assalamu alaikum, batyr-aga!'

'Wa alaikum as-salam, my dear Khan! Welcome to your kith and kin! Please come through.'

The elders Azhibai-biy, Aral, Altai, the batyrs Shotan and Myrzatai parted to let the other guests into the luxuriously decorated yurt, but Abulkhair let Bopai pass ahead and, without heading for the seat of honour, positioned himself a little lower, on the right side of the *tor*.

The old men from the Tabyn clan and the younger men too were shocked by Abulkhair's gesture, but the master of the house, Tegisbai, remarked,

'Brothers, dear Adai folk, our Khan always takes the seat of honour among his people, but for the Adai, he is a son-in-law! Abulkhair knows the customs! So, you elders of the Alim and Tabyn clans, dear Eset-Batyr, Boke, come through and take your places of honour!'

'Well, that told us!'

The distinguished elders conversed while the delicious shubat and koumis, fresh from the morning, were being served, with tea at the abundant table spread. Abulkhair spoke only occasionally, most of the time preferring to remain silent and listen. He wanted to hear the words that would help him understand the mood of the people and their thoughts on what was happening in the steppe.

'We are concerned about the well-being of the land of our fathers, our vast steppe that begins on the banks of the Zhaiyk and the Edil and ends at the Ustyurt Plateau at the other end. And we are not talking solely about our pastures but, above all, about the fate of all twenty-five clans of our people, including the Argyns and the Kipchaks, who have joined us from the north. How has it come to pass that everyone is now experiencing such difficult times?!' Azhibai-biy paused briefly and cast his eyes over everyone seated around him. 'Is this really to be the fate of the Kazakh people, that we are destined to fight continually for our lands and live in constant battles with our enemies?'

'Oh, Azh-aga, these conflicts and clashes have been going on for a long time, since the beginning of human history. Some want to dominate and fight to seize land and subjugate people. Others strive not to surrender to these invaders and make every effort to stand their ground. This is the law of life. This was how it was before us and so it will be after we have gone, so what can we do in the face of this eternal struggle?' Shotan's pleasant voice sounded calm and even. 'Only one thing worries me: what kind of state will we leave for our descendants? We should be able to show courage and make the right decisions, so our enemies would not laugh in our faces and our friends would not gloat.'

'That is the case, and who would doubt it?!' Sakinbai-biy replied, turning to face him. 'Everyone has these thoughts, Shotan. And we understand and feel your words and thoughts, Azhibai. So, what can we do about it? It is not for all of us simply to shift this burden onto Abulkhair's shoulders and sit and wait. How can we support our young Khan, who has brought all the Kazakh people together and who does everything possible to preserve its unity? How can we properly unite and preserve the very foundations of our state? Will we allow our enemy in the north to place fetters on our people, who are exhausted and have shed so much blood in wars with the Kalmyks as it is? Or is there still a way to resist and prevent our destruction?! Let us all think about what we can advise our Khan, who is pursuing a policy with the Russians without war while at the same time trying to preserve our independence.'

Since Abulkhair was a sultan, Sankibai, known for his generosity, was his faithful companion and friend and helped him by supplying the army with hardy horses suitable for the difficult marching conditions. The many herds that belonged to Sankibai were grazing back then in a vast fertile valley in the floodplain of four rivers, the Zhem, Sagyz, Temir and Oyl. Bopai knew well that Abulkhair had great respect for Sankibai-Biy and valued their long-standing friendship. Even now, Sankibai was one of the wealthiest owners of thousands of horses in these parts. However, he was also well known for having fought numerous times — alongside Azhibai, Aral, Eset, Shotan and Esbolai — against the Torgauts who would rustle horses from spring to autumn and attack the auls of the local Alim, Adai and Zhetir people from the lower reaches of the Zhem. It was for this that Abulkhair particularly respected Sankibai. On this occasion, too, Abulkhair listened attentively and respectfully to Sankibai's concerned words at the dinner in Tegisbai's yurt.

Tegisbai-Batyr also very much liked the thoughtful and sensible words of Sankibai, a man who held considerable sway in the Shekhti clan. However, he kept his feelings to himself, deciding to wait to hear what the Khan would say.

Bopai had not missed a single word or gesture of the elders and looked at Abulkhair, who was seated by her side. The Khan was silent for a while, evidently deep in thought. Without doubt, the distinguished nobles who had gathered there had accurately pointed to the problems with the current domestic and foreign policy of the Horde, of which he was the Khan.

'Distinguished elders, I thank you on behalf of the people and personally for your words. You know well that I have strengthened the Khanate over all these years, not for the sake of my power over the people alone. When the Dzungars invaded from the east, it was not in vain that we bloodied their crafty noses. The point was not to destroy the integrity of our land and people. When we maintained our unity, we crushed the enemy. Our task now is to safeguard our land by peaceful means, never to bow our heads and never fall to our knees. However, if anyone dares to obstruct this path or apply undue pressure from the outside, we will fight back and put up a merciless resistance! We are faced with a difficult choice. We might need to make sacrifices, but I am confident we will not shed tears or display cowardice! And we will leave this covenant for our descendants, brothers!' Abulkhair paused before continuing: 'As for me, this is what I have to say to all my relatives gathered here. Dear kinsmen, could I really remain at peace, happy only with the title of Khan, shirking the responsibility that was entrusted to me by the Kurultai? Turning my back on the aspirations of the respected elders, biys and batyrs of the three zhuzes? If I could do that, it would be a display of unacceptable weakness. I am not capable of such a thing — neither my lineage nor my conscience would allow it!'

'Well said, Abeke!'

'You have perfectly expressed our innermost thoughts!'

'Such words!'

Once the elders had voiced their approval of Abulkhair's words, Tegisbai also decided to speak.

'Well, most-respected Azhibai-aga, honoured descendant of Alim, the eldest clan of the Junior Zhuz, you shall recite the *bata* blessing over today's special meeting of our guests.' Saying this, he turned his outstretched palms upwards.

Azhibai-biy stroked his thick white beard with long fingers, also opened his palms and turned his brightened face to Abulkhair.

'May Shadiyar be your friend, Muhammad be your support, Kyzir be your companion, Lukpan, your faithful comrade, and may the spirits of your ancestors guide and support you wherever you go![17] May good fortune accompany you on your journey! Almighty Allah, our praise is due to you alone! Accept the sincere prayers from the pure intentions of all those seated here beneath the shanyrak of Tegisbai, the noble son of the Adai people! Allah Akbar!' With that, Tegisbai placed a hand on his chest, an expression of his gratitude to Azhibai for his blessing.

'Friends! Brothers! The ceremony to mark the arrival of our honoured guests — our son-in-law Abulkhair-Khan and daughter of our clan Bopai — will continue with various contests. *Baiga* horseracing! *Audaryspak* horseback wrestling and Palauan wrestling! The undefeated strongman Balta from the Ali-Adai clan will fight here today!' Tegisbai declared loudly. 'Well, Myrzatai, escort our guests, if you will.'

The young Palauan wrestler Balta, barely older than twenty, was on the summer pasture of Syuindyk's aul that day purely by chance. Having no animals of his own, either for riding or for carrying, Balta was pulling a four-wheeled cart by its short handles along the road that ran parallel to the Amu Darya. The cart was laden with a two-camel load of ten or so sacks of flour and some other provisions, which he had received in exchange for wool and leather. Not far

---

[17] Shadiyar — an Egyptian sultan revered by Muslims; Mohammed — the main prophet of Islam; Kyzyr — a mythical character of the Turks, the patron of all people and a holy elder who gives blessings; Lukpan, or Lukpan Hakim — an artistic image in the folklore of Eastern peoples, a defender of his people who upheld justice and truth.

from the lands of the Mangyts and the Turkmens, Tegisbai had stopped him.

'I will give you a camel to harness to this cart; only linger a few days with me! You will demonstrate your strength and skill to the Khan. Wrestlers have been specially invited from the Esteks and Turkmens, and you will also be able to compete with the famous Palauan Kara from the Tabyn. You'll show what you're made of and, Allah willing, Balta, fortune will smile down upon you.' Tegisbai thus persuaded Balta to stay; he could hardly have refused.

'Let it be as you say, Tegisbai-aga! I will fight with anyone you like! You well know that if there is anyone who does not quail at the opportunity to fight me, then there is no way I can back down!'

'Oh, don't I know it, Bata! Make your preparations from today. We have already slaughtered a two-year-old lamb for you, with two large goatskins of koumis, sweetened with smoked *kazy* sausage, just for you! Tomorrow, you shall show off your courage and might before the Khan.'

'If necessary, I will fight with the Khan himself!' Balta replied, stretching his mouth into a broad grin and flexing his biceps for effect.

'You are most certainly a fearless batyr, Balta, and no mistake!'

'Well, and what did you think?!' Balta said, puffing out his chest and laughing out loud.

Having eaten half of the cooled meat in the morning and having tipped half a large goatskin bottle of cool koumis, Balta was full to the brim and, twisting his thick neck, with the words: 'Oh, Almighty Allah, in You alone I trust!' he jumped up from his seat.

The assembled guests, overtaking Abulkhair and his group of dignitaries, flocked from both sides to where the Palauan wrestlers were to fight. Bets were placed and soon, the famous, undefeated fighter Kara strode majestically into the centre of the circle, flexing the powerful muscles on his arms and thighs to face the young Balta in the first bout. Balta deftly fought off the over-confident, arrogant Kara's strong arms as he tried to grab him around the waist. The broad-shouldered, muscular Kara, who was an inch shorter than Balta, had not expected such a response from the young fighter, and his eyes flashed angrily, taunting his opponent.

However, just as he was about to grasp his opponent's right shoulder and bring him down, Balta twisted around and grabbed him by the hip, causing him to stagger. Kara quickly managed to regain his footing and took up his stance once more. Realising that he was facing a serious opponent, Balta summoned all his strength and, at the moment the angry Palauan rushed at him, he grabbed him under the arms at lightning speed, lifted his wide feet from the ground and brought him crashing down onto his back. Kara was laid flat on his shoulder blades. The famous wrestler punched the ground in frustration and, crushed by his first defeat, took a good while to recover, kneeling on the ground with his head down.

In the next round, a confident, strong Turkmen could not get the better of Balta either.

The final came and a Bashkir Tatar wrestler called Baishagir entered the circle. He was slow but very strong and, thus, looked rather like a bull. He had no doubt he would take the first prize in the contest, organised to mark the arrival of Abulkhair-Khan. Showing off his broad shoulders and puffing out his chest, Baishagir stared defiantly at Balta and screwed up his nose disdainfully. Then, rubbing his hands together, he rushed at Balta, standing opposite. He grabbed him around the waist and tried to throw him to the ground but could not even move him. The very next moment, Balta struck the clumsy man sharply on the knee, making him stagger but not fall. The bull-like Baishagir jumped out of the way, ducked and confidently advanced towards his opponent. Balta extended his right arm, suddenly grabbed Baishagir under the arm and threw him over his shoulder. The bull-like man was unable to control his heavy body and fell onto his back; Balta pinned him down with all his weight, giving him no opportunity to move.

Balta stood in the centre of the circle with his feet firmly planted on the ground, and that was the moment of his victory, to the great joy of Tegisbai and all the Adai people who were cheering for him.

Abulkhair and Bopai truly admired this young Palauan, who had taken down his opponents, one after the other, with his strength, energy and agility.

'Abeke, give a special prize to the victor, your Adai brother!' Bopai said, looking at Abulkhair with a kindly smile. 'This young man has proven himself worthy of the first prize, so let the Khan's offering elevate and glorify him before everyone!'

Abulkhair-Khan stepped forward and, surrounded by cheering spectators, placed a green velvet chapan gown with a beaver collar on Balta's shoulders and a beaver hat on his head.

'My people, there is another gift — a *tai-tuyak*[18] of sorts from our family to the best wrestler, who has brought glory to his clan. My wife, the daughter of your clan, will present the prize.

Abulkhair looked over at Bopai and nodded her over. Bopai entered the centre of the circle with a nugget of gold the size of a horse's hoof in her extended palms. Taking the tai-tuyak, which glistened in the rays of the sun, Balta bowed his head before the Khan and Khanum, placing his right hand on his chest in reverence... In just a few days, the stories of the respected elders and nobles about the honour that the Khan had granted the young Adai wrestler and

---

[18] A percussion instrument made from the hooves of animals

about Abulkhair's fiery speech at Tegisbai's home spread to all corners of the vast steppe.

***

During the final days of his stay with his wife's relatives, Abulkhair decided to visit the holy sites and honour the memory of his ancestors at Saraishyk, two days' travel towards the Naryn sands, just beyond the town of Uishik on the banks of the Zhaiyk. They left their wagon and travelled on horseback, and they were joined by a group headed by Shotan and Myrzatai from the Adai aul.

Nearing noon two days later, the town of Saraishyk appeared beyond a bend in the right bank of the lower reaches of the Zhaiyk.

'And there is Saraishyk! There, look, beyond that bend!'

Myrzatai's loud voice startled Bopai, who was riding her piebald colt on the other side of Abulkhair.

Abulkhair pulled the reins on his grey-white stallion and came to a halt. The others also brought their horses to a stop.

'Here we are at this sacred place, where we will offer a prayer in memory of our ancestors,' Abulkhair said, gazing across the deep Zhaiyk to the opposite side. 'We are standing on the threshold of an ancient city founded by the Golden Horde more than two centuries ago. Both the Kazakhs and the Nogai people lived here. It was from here that Edigei and Kasym Khan ruled — if we delve deeper, then even Zhanibek raised his standard here.'

Trying not to deviate from the route that once led to a bridge from the eastern to the western banks, the travellers followed their mounted guides to the opposite side, where the waters were shallower and the course narrower.

Barely visible against the greying soil, light-coloured hillocks were all that remained of the city walls. Abulkhair was truly dismayed at the sight. Bopai's heart ached from the feeling a child gets when orphaned. Myrzatai, Shotan and the other fellow travellers also looked at this image with a sense of melancholy. This city, once resplendent in luxurious mosques with blue vaulted domes and tall minarets extending their splendour to the heavens, with wide streets and narrow alleys alike, all bustling with life, now stood before them as nothing more than small heaps of earth. There was a time when overseas travellers compared Saraishyk to the paradise that was Baghdad — it was a major trading centre on a crossroads on the Silk Road that joined East and West, and now it was a mere mirage, shrivelled and haggard in deathly silence, weighed down by the cruel passage of time.

'I once heard from my late father Kazhy-Sultan that the body of Kasym Khan was buried at the site of his Khan's seat in Saraishyk, in a mausoleum with a beautiful vaulted ceiling. As a child, he and his father, Oseke, my grandfather, used to visit this elaborately designed mausoleum. It is most likely located somewhere in the centre of the town,' Abulkhair said, turning to Shotan and Myrzatai once they had come right up to the hillocks where the town had once stood. 'If that is the case, it must be somewhere on that side. Let's go and take a look.'

They found a mound shaped like a high dome and knelt around it in a circle. Bopai knelt next to Abulkhair, half a turn of the circle from the other men, her lean, sun-tanned face turned a little to one side.

Myrzatai began by reciting *Al-Fatiha* and continued with the long verses of the *Ayatul Kursi* before nodding to Shotan and asking him to give the blessing. Opening their palms before them, all those kneeling around the site offered a prayer in memory of Kasym-Khan and Edigei. For a moment, the pilgrims gave themselves over to reflections, inspired by this legendary place that had now sunk into the ground with its vague memories of years gone by and the people who lived here.

Suddenly, a barely audible *kobyz*[19] melody reached Bopai's ears. She imagined the city gates opening wide to let in Edigei's warriors, whose return was heralded by a fanfare of trumpets. Through the depths of time, through an invisible yet palpable air of centuries gone by, the city rose proudly before her in all its beauty. Edigei himself, seated on his stallion, appeared before the travellers and, pulling on the reins, said, *Abulkhair, Bopai! You have come to these holy places from afar, to where my warriors and I once trod. You bow not only to my spirit — you offer a prayer and pay tribute to the memory of the capital of all the Nogai people! I charge you, my worthy descendants, to take your revenge on our old enemies who destroyed the city of Saraishyk. Do not consign this special place to oblivion — this place where your ancestors had their seat and where your fathers proved their heroism to all. May the eternal spirit of our forefathers never be erased from history's memory, to remain for centuries to come! May my eternal Saraishyk be a haven for you and a source of strength. May Allah help you!*

Bopai shuddered from this incredible vision, and she felt a truly thrilling sensation. The breath of that distant past touched her sensitive nature for only a moment, but that moment was enough to turn her heart completely upside down. Bopai's face was burning and a cold sweat broke out down her back. It seemed that the gift she had been given in her youth was making itself known again. Unnoticed by the others, Bopai turned to the west, in the direction of Holy Mecca, and uttered a *kalima*.

'This city of the Nogai, the clan of the famed Edigei, who took the people under his patronage, was destroyed by the Don Cossacks and razed to the ground by the cruel Russian Tsar Ivan, known for murdering his son. Neither our generation nor the generation to follow it can ever forgive such an act!' The companions could only sigh in sadness

---

[19] An ancient Kazakh string instrument with two horsehair strings. The resonating cavity is usually covered with goat leather.

when they heard Abulkhair's remarks, so full of bitterness and so heartfelt.

'Abeke, you say that our generation cannot forgive?' Bopai said in a quiet, trembling voice. 'Yes, that is true. But what is also undoubted is that our descendants will not be able to forgive such cruelty even two or three centuries from now! It is not possible to erase such things from the memory of those who strive with all their might to protect their land and their people. Unless we lose our unity and fall under a yoke that destroys our present, then this pain will remain in the memory of our future generations!'

Tears appeared in Bopai's sad eyes and slowly rolled down her delicate face, reflecting the surge of feelings that now engulfed her.

Returning to the Khan's seat after visiting relatives and then Saraishyk, Bopai understood and sensed like never before the true thoughts and feelings of Abulkhair, of which he spoke only seldom but always carried deep inside. His sole, cherished aim was to preserve the integrity of his people and his native land. In all the years they had been together, she had perhaps never felt so poignantly the heartache of this man who was so dear to her heart.

* * *

By the time the outline of the high mountains had appeared in the distance through the bluish haze, it was already past midday. The travellers had been on the road for a week but, so as not to become overly tired by the long journey, they had stopped for a couple of days and were now heading to the south-east, towards Temirastau Hill. Bopai left her light wagon, which was trundling along slowly yet swaying violently, and mounted her grey-white colt horse, led by Temir, one of the Khan's guards. The empty wagon and the other transport with the load for the journey were sent to the Khan's seat in the lowlands at the foot of the mountains.

Abulkhair steered his broad-chested piebald stallion towards Temirastau and moved on with several companions and Bopai, who had now joined them. Bektore trotted at the head of the group on an enormous roan steed with a white forelock. He was a tall man, sturdy yet mobile, despite being in his fifth *mushel*[20], and he was already sporting grey wisps at the end of his whiskers and beard. Bektore, their constant companion and guide on their long journeys, led them to Mani Aulie Hill, known as the Peak of Meaning.

Since the time of Genghis Khan, the horses of so many have left hoofprints on these tall hillsides along the Irgiz, from where a view of a boundless valley in bloom opened out on all sides as if it were in the palm of your hand. Committing to memory the first bloody attacks of the Kalmyks and the Dzungars, this elevated point, known as the Peak of Meaning, became a symbol of a mournful yet sacred period in the history of this land. This was the site of the Mani Aulie necropolis, the final resting place of a girl called Akbilek.

The higher the companions climbed the serpentine road, the more they felt the steppe wind from that holy land on their faces, a wind that filled Bopai's heart with its aura. The legend that reached her from the depths of time resonated like a distant melody in her memory. The necropolis, constructed from wide, flat black stones into a cone shape, much like a wedding headdress, rose from the hill where the young yet brave beauty Akbilek found her last shelter, and it seemed that her spirit was carried on that gentle breeze to caress Bopai's face.

Images appeared clearly to Bopai, one after the other, of that ancient legend that had been passed down from mouth to mouth through the generations.

---

[20] Equivalent to a 12-year period.

In those distant, cruel times, a supreme leader of the Dzungars, a *khuntaiji*, unleashed war and attacked the peaceful, defenceless people. Having laid waste to the people, he executed their leader and took his widow, with a child in the womb, for himself.

When the time came, the woman, now a concubine of her sworn enemy and in a foreign land, gave birth to a girl. The mother named her Akbilek. When the girl turned sixteen, her mother's heart, exhausted by years of sorrow and humiliation, began to ail from a serious illness. Realising that her time was running out, the woman decided to smuggle her only daughter back to the homeland of her fathers. One night, when the Dzungar leader had left on a hunt with his nökers and warriors, the poor woman, with help from a few decent people, released a young lad from his dungeon and gave him her final will, saying,

'My dear boy, I entrust my daughter to you! Please take her safely to her native land. I bless both of you on your journey home!'

They set out without delay on prepared horses, heading to the west. Knowing not how long they had travelled, when the fugitives had crossed the Turan Plain, leaving them just one day to the banks of the Irgiz, they noticed a pursuer drawing ever nearer.

'That is my Dzungar stepfather! He is riding his war horse, which can gallop tirelessly for three days. No other horse could have caught us so soon. I will hold him off and you carry on. Don't you think about me, just go!'

Akbilek placed an arrow in her bow and drew the bowstring back. At that moment, the Dzungar leader pulled on the reins and stopped his steed.

'Don't stand in my way! Turn your horse and return from whence you came! If you come any closer, this arrow will fly straight into your heart!' the girl cried out.

'I taught you archery when you were a child and now, I see your mother's blood runs hot through your veins! So, you've decided now to launch your arrow?!' Her Dzungar stepfather's face contorted with anger. 'If I had known things would come to this!'

He lowered his spear and, hooking it to his saddle, he turned his palms to Akbilek.

'May your hands never touch what your eyes ever see!' As he uttered his curse, he turned his restless horse sharply, dug in his spurs and galloped away.

Very soon after that, the warrior who had accompanied Akbilek returned.

'Oh, you should not have done that! You should not have returned. Anything could have happened on the way!'

The agitated Akbilek sadly cast her large, radiant eyes at the batyr who was looking at her ardently. Forgetting her stepfather's curse, she allowed this pure feeling to engulf her. Once things had calmed down, they were returning to their homeland to fulfil the innermost wishes of Akbilek's unfortunate mother. Once they reached the Irgiz, the fugitives stopped by a lake with banks densely covered with reeds and willow. They let the horses out to graze in the lush meadow and decided to rest and bathe. Hiding from the eyes of the smitten dzhigit, the innocent girl, full of youthful beauty, bathed in the shade of the reeds and rushes and failed to notice an enormous snake approaching her from the shore. It sank its venomous fangs into her breast and coiled itself around her snow-white, fragile body. Hearing the girl's frightened cry, the lad rushed to her and slashed the snake to shreds with his dagger. However, with the poison spreading all over Akbilek's body, she was losing strength and all she could do as she fell into unconsciousness was impart her single, final wish to the warrior who felt so passionately for her: 'Leave me here and place a sign over my grave, but do not give my name...'

And that is the legend, as passed down from ancient times. The warrior, they say, doomed to suffer eternal sadness, made a necklace from the spine of that cursed snake and wore it around his neck until his dying day as a symbol of his tragic love. To anyone who asked, he would always answer that there was a particular meaning. Who knows, perhaps the name of that hill Mani Aulie, the Peak of Meaning, has made it through to today from a legend that was very similar to the truth.

After Bektore had read the Surah *Yaseen*, Bopai, with palms facing up, repeated the *Amen* to herself and she could picture the beautiful girl who had died so young and innocent and who had made this place so sacred.

As the travellers descended from the Peak of Meaning, Mani Aulie, and continued to the Khan's seat, Bopai repeated her prayer over and over, from the depths of her heart,

Oh, pure and noble spirit of Mani Aulie, help our Khan in this troubled time to fulfil his honest deeds for the good of his native land and his sincere intent to achieve the cherished goal of the people! Let it be so!

CHAPTER 5

From early that morning, Governor-General Ivan Neplyuev had been feeling uneasy. He paced back and forth in his vast office, from the doorway to the tall, ornate windows that looked out onto the sunny side, but he simply could not rid himself of the thoughts that troubled him. Since early autumn, Abulkhair-Khan had clashed periodically with Ural Cossack detachments, once even attacking the fortress at Uishik, and it was clear he was in no mood to compromise. Neplyuev clearly understood that the Khan had no intention of submitting to the authority of the Tsarina and everything he was doing was nothing but a display of irreconcilable enmity. The Governor also knew that Abulkhair would do everything possible to return his son Kozhakhmet, who was in Orenburg under pledge. It was obvious that breaking that pledge agreement would aggravate the conflict. Of course, it would be Neplyuev who would be held primarily responsible for all of this.

The recent increase in the Kazakh Khan's military activity had forced the governor-general to give these matters serious thought. So, what was he to do? Neplyuev knew that dispatching Cossack detachments into open battle against Abulkhair's warriors would not help to break the Khan's seat. And yet, although he knew this, he did not consider alternative means because he could not turn away from his decision to conquer the nomadic people and subjugate them to tsarist authority. Not only that, but the general believed that the powers-that-be in Saint-Petersburg would likely support his idea to use an additional detachment of armed Kalmyks against Abulkhair — the Kalmyks who dreamed of annexing the Khan's lands to their Dzungaria.

At lunchtime, a neat-looking adjutant, Staff Captain Makhorin, interrupted the general, who was deep in thought, and explained to him that two Kaisak envoys had arrived from the Khan's seat — the Alim batyr Seitkul Kudaikulov and the Kereu biy Kuttimbet Koshtayev — asking that he receive them as a matter of urgency.

'What's the urgency? What is it they want? Have they been sent here by Abulkhair himself? Find out, Staff Captain! And stop your dithering, man!'

Neplyuev looked at his adjutant with an angry frown.

Makhorin, accustomed to living on a knife's edge, had already prepared an answer:

'I have, Your Excellency! They say they are envoys sent personally by Abulkhair-Khan. I have also ascertained through the interpreter that they have with them a letter from the Khan addressed to you.'

'I se-e-e!' the general said, stretching his words in a harsh tone before hesitating with an answer for the adjutant who was awaiting instructions. Then he spoke, pale with rage: 'If they are here on the same matter — I am talking about the Khan's son Kozhakhmet — then there is no need for them to await my reception!'

'Understood, Your Excellency! However...' the staff captain said and then stammered something more inaudibly. The general looked back at him questioningly.

'What do you mean, "however"?'

'Judging by what they say, they have something that they must verbally convey to you personally from the Khan.'

'If that is the case, then the Khan should come himself and not relay this and that while sitting importantly at his Khan's seat. You send those men back right away; I will not receive them! Get to it!'

Neplyuev saw the arrival of the envoys as a threat from Abulkhair, the latest demonstration by the Khan of his unwillingness to bow before the Russian authorities and even disdain for Neplyuev's high-ranking position.

For a good while, Neplyuev was unable to recover his senses. *As long as the power at the Khan's seat remains in the* hands of this Abulkhair, the threat they pose is serious, which means that something must be done urgently to remove him. If these wild nomads suddenly rise up and begin attacking, it won't be easy to stop them. We need to find someone among the Kaisaks whom we can set against Abulkhair; we need to establish ties with the sultans who are vying for power, for if we don't, these bloody confrontations will never end.* Looking out of the huge window at the clouds floating low in the autumn Orenburg sky, the general finally made up his mind about what he would do.

* * *

Somewhere nearby, the young sultan Kozhakhmet heard a girl's voice singing a sad song.

*The Ural's been stolen, the Emba too,
Deprived of the Volga and my friend.
So what is there left in this life so blue?
Tell if you know, when will this all end?*

Kozhakhmet had been transferred for on business to the office of Ataman Alexei Sokolov in the town of Sorochinsk, which stood at the confluence of the Samara River, which originated in Orenburg, into the Volga. He lived in conditional captivity, more or less as a pledged hostage near the military garrison in a small wooden house with two little windows.

The warming song stirred the young sultan's heart and captured his attention. *I wonder who that could be?* he said to himself and looked out of the half-open window into the courtyard, but he could see no one. It was a fine day in May and a pleasant breeze was blowing. The song's sad words caused him even greater consternation, for the girl's voice was so full of sadness.

They'll take the Volga, and with it my home,

> *So, will I then be left all alone?*
> *My soul will die, if the Ural you take.*
> *Who will then help when my life's at stake?*
> *Once the Oyl is gone, memories will fade,*
> *So pity the lost; come to our aid!*

Emerging onto his threshold, Kozhakhmet noticed a very young, slender Nogai girl with a fair, charming face fetching water from the well on the other side of the street. It was she who was singing the melancholy song, swaying slowly, leaning on the well beam.

> *Dressed in the black velvet of the forest*
> *Our lands they will just fade away,*
> *And lauded by their cunning words,*
> *Our lads will march into the fray.*

Catching sight of the young dzhigit with the wispy moustache, looking at her with confused and bashful eyes, the young songstress abruptly stopped singing and let the pail attached to the wheel clatter down to the bottom.

What a delightful voice she has! She probably serves one of the local wealthy Cossacks or Russians, no doubt, Kozhakhmet thought to himself. With a tingling sensation inside and filled with longing for his homeland, the young sultan involuntarily walked over to the girl without once taking his eyes from her.

Her large eyes glistened in anticipation and she blushed. She didn't know what to say to the shy lad who silently helped her pull her pail of water from the well. Kozhakhmet himself could find no words himself. They gestured in silence and both understood one another perfectly — suddenly, they smiled at one another, unable to find another way of conversing.

'I am Nafisa. And you are?'

'Kozhakhmet. You know, you sang just like my other;

your voices are so similar!'

'It is a sad song and I cannot sing it when my masters might hear, so I sing whenever I am alone.'

'So, they don't like it, do they?'

'That's right because they don't like the Nogai. Because of this hatred, way back when, they took our native lands and dispersed the people.'

Nafisa bent down, hooked both pails of crystal-clear water to her yoke, glanced with a smile at Kozhakhmet and hurried off along the street.

That chance meeting with that young Nogai girl stirred the heart of the young sultan. He might not have been a prisoner under house arrest, but he had been under the watchful eyes of the Russian authorities, far from his native land and his loved ones, and deprived of his parental love and affection. All this tormented him with longing and sadness, and Nafisa's singing reminded him of the voice of his beloved mother, Bopai. Kozhakhmet had been a child at a conscious age when he had heard those tender melodies from his mother and now those songs had echoed once more in his memory.

The term for the return of the pledge had been postponed with each passing year and Kozhakhmet could not help thinking that relations between Orenburg and the Khan's seat must have come to a head, something that did not improve his mood. The image of the attractive Nogai girl, singing about the sadness of her people, had at least brightened the grey of the humdrum life, like a ray of sunshine in those seemingly never-ending dreary days. From that moment on, Kozhakhmet made it a habit to look from his window the moment he awoke, excited in anticipation of another meeting. Wishing so dearly to hear Nafisa's pure voice again, he could not shake off his sense of longing for her. However, the bright-eyed maiden never returned to the well for water. Soon, the town ataman received an order from the Orenburg general to transfer

Kozhakhmet to Kazan, where he would henceforth fulfil his duties as the *amanat* pledge. The young sultan realised that he would not be returning to the Khan's seat any time soon and the fact that he was hardly likely ever to see that fair-faced girl with the melancholy again only added to his sadness. How could he possibly find Nafisa, who served in one of the wealthy houses of the Russian Cossacks in this, albeit small, fortress town? And even if he did find her, how would he get to meet with her? Kozhakhmet was quite beside himself because of his feelings for the sad beauty who had disappeared just as suddenly as she had appeared across the street. He so wanted to see her again, talk with her and get to know her better. All of his desires were now focused on that wonderful songstress, who had illuminated his monotonous life and excited his heart.

Ataman Sokolov wanted to send the Khan's son to Kazan as soon as he could, but Kozhakhmet kept finding reasons to postpone his departure. Under the pretext of having to gather his many things for the journey, he had managed another couple of days of delay. However, he still gazed out in vain across the street to where the well stood. For an unknown reason, the Nogai girl for whom he had fallen quite passionately never did return to that well for water. Day and night, Kozhakhmet would visualise Nafisa in his mind's eye. As for her, having bewitched the young lad with her radiant smile, she did not even guess about his feelings. Gradually, Kozhakhmet's dream of meeting Nafisa again began to fade. The songstress never did grant the sultan the happy opportunity to see or hear her again.

And so, the day of his departure finally came. The wagon, drawn by four pairs of choice stallions, accompanied by a mounted guard of honour on either side, took the young sultan away to the distant, glorious city, and Kozhakhmet had never seen his sad beauty again, having fleetingly touched his heart and stirred his soul with sweet longing.

***

Abulkhair, who had been in a bad mood since the morning, sat alone in his large yurt home and only occasionally asked Bopai to bring fresh koumis, prepared the day before from the evening milking of the mares. Seeing that the Khan was perturbed by something and was deep in thought, Bopai forbade the servants from entering the home unless essential so as not to disturb him.

The Khan was seriously concerned by the alarming news about Turken-Zhaumites, who were unrelenting in their aggression at the border on the southern side of the Ustyurt Plateau.

The Turkmen batyrs Bori, Kakhar, Kylysh and Berdioglan intended to return the lands that had belonged to them before Genghis Khan's conquests — the valley stretching from the eastern edge of the Aral Sea to the Mangystau peninsula, which was under the authority of the Khan. This was why armed Turkmen detachments had ventured on their campaign. Bokenbai, now in his seventies, asked for the Khan's support to send multiple detachments of Adai and Tabyn warriors, led by his son-in-law Eset from the Tama clan and the young Batyr Baikozy, sent specially from the Argyns by Shakshak Zhanibek, as a matter of urgency to the other side of the Ustyurt Plateau, from the sands of Sam and the Matai saltmarshes. It was this news that had caused Abulkhair to think so hard. He was well aware that Bokenbai, whom he had known for many years and with whom he had fought shoulder-to-shoulder in battle, would have good reason to become so wound up and prepared for battle despite his age. Although he understood this, who could guarantee that the Volga Kalmyks and the Cossacks, relying heavily on the Russian authorities, would not take advantage of this moment? The Khan shared his thoughts with Bopai that there could be no indiscretion here.

'My Khan, Abeke, our Bokenbai cannot but know or sense that there will be no peace for the people until we have repelled the Turkmens from the South. Our enemies from the north-west, who are ready and raring to rush in to attack, will most likely exercise caution too, for they know that the Turkmens will not let them get away with it if they were to go in, along the Edil, the Zhaiyk and the straits of the sea. If they are in their right mind, they will think twice before attacking us at this time. As you well know, the borders and the rearguard of the Khan's seat are strengthened by batyrs led by Nuraly and they do everything to protect us. We will ask Allah for patience for the valiant Bokenbai, whose honour never waivers.'

'Yes, my wife, we will ask Allah for his patience. That is what we will do. I know Bokenbai well — he will not falter in this campaign. Let us take the risk and hope for victory!'

At dusk, a messenger galloped from the Khan's seat with a positive response for Bokenbai.

Receiving the Khan's message, Bokenbai's thousand-strong army moved forward and, just past midnight, crossed the Ustyurt Plateau. With the first rays of the sun, the warriors descended to the lowland plain spread out before them on the western side of the plateau.

Bokenbai was already feeling his age — he was tired from riding in the saddle for so long, unlike in his youth, and his body had become heavier. However, the annoyance from his fatigue would not stop him. His burning desire to reach his goal and his fierce determination drove him on. An experienced and proud warrior, Bokenbai was more confident than ever that he would crush the enemy that stood bristling in anticipation of its prey, and there was nothing that could stop him. There could be no doubt that it was this unshakeable confidence that spurred him on and kept him going the entire journey.

Eset-Batyr noticed the still fiery glint in the eyes of the elderly Bokenbai-Batyr, who had never lost heart, even in the bloodiest of battles. Bokenbai, full of his warrior's passion, was like an eagle searching for its prey. Eset concluded from this that no one else could emerge victorious in the pending battle — he might be older, but he was still an immensely powerful batyr.

The Turkmen guards and scouts, who had carefully watched over their surroundings from their elevated position, first heard the rumbling of hooves from the north, followed after a short time by a mass army of Kazakhs advancing towards them in thick clouds of dust.

Armed to the teeth and ready for the fight, the warriors Kylysh and Bori bided their time. Splitting into two flanks, they decided to strike from both sides simultaneously.

From the very outset, the Turkmen batyrs knew that Bokenbai would command the Kazakh army. Deep inside, they had been hoping that the ageing commander had lost his former power and would be wholly unable to overpower them. However, the rapidly advancing Kazakh army made them anxious.

The warriors from both sides brought their war horses to a stop, facing one another just an arrow's flight apart.

'Hey, Bokenbai-Batyr! Come closer! Come on out! Come on!' the Turkmen batyr Kylysh shouted curtly with unrestrained anger in his voice, shaking his steel spear above his head.

The consolidated Kazakh army under Bokenbai was now right up close and it wasn't long before they were engaged in a fierce battle once the Turkmens had rushed at them in a furious attack. In the first moments of the battle, the ears rang with the wild roars and squeals of horses, the clanging of spears and sabres, and the shouts and groans of the soldiers. It seemed that the steppe itself, which had been lying not that long before in peaceful silence, was now screaming in terror, awakened by the thunderous noise of a cruel and bloody battle.

The Turkmens, initially bold and full of vigour, soon

became confused by the direct and powerful Kazakh onslaught that pounded them from all sides. They fought off attacks and evaded encirclement, but they could not make a decisive rebuff. Kylysh realised that he had almost no chance remaining to kill Bokenbai himself, as he had wished from the very outset, so he circled the formation and rushed right at the Kazakh batyr, who was fighting in the centre of the fierce fighting on his dapple-grey stallion. At that very moment, aiming his long spear at Bokenbai, the bloodthirsty Bori had sneaked up in a lowly fashion and thrust his spear into the Kazakh's thigh as he was busy fighting off Kylysh. Bokenbai swayed a little, sat back upright, took his sharp sabre and sliced the tip of the spear that had pierced his body and was tearing at his flesh. Eset-Batyr suddenly appeared before the complacent Kylysh, engaged him in a battle of sabres and, with a swift and dextrous movement, sliced his head from his shoulders. He was about to rush at Bori when Bokenbai stopped him short: 'Hold it right there! Leave him to me! I'll finish this damned jackal off myself!'

Sensing Bokenbai's fury, Bori turned to launch another attack but only managed to see the large grey horse coming at him at full speed and the glint of a blade. Bori's head dropped to the ground and rolled away.

Bokenbai did not even notice in the heat of the battle. At one moment in the battle, an old Adai warrior and healer managed to pull the almost ten-centimetre-long tip of the Turkmen spear from Bokenbai's thigh and, applying ash-treated felt to the bleeding wound, bandaged it with a clean white cloth. Wiping the cold sweat from his brow, Bokenbai walked to his horse, put his foot in the stirrup and jumped into the saddle as if nothing had happened.

'Almighty Allah, grant out priceless batyr and valiant Bokenbai the strength and resolve!' the warrior-healer said in prayer, passing his hands over his face and twirling his sparse, short beard. 'Give him strength!'

Bokenbai spared the sole remaining Turkmen voivode Berdioglan and his now battle-scarred cavalry, now no more than a hundred in number. Eset and Baikozy appreciated this shrewd move by the batyr.

'Hey, Zhaumite-Turkmen Berdioglan! I know that you simply don't have any arrows left to kill me right here. I respect your sense of dignity; believe me. You are lucky to be alive. So, just don't think about vengeance, for it is you who attacked us because of the ancient history surrounding the lands here. We didn't touch you. In the end, what happened is what happened. I hope that you will pass on to your people that we do not tolerate others encroaching on our land and trying to dominate and rule us. Now, return to the place from whence you came and do not dare to bring your war to us again!'

In the sunny April days of 1742, Bokenbai's army, after crushing the Turkmens, headed off in a large nomadic party, with horses and camels, to the native lands of the Tabyn, to the north-west of the Ustyurt Plateau. The detachment — after losing a number of its brave warriors but with honour and dignity intact — was led by Bokenbai himself despite being badly wounded in that battle.

Although Bokenbai tried not to succumb, the wound from the spear did not heal and his condition steadily worsened. Two months later and the batyr passed on from this life. All the people from the Tabyn, Adai and Alim clans mourned the loss of Bokenbai, who lost his final battle — the battle with his wound, and no one felt this grief more than Abulkhair and Bopai.

The loss of his elder comrade and faithful colleague Bokenbai weighed heavily on Abulkhair; they had been brought together by the great Karakum Council thirty-two years before when the fate of the Kazakh people, worn down by battles with the Dzungars, was finally decided. Bokenbai had always been by his side in all important events to ensure the unity of the people: at the Battle of Anyraqai, where he led the army of three zhuzes and defeated their sworn enemies, bringing them to their knees, and in the most complex dealings with the Russian authorities, when they had needed to resort to all manner of tricks to reach an agreement. He was a brave warrior and a wise counsellor; who now would be able to fill the void left after Bokenbai's passing? Who else was there in this world and at that time who could offer him that level of support? Bopai alone could feel with all her heart how deep the loss was for Abulkhair and how difficult it was for him to cope with the burden of his grief.

During this time, the Khan's seat, based that summer on the banks of the Irgiz in a fertile valley at the foot of the Peak of Meaning in Temirastau received more visitors from all corners of the steppe and its remotest parts than anyone could count. The elders and batyrs, who came to share the Khan's grief and pay tribute to the memory of Bokenbai, were met by Nuraly-Sultan's men and accommodated according to status in specially erected, snow-white yurts of various sizes. Only after this did Nuraly himself bring them in turn to see the Khan.

Only Shakshak Zhanibek, accompanied by well-known biys and batyrs from the Argyn clan, were brought straight to the Khan. Bopai had instructed Nuraly to do this. Learning that Zhanibek was already nearing the borders of the Khan's seat, she summoned her son and gave him strict instructions:

'You can take this as an order or a wish of your father, but bring Zhanibek-Batyr directly to the central yurt. Nuraly, you know very well how highly your father reveres Zhanibek. The Tarkhan, who shared the hardships of battle with the Khan and with Bokenbai himself, must be received here. You will personally see that this is done.'

And the Khan's wish was fulfilled. A beautiful Bukhara carpet was laid out in full before the tall doors to the central yurt that were decorated in silver ornamentation. The moment Zhanibek stepped onto this carpet, two guards bowed their heads to the batyr as a sign of their profound respect, placing their hands to their chests.

Having crossed the threshold and standing under the shanyrak of the central yurt, Zhanibek greeted the Khan in a warm, low voice, 'Assalamu alaikum!' His companions, placing their hands to the right side of their chests, paid their respects to their hosts in a reserved fashion.

Abulkhair sat in the seat of honour on his throne in the sixteen-panel yurt. To his right, behind a curtain of fine white silk, sat Bopai on a smaller oak bench. Seeing the guests, she immediately rose to her feet. After an exchange of greetings and a brief embrace, Zhanibek took a seat beside the Khan, while nearby, they seated Baikozy, a young batyr from the Tarakty clan with a shrewd look from sparkling eyes and strong features.

After clearing his throat and then holding a pause, Zhanibek spoke:

'Oh, Abeke, we are like orphans now we have suddenly lost our protector, Boke. Bokenbai never once lowered his spear; he was born of the honour and conscience of his people and remained courageous until the last minute. He never ceded his native lands to the greedy Dzungars; he raised his thousand-strong army in the battles of Anyraqai and Bulantin and launched fearless attacks with a battle cry in the name of his people. And now this faithful elder comrade-in-arms has left us. Like you, Abeke, we feel your pain like eagles with clipped wings. Bopai felt with all her heart the sadness and bitterness of the loss conveyed in Zhanibek's muffled voice.

The batyr was holding back the emotion, his cheekbones moving up and down and his broad chest heaving.

Looking at Zhanibek, Abulkhair realised that the batyr needed a pause to be able to continue, so he did not interrupt.

'What can we do when faced with the fate that is predetermined for every mortal man? However sad it might be, Abeke, it appears that Bokenbai's time had come. And I suppose you must now be thinking who will be your true counsellor and faithful aide in your hopes and cares. Especially now, when all of your efforts are directed at protecting your people and land from the cunning tricks of our enemies and, most of all, from those in the northwest who give us no peace. After all, you must be thinking how things will be now that Bokenbai is no longer among us, am I right?'

Zhanibek had hit the nail on the head, naming precisely the problem that had been tormenting the Khan most of all, and Bopai was struck by his subtlety and depth of understanding.

Without waiting for Abulkhair to reply, the batyr concluded,

'You people stand behind you. And we are here, always prepared to support you. Abeke, we have endured so many trials and tribulations together, and we have always been together, and these things have only brought us closer together, you know that. Can I not be your unwavering support, one who has stood shoulder to shoulder with you to defend our native lands of Saryarka and Syr Darya, Sauran and Zhetysu?! I want you to remember this and never forget it!'

'Wow! Zhanibek, the strongest and most worthy son of the great Argyns, you could not have put it any other way!' Abulkhair spoke, his voice slightly lowered and leaning a little towards Zhanibek, thus displaying his sincere respect and gratitude to the batyr. 'My dear Zhanibek, I wholeheartedly accept your devotion as a true friend who has come at this difficult time to share the pain of the loss of our elder brother Bokenbai. We have known one another since our youth and I have the greatest respect for you. I thank the Almighty that I have such a batyr by my side, fighting for his people with valour and courage and never yielding to our enemies. And you were with Bokenbai in supporting me in defending our honour in a difficult struggle against foreigners trying to subjugate my people and ensuring I was never satisfied with the title of Khan and ruling in my Khan's seat alone. Be it yesterday, today or tomorrow — you will always be by my side, and I do not doubt that!'

Bopai noticed that Nuraly-Sultan, who was sitting alongside, was paying close attention to what his father was saying to Zhanibek, that he understood the depth of their meaning and sensed the excitement that had seized the Khan. It was for good reason that the Khan wished that his eldest son, the heir, should always be present at such important meetings with the nobility and respected elders.

Half-turning to face her son, Bopai reminded him that the conversation would continue over dinner and she instructed him to take care of the honoured guests and make sure everything was in order with their accommodation.

CHAPTER 6

One afternoon, two travellers arrived at the Khan's summer camp on the banks of the Irgiz. The two were batyrs — Altai from the Ak-Kete clan and Karak from the Karakalpaks. They stopped a short distance from the white yurt of the Khan, which stood out from all the rest.

'Who could it possibly be?'

Bopai looked questioningly and gestured subtly to Mandi, who was busy with her chores. The maid understood and headed straight to the exit. Loud voices were heard as the guests approached the threshold.

'Would it be convenient if we come straight in? It appears we are barging in without an invitation... Perhaps if we had let people know, someone would have met us...' Karak-Batyr said hesitantly.

'Oh, come on, we are not common folk here and the masters of this most honoured home will recognise us and will not shun us, you'll see.'

Bopai stopped Mandi, who was about to open the expensive and ornately carved double doors and instead went out herself to meet the esteemed guests.

'I am delighted to welcome you, most honoured batyrs! Please, do come through.'

The guests, sincerely grateful for Bopai's warm welcome, replied, 'Assalamu alaikum!' and entered the home.

Placing her right hand on her chest, Bopai accepted the traditional greeting and homage of the guests to the central yurt. Passing through to the seat of honour, the guests settled themselves on embroidered velvet quilted blankets while Bopai knelt a little lower.

'Welcome!' Bopai welcomed them warmly again with a charming smile. Turning a little, she said to Mandi, 'Bring some fresh koumis from the large goatskin.'

Tired from his morning journey, Altai drank down the cool koumis with great pleasure, carefully and without hurrying, so that not a single drop fell on his thick moustache. The delightfully cool taste of lush grass instantly cheered him up.

'Our Khan set off before noon yesterday to the caravan route to Tashkent, in the lower reaches of the Irgiz, with his warriors and nökers. Nuraly-Sultan went with him. The Russian trade caravan from Orenburg and the fortress on the Zhaiyk is following that route and on the way back, it should stop over at the Khan's seat. It is about this that the two sides need to agree. I also think that they will do some hunting,' Bopai began to relate, ensuring the guests were fully aware of the situation. 'Allah willing, they should make themselves known by nightfall, perhaps even sooner.'

'Well, and our visit is linked with the fact that Karak-Batyr would like to ask the Khan's permission to migrate and stay with his people, the Karakalpaks in the south,' Altai-Batyr explained. 'As far as I know, Abulkhair, he will approve this intention. So, we came here together so as not to send the batyr out alone on this business. He once fought with honour and valour in battles against our old enemies in the same ranks with me, with your father Syuindyk and your brother Myrzatai.'

'How could one forget such an example of courage and bravery, for this batyr is a legend among the Kete and Adai clans, and indeed all the lands between the Saguz, the Zhem, the Oyl and the Kiil! This is the man who taught me to shoot with a bow and arrow and spear-fighting when I was just a girl, more like a boy, training alongside Myrzatai's warriors!'

Bopai's face brightened at the memory of her distant youth and she smiled fondly.

The usually reticent Karak-Batyr, seemingly occupying a good half of the seat of honour and towering over everyone else, shuffled in his seat, softly cleared his throat and changed the subject of the conversation.

'If we are to await our Khan, we should really unsaddle

the horses and...'

'What are you talking about, my dear Karak-aga! Please do not worry about that — we have someone who can tend to your horses,' Bopai said and walked out to issue an instruction.

That night, Altai and Karak stayed over at the Khan's seat while waiting for the Khan.

Upon his return at nightfall with his entourage of warriors, personal guards, hunters and escorts, Abulkhair left his guests undisturbed. Having enquired from Bopai about the reason for the batyrs' visit, he decided to leave the meeting with them and their unhurried conversation until the morning.

The following day, everyone gathered for morning tea at a rich spread in the central white yurt with a high vaulted ceiling, specially designed for receiving important guests at the Khan's seat. Having asked about the well-being of the people and having chatted about everyday affairs, Abulkhair finally turned to his guests with a questioning look, waiting for the discussion of the most important topic.

'It is this that had brought us to the Khan's seat...' Altai said, then paused before continuing, 'Here he is — Karak! A descendant of Abdirali, who, in his turn, hailed from the famous batyr Baikaragan, well known among the Karakalpaks of the Teristamgaly tribe. You know this very well yourself, Abeke! During those difficult times in the fate of our people, when we fought the Dzungars from one side and the Edil Torgauts from another, he has been in your ranks from the very beginning. What is more, this is the batyr who, in fighting the Russian sycophants and the Turkmens, took on more than his fair share. Abeke, I believe you should hear from him directly as to the reason why he is here.'

Rather like a steppe eagle before a swift flight, Karak-Batyr puffed out his chest a little and straightened up.

'Gracious Khan, I think it would be no exaggeration to

say that we share the same roots. We are Karakalpaks and since we moved from the Sauran and settled in the valley along the lower reaches of the Syr Darya, on the lands of Sara and Almasek, together with the Kete and Adai clans, we have lived together, communicated closely, raised our children and shared both joys and sorrows. Now, Abeke, your subjects, the Karakalpak people, intend to migrate to the land of their ancestors. And I have come to relay this message to you personally. This does not mean that we intend to break away and distance ourselves from you. Quite the opposite: we will remain your faithful companions and will always be by your side whenever you need us. I want you to know that!'

The batyr spoke in an even, pleasant voice, both seriously and thoughtfully, the spark in his piercing eyes reflecting the resolute and brave warrior that he was. His words touched Abulkhair. Bopai, seeing the batyr's trepidation, thought that his words, so meaningful and heartfelt and from such a close comrade, would not leave the khan indifferent.

'Batyr, I have listened to you attentively. You have spoken as befits a real man who knows the traditions and honours all customs, and your words are much to my liking. I can see the purity of your intentions and your sincerity, which only reinforce my faith in the inviolability of our unity. What can I say but wish you a safe and pleasant journey?!' Abulkhair then addressed Altai-Batyr: 'I think that, before you embark on this significant and virtuous journey, it is important that our brothers receive the blessing not only of the biy of the Kete clan but of the biy of all the people in the horde — Azhibai! Send word today!'

That same day, even before noon, messengers hurried out to all corners of the vast steppe. Very soon, masses of well-wishers gathered at the Khan's seat to see off the Karakalpaks with their blessing and best wishes. Every clan came with its own *sybaga* — a sign of respect for those preparing for their long journey to their historical homeland. Cattle were sacrificed for meat for the travellers and boxes were brought stuffed with all kinds of food. Additional livestock for the long journey was also provided, all ready to move out after the caravan.

The festivities continued for two days at the Khan's seat. On the third day, as soon as the sun's first rays flashed over the horizon, the thousand-strong nomadic caravan of Karakalpaks, headed by Karak-Batyr, moved south from the banks of the Irgiz. Barely able to hold back their tears, the brotherly people said their farewells after years of clinging to one another. It was the hot mid-July of 1744.

* * *

Immediately next to the central yurt stood the home of Nuraly and it was from there that the five-year-old Taykara came pattering along, following Bopai. She was forever asking her grandmother things and nestling up to her, which made Bopai even more delighted with her granddaughter, that little girl with dark, currant eyes and a pigtail protruding from her head. Lifting the little girl in her arms, Bopai clasped her to her bosom, kissed her soft white cheek, and inhaled the child's delightful milky scent.

'Oh, my sweet child! My bundle of joy!' Bopai poured inexhaustible affection and tenderness on her favourite Taykara. 'My little ray of sunshine!'

'Like that one way up there?' the little girl asked, squinting her eyes and laughing infectiously with her finger pointing at the sky. It was almost noon and the sun was taking its place of honour in the clear June sky.

'Ah, but you are brighter and hotter, my darling!'

'If I'm really hot, then I'll burn you, Granny!'

Bopai melted with delight and kept talking with her granddaughter, enjoying everything that Taykara said to her.

'You won't burn me, silly, but you will keep me warm!'

'So, I'll keep you warm, will I? Really and truly?'

'Of course, it will be like that, really and truly, my dear!'

Feeling completely happy, Bopai and her granddaughter entered the central yurt. The maid opened the door wide, courteously letting her mistress inside.

Abulkhair was preparing to travel to see the Karakalpaks the following day and he was assigning tasks to Nuraly, bringing him fully up to speed with the internal and external affairs of the Khan's seat. They also discussed the details of the trip. So as not to disturb their conversation, Bopai quietly took Taykara through the side door into the dining area that adjoined the main yurt.

'If while I am away, any news comes suddenly from the messenger Mambet, be sure to meet him personally. Based on what I have been told, he left Kazan a good while ago.'

As a rule, Abulkhair did not reveal his feelings to others, but he had been overtly anxious about something recently as if he were at a crossroads. Nuraly, who was sensitive to such things, had noticed this and was growing increasingly worried about his father. Nuraly listened attentively to his instructions and nodded silently in response, but he could see from his father's face that he was seriously troubled by something.

'I have to settle the affairs of a clan in the lower reaches of the Syr Darya, so I am preparing for the journey. I am taking a small group of trusted warriors with me, headed by Bektore; they are fast and experienced in campaigns of this kind. If anyone from outside makes enquiries, don't tell them anything. As far as internal affairs are concerned, you'll sort them out yourselves.'

Abulkhair did not tell any of his close advisers about his intentions to keep Karak-Batyr's army closer to the border of the Horde or about the purpose of his current trip. Having long since learned that it was always better to be wary of hostile brethren, with aspirations for the Khan's seat and with the support of the authorities in Orenburg,

Abulkhair made sure that no one knew about his affairs. He warned both Bopai and Nuraly of this, too.

Heading south from his seat, Abulkhair-Khan rode with a small group of men a reasonable distance from the Irgiz until they reached the sandy valley of Ayyrkyzyl. Nearer to lunchtime, they stopped for a rest and released the horses to graze.

'Bektore, I get the feeling you sense there are all manner of beasts living in these sands and undergrowth. We could try to catch something. The main thing is not to deviate from our course,' Abulkhair warned, noticing the excitement of a potential hunt in his companion's eyes. 'It would be good to have a bit of roast gazelle this evening, I must admit, but warn the lads not to touch the females or the offspring. If they come across a trail, then they should only go for the male.'

No sooner had they heard the Khan's approval than the warriors, excited in anticipation of a hunt, split into two or three groups and set off into the sandy hills in search of gazelles.

Leaving five or six warriors to guard their camp, Bektore spurred his roan steed with its white forelock to catch up with the other dzhigits. He reckoned that the now-grown bucks would be grazing between the sandy slopes in the hollows, where the grass was at its most lush, and it was to there that he steered his horse. Bektore had no wish for his warriors, keen hunters, one and all, to get lost in those sands for nothing.

Abulkhair assumed that, by stopping for rests and overnight stays, they should reach their goal in a couple of weeks by marching at a decent, steady pace. However, before that, they had to pass through the wave-like sands of Ayyrkyzyl, to the edge of the boundless sandy Karakum Valley and then through the western bend in the great Amu Darya to the borders of the lands of the Karakalpaks. *The most important thing is not to deviate from the route and to keep to the timeframe. To ensure the men don't get bored and to keep them on their toes, I see no reason not to allow them some time to go hunting,* Abulkhair thought to himself. Left alone with his thoughts, Abulkhair lay on his side, leaning on his arm, and his attention was drawn to the individual snow-white clouds passing slowly across the clear sky like curly balls of camel hair.

To where, I wonder, is this leisurely white caravan making its way? Where will it find shelter? In which corner of the vast sky will it finally come to a stop before melting away forever? So, if these clouds eventually disperse to leave no trace, does that mean that the whole point of their existence is simply this? What is the point of such an existence if their traces simply disappear in the end? And if, in this corruptible world, man leaves no trace behind him, how is he better than these clouds?! And what, then, is the point of his life spent in battles, disputes and constant struggle? Where is the truth — in victories achieved over endless days and nights in an irreconcilable struggle with one's enemy or defeats so full of shame and regret? How can we know for sure for whom and for what we are fighting? Is our illusory life really as meaningless as those clouds that drift quietly in the blue sky above us, to then become nothing but vapour and water?

The Khan was not overly tired from riding in the saddle, but now, relaxed and lulled by the peaceful silence, he succumbed to his usual light, bird-like sleep. Even in his grand military campaigns and long journeys, he had grown accustomed to sleeping in the saddle, leaning his chin on his whip. During such a short and light sleep, Abulkhair had time to refresh himself and wake up rested. On this occasion, he was awakened by the merry chatter of his men returning from the hunt and he could tell from their murmurings that they were pleased.

Bektore was riding with the spoils: a beautiful male gazelle with curved horns lay across his saddle.

'Abeke, if you allow it, the lads will flay and butcher the

gazelle before we head on our way. We'll try a roast from it when we reach our overnight camp.'

Bektore then threw the carcass onto the ground. Two of the dzhigits took their daggers and, as quick as a flash, they skinned the fat gazelle, butchered it, scored the pieces of meat for further preparation later and placed it in a special food bag.

* * *

The July heat was unbearable when Abulkhair reached Karak-Batyr's settlement precisely on the scheduled date.

Karak-Batyr's modest people had settled to the south of the Aral Sea, on fertile lands at the mouth of the Amu Darya, where they lived a peaceful life. The respected nobles and elders of the people greeted the Khan with special honours, while Karak himself emerged to meet Abulkhair with open arms. The welcome of the esteemed guests soon became a full-blown celebration of festivities to mark Abulkhair's arrival. Poets and storytellers performed, each according to their particular style, while the mighty Palauan wrestlers squared up to one another. Karak-Batyr's warriors competed in archery to strike a silver nugget from a distance and tried their strength and agility in *kokpar*[21]. Throughout the evening, the special guest storyteller and poet Zhien from Chimbay performed the legendary epic tale of *The Forty Maidens* in the luxurious grand yurt with its twenty-four ropes. Seating himself on a round Bukhara mat, the poet first tuned his *kobyz*[22] and, turning his plump, red-cheeked face to Abulkhair, spoke in a smooth and soft voice:

'Most honoured Abeke, we are related peoples, our origins hailing from our ancestors Kazakh and Sozak! The story that the strings of my faithful kobyz will tell is merely

---

[21] The Central Asian sport in which horse-mounted players attempt to place a goat or calf carcass in a goal.
[22] An ancient Kazakh string instrument with two horsehair strings

an episode in the common history and destiny of our people. This is the legend of the beautiful Gulaim and similarly brave, charming maidens who defended their people and their native lands, has been preserved in the memory of the Nogai people and passed down the generations to us.'

The lingering, piercing sound of the kobyz, the melody that introduced the epic tale and the voice of the poet relating the tale of times gone by seemed to transport Abulkhair to another world.

> *The centuries since then have passed,*
> *The people then were shackled fast.*
> *Our ancestors they always lived*
> *On their native lands of Nogay.*
> *By the Mountain of Alymkhan,*
> *By the Zhana-Darya River,*
> *Stood Sarkop, a city most fine,*
> *Where Kargaly waters once flowed.*
> *Once a man had wealth aplenty,*
> *Of many lands the master he*
> *By the banks of Zhana Darya,*
> *In the lush coombe of Kargaly.*
> *For its title, a label so high —*
> *They gave it the name Burabai.*

The sound of the kobyz floated in the air, exciting every listener, and its strings sang piercingly and mysteriously. Zhien continued in the Karakalpak language, which the Kazakhs could understand and see as almost their own.

> *But sorrow there was but one —*
> *Posterity the bai had none,*
> *Now past sixty and on his tod,*
> *No child to him did grant his God.*
> *And then his youngest wife did bear*

For the bai, a daughter so fair!

The entire being of the storyteller seemed to blend as one with the tune from his kobyz, while Zhien's expressive and melodious voice seemed to bring the poem's heroine to life as he related this wondrous legend, painting first a young beauty, then a headstrong and courageous warrior!

> *Gulaim and men on side*
> *Push ahead, their war steeds ride*
> *'Cross the deserts of Ormiya*
> *And from their steppe home so vast*
> *The Kalmyk enemy they cast.*
> *Some choose rest once fighting's done.*
> *But not this lass, for off she runs*
> *To the steppe, to stalk more prey*
> *Saiga, deer, such is her way.*

To conclude his lengthy poem, Zhien played more slowly, and the melody from his bow sounded as soft as the rays of the morning sun.

> *So Gulaim and Kyran too*
> *Lived in their homeland in peace,*
> *Two heroes, the price they knew*
> *Of happiness that will not cease.*
> *Forty maidens now live free*
> *And blossom to delight us all,*
> *Proudly wearing trinkets shiny*
> *And nothing else can so enthral!*

Abulkhair was most pleased with the warm welcome he was afforded and the respectful attitude of his brotherly people. He expressed his particular appreciation to the storyteller Zhien:

'Zhieke, you have brought us all much joy by so

wonderfully telling the story of the beautiful Gulaim who displayed such valour and who became a leader of warriors in the battle against her enemies. You have left a lasting impression and I am most grateful to you for that. Your talent as a storyteller has long been spoken of among the people, so it was such a pleasure for me to see and hear you perform!'

Karak-Batyr could not but respond to Abulkhair's words, so filled they were with gratitude and reverence.

'How beautifully put, most honoured Khan!' he said and bowed. 'The craft of our esteemed Zhieke was all in your honour! We thank you for your kind words!'

Night had already fallen when the evening drew to a close and Abulkhair, deciding to take the air before turning in, went outside, throwing a light cloth gown over his shoulders. Karak and Bektore followed him, and the three of them walked for a while in total silence to the light of the bright moonlight. Without breaking the silence, Karak-Batyr pondered the essence of the matter, which he guessed would form the subject of the following day's conversation with Abulkhair. During the past two or three days, while he had been by the Khan's side, they had managed to discuss the current state of affairs. Karak had noticed that Abulkhair was concerned about the news that the Khiva Khan Kaip planned to ask for the hand of Barak-Sultan's youngest daughter and take her for his youngest wife. The fact that Barak-Sultan, who harboured a grudge, was cementing his alliance with Kaip Khan alarmed Abulkhair, whose power extended not only to the Junior Zhuz but to Argyns and Kipchaks as well. That was why the Khan needed to be sure that Karak would be his reliable support and aide, for only then could he safely return to his seat. Knowing that Abulkhair had lost his most faithful comrade and adviser, Bokenbai, Karak-Batyr understood why the Khan had come. He was also sure that this was what he would hear the next day from Abulkhair himself. The entire elite had gathered at Karak-Batyr's to see the Khan before he left, all the biys and elders included. Everyone was served the morning's koumis in large bowls, flavoured with sweet Samarkand raisins, smoked kazy sausage and smoked fat from a camel's hump. Abulkhair began his speech with the importance of preserving the integrity of the nation, fulfilling the sacred duty and defending the vast territories of their native land from enemy attacks from the north and south alike. He also said that he was returning to his Khan's seat, knowing that his brotherly people were united with him and that he was confident of the reliable support of the Karakalpaks.

'If our neighbours from the north do not stop provoking their henchmen and performing despicable deeds, there can be no peaceful alliance with them. And we have repeatedly made this clear to them in open warfare, where so many of our young warriors have perished. The Turkmens and the Khivans that neighbour your lands wish to take possession of your territory and threaten our amicable, peaceful existence, as you, under Karak here, well know. There is no way we can persuade them not to encroach on each other's lands and establish trade relations and mutually beneficial exchanges. And to live in peace and accord. Another reason why it is not easy for us is because some of our very own appear to hold a grudge, perceiving all we do as evidence of our submission to the stronger side. And that is why the only thing I want to do now is to strengthen our amicable relations with you.'

'Too right!'

'I couldn't agree more!'

'Well said!'

'Abeke, you have spoken important words for our peoples, whose roots are united!'

Hearing the Karakalpak elite approving Abulkhair's words, Karak-Batyr also expressed his opinion, ending with a farewell:

'Abeke, I sincerely wish you every success in your coming negotiations with the Orenburg general, who represents Tsarist authority here. I trust your authoritative nature and the glorious name of the Kazakh Khanate will shine through!'

The next day, before dawn had broken, Karak-Batyr and his warriors accompanied Abulkhair, who was departing on the return journey to the northwest from the bend in the Amu Darya. The escorts remained where they were until the Khan's group had completely disappeared from view. It was then that the disc of the sun began slowly to rise in the sky, bathing the horizon in a scarlet light.

* * *

No sooner had Abulkhair returned to the Khan's seat than he and Bopai had to set out once again as a matter of urgency. They took with them reliable warriors led by Bektore as their escorts. Their destination was Sankibai's aul, which lay to the south-east of Zhem.

The Kalmyks had launched a sudden onslaught on the unsuspecting Shekti aul and, in the battle that ensued, Sankibai's beloved daughter Akbota, the youngest in the family and the only girl among four brothers, was killed. Receiving this sorrowful news, Abulkhair immediately set out to offer his condolences. The death of his only daughter at the hands of the Torgauts had broken Sankibai, and Abulkhair could not remain at home and not support his friend at such a difficult time.

And so, he had set off on this long journey without a second thought. Bopai understood what the Khan was feeling and sensed how he empathised with his friend's inexpressible loss. At noon, one day in August, crossing the eastern side of the Ustyurt Plateau and before reaching the valley by the banks of the Zhem, past a small range of hills, they approached the foot of a snow-white mountain whose outline resembled the figure of a girl in a frilly dress.

It was here, on the outskirts of the small aul, that Abulkhair and his companions were met by Sankibai's middle son Bakesh. After the usual greetings and asking how the travellers were after such a long journey under the scorching sun, Bakesh escorted them to the central, sixteen-rope yurt that stood out from the others with its elevated shanyrak and white canvas.

Inside and to the right, seated a little lower than her mother-in-law, was Bakesh's young wife, mourning her sister-in-law Akbota, comparing her pure beauty with the morning star and recalling her key virtues — courage and fearlessness. After a long memorial song, the aul mullah began reciting prayers from the holy Qur'an in a melodious yet sad voice, starting with the Surah *Al-Fatiha*.

During the memorial dinner, when condolences were passed to Sankibai, he only occasionally sighed and related how his Akbota and engaged the brazen enemies in battle and had been killed.

That day, Akbota had decided to take a walk on the slopes of the ornate mountain that towered not far from their aul. Leaving her piebald three-year-old down below — a direct descendant of her father's white-hoofed mottled stallion — she climbed to the top of the mountain as she often did to admire the valley that spread out below as if in the palm of her hand before disappearing beyond the distant horizon. Suddenly, quite by chance, she caught sight of Kalmyk warriors crossing to their side of the river in small groups. Akbota immediately ran to warn her aul to save the people and their livestock that was so vital to their livelihood. Gathering all the young men who remained in the aul, she put on her brother's armour and helmet, took a spear and a bow with arrows, and they went off and hid that same evening near the mountain to await the Kalmyks. Their insidious enemies intended to crush the peaceful Kazakhs by attacking them unexpectedly. However, the first ranks of the advancing fighters found themselves ambushed by Akbota's detachment. The Kalmyks were defeated that evening and the survivors retreated and scattered. They had been especially frightened by the fearless young batyr, whose war horse, like the mythical winged spirit that had carried the Prophet Muhammad to Mecca, flew across the field yet remained unscathed. They took a while before attacking again. Waiting for reinforcements, they prepared their next offensive for a quiet predawn hour.

Akbota did not doubt that the Torgauts, having lost the first battle, would be back to attack once more, this time with greater numbers, and so her young warriors slept in shifts, keeping their horses close and remaining alert. As soon as dawn had broken, the snorting of horses and the barely discernible whispering of the advancing Kalmyks could be heard in the morning quiet. The keen hounds of Sankibai's aul, hearing the unusual sounds for that time of day, began to back from all directions, awakening everyone around. Akbota's warriors leapt up and mounted their horses.

The Torgauts had hoped to take the sleeping Kazakh fighters unawares and quickly massacre them, but their plan could not be realised. They were forced to engage in a brutal battle with Akbota's warriors, all armed to the teeth.

After their evening defeat, the new reinforcements, headed by a khuntaiji, had been given strict instructions to kill the Kazakh leader at the first opportunity. Therefore, during the battle, they focused all their attention on Akbota. This *young batyr* moved with lightning speed, letting no enemy fighter near and repulsing every attempted attack. The khuntaiji and his now depleted detachment of Torgauts then retreated and, climbing a nearby hill, aimed his bow and arrow at the unprotected head of the *young batyr*, who was beating off enemy fighters left, right and centre. The first two arrows, fired in quick succession, failed to hit their target, but the third plunged right into the shoulder of the young warrior who had struck such fear in the Kalmyks, and the head of the invading force launched a fresh attack with a triumphant roar. However, the majority of the Torgauts were no longer able to continue the fight — some of them lay motionless, having perished in the battle, while others were using the last of their strength to flee the battlefield. The bloodthirsty khuntaiji, who was rushing back into battle, did not remain jubilant for long, for one of Akbota's warriors caught up with him and stabbed him through and through with his spear.

After two failed attacks, the remnants of the Torgaut detachments failed even to cross back to the other side of the Zhem, and they all perished in utter ignominy.

That was how the young Akbota, the young batyr fighting on the slopes of the snow-white mountain, had died, and Sankibai's family and all their brothers and comrades were in mourning. Sankibai buried his Akbota, his *white camel*, as he called her, on the same mountain that looked like a girl in a white dress. The high, picturesque peak accepted the innocent body, offering eternal shelter to the brave daughter of her people.

After the funeral prayer, Abulkhair and Bopai looked down from their elevated position over the vast steppe in bloom that stretched as far as the eye could see. They remained silent for some time in sad silence.

'This mountain top, now the eternal resting place for a young beauty, has now become Akbota's Mountain!' Bopai said and sighed sadly, wiping a tear from her lashes with her little finger. 'The mountain of Sankibai's daughter Akbota! Akbota Sankibai Mountain!'

At that moment, Sankibai's piebald horse gave a roar and the echo reverberated all around Akbota Sankibai Mountain.

* * *

Having received an urgent note from the messenger sent

by Myrzatai, Abulkhair was forced to leave the Irgiz in a hurry and head for the Zhaiyk with a hundred warriors and his Nuraly. Bopai turned cold from the disturbing news and was gripped with fear. All the land where the Adai, Alim and Tabyn people lived and grazed their cattle was at the mercy of a great fire — the steppe was burning. It was unknown where and how the fire started, but one thing was clear: they had never known such a horror before. The realisation of this distressed Bopai and made her truly frightened.

'Abeke, my Khan, I entrust you to Almighty Allah alone. May the spirits of your ancestors watch over you!'

Bopai tried to remain strong, although the tears were flowing, there was a lump in her throat and her eyes betrayed anxiety.

Moving quickly, Abulkhair and his warriors reached the Zhaiyk river valley by the evening of the third day. Spending the night there and giving their horses a chance to rest, they set off once more early the next morning. Myrzatai met with them in the appointed place, a little upstream along the Zhaiyk, by the banks of the Elek.

'This nightmare is down to the authorities in Orenburg. We think this is their evil-doing, Abeke! People saw with their own eyes: the Cossacks set the steppe alight! It is their way of depriving an entire nation of shelter and livelihood. You see, they understand that you can't escape from a fire quickly, gathering all you own and moving to a safe place. They cannot defeat us in an open, honest battle, the cowardly villains, so they resort to dirty tricks like this!'

Abulkhair was sure that what Myrzatai was saying had to be the truth. The peaceful steppe, yellowed by the noble shade of the feathergrass, was now at the mercy of an enormous serpent, slithering relentlessly forward. The land was burning mercilessly, turning black before the eyes, the purple tongues of the flames from the raging fire rising upwards to lick the sky, mixing with thick smoke that turned to dark clouds that blacked out the light. The fearsome flames had engulfed the entire area and burned the faces of the warriors with their hot breath as they stood dumbfounded.

Hares, foxes, corsacs and other small animals ran about, not knowing where to find shelter from this attack. It seemed as if these unfortunate creatures were prepared to seek protection from the people, for they ran towards them, ready to hide behind them to avoid the calamity.

Not only the animals had been taken by surprise and frightened to death, for the people, too, who had settled in the autumn pasture ground, were now forced to leave urgently and migrate elsewhere to save themselves. Abulkhair, too, was frightened by this dangerous, uncontrollable event. Having survived many fierce battles with the Dzungars and seen the atrocities of ruthless enemies in the settlements they had conquered, this was the first time he had encountered such foul play. His neighbours, filled with enmity, were burning to the ground the land that was home to his people and which fed them. The only solution available was to take the people from that dangerous place as soon as possible and lead the livestock away from the fire. The warriors under Myrzatai and Nuraly split up and rushed to fulfil the Khan's instruction. Gasping not so much from the fumes as from rage, Abulkhair looked out over the burning steppe and swore never to forgive this cruelty of the malicious Cossacks and not to leave this evil unpunished.

Abulkhair and the warriors who remained with him were unable to stop the fire, so they simply followed after the other people who were leaving. The anxious night was spent shrouded in the smoke from the raging fire. It seemed that hope was fading more and more.

Just before dawn, gusts of a harsh wind blew from the north and dispersed the clouds of thick smoke that had covered the space between the land and the sky throughout the smouldering night. The flickering fire had changed direction and was now on the right-hand side. The now grey steppe had a morose appearance, and the tongues of flame from the dry wind were burning even more intensely. For a moment, the distant sky, barely visible through the curtain of smoke, seemed to have fallen lower as if it were about to collapse. Suddenly, the wet breath of autumn could be felt from the succession of purple clouds floating across the sky and the penetrating wind was soon replaced by heavy rain.

Abulkhair's dark mood, crushed by the gravity of the situation he faced that early morning, was dispelled, at least by just a little, by that unexpected autumn downpour. Whether it was the great power of nature or indeed because of the will of Allah Himself, a mighty obstacle was placed on that monstrous event, which had scorched not only the land but also the world of those who live on it.

Perhaps it was the spirits of the ancient ancestors — who once roamed freely on these beautiful steppe lands and found their eternal rest here — who had protected their lands in this way.

In spite of his considerable fatigue, Abulkhair never once dropped the pace on the journey back to the Khan's seat. Deep inside, his anger and desire for revenge against the Cossacks were intensifying, much like the cold rain that late autumn. Knowing he could not reconcile differences with his old enemy after this weighed heavily on the Khan's shoulders. Abulkhair did not know of the Tsarist order of 11 May 1747, which stipulated that the steppe from the Volga to the Urals was to be set on fire that autumn. This was a method applied to subjugate and establish the authority of the Russian Empire over the western lands of the Khanate. Of course, the Orenburg general did not see it as necessary to notify the Khan's seat of this; after all, he believed that these were the internal affairs of the empire. However, the governor could not know that Myrzatai-Batyr from the Adai clan, the Khan's faithful associate, would come to learn of the actions of the Cossack soldiers.

* * *

For some time, dissatisfaction regarding the Khan's authority had been growing in all corners of the steppe. Eventually, these conversations reached the Khan's seat. Was this really the peaceful life in the open air that had been agreed with the Russian Empress? The fact was that the pastures were shrinking in size and attempts to take them away had not ceased in any way. So, what was the Khan's objective — to hand over all their lands to the Russian authorities? In order to preserve his title and position, has he decided to bring all his people on bended knee to subjugate us all to the Russian Empire?

These harsh accusations, voiced by individual elders and biys, wounded Abulkhair and caused him great pain. In their words, it seemed that all his efforts to protect the people from bloody massacres and senseless sacrifices, all his endeavours to unite the people and preserve their integrity and all his constant anxiety were nothing more than a means to protect his interests! It was as if he had entered into agreements with the influential Russian authorities for the sake of his status and his own well-being! More than ten years had passed since he had signed that piece of paper from the Russian Tsarina that was supposed to prevent conflicts and strife between her subjects and the Kazakhs. Did this mean, therefore, that the continued provocations and clashes with the Tsarist henchmen, giving no opportunity to lay down arms and rest awhile, were merely concealing the Khan's personal interests?!

Abulkhair decided to discuss this problem openly, summoning all the biys and elders to a council at the Khan's seat. Bopai understood and supported him in this intention. Correctly sensing the Khan's mood, she took it upon herself to prepare for the meeting of the nobles. Erecting separate yurts for the heads of clans and the biys, who were to come from all corners, preparing sufficient food and drink, and making sybaga for each guest — Bopai did not miss the slightest detail and personally oversaw the fulfilment of all instructions.

It was the middle of June. Some five hundred people arrived at the Khan's seat from settlements near and far in just the first days. The Alim and Kete, headed by Azhibai and Altai, the representatives of the twelve families from the Baiuly clan, together with Myrzatai and Shotan, the seven clans under the Tama Eset, Barky-Biy with the Argyns and the Abak Kerei, Syrymbet-Batyr, and the elders and nobles from various clan unions all arrived one after the other and settled in their respective yurts.

Finally, everyone was assembled for the grand council; they had not simply come to visit, for each of them had something to say to the Khan. The following morning, the arrivals all gathered on the clearing before the Khan's yurt. Abulkhair sat in the centre, under a specially drawn awning, both sides of which were fully open. Bopai sat to his right. To his left sat Azhibai, Altai and Eset, followed by Barky-Biy, the thirty-year-old Otei-Batyr from the Argyn clan, and Nuraly-Sultan.

According to the tradition at such important councils, the first word was taken by the eldest of the Junior Zhuz elite, Azhibai-Biy.

'Dear brothers, greetings to all of you who have made the special journey, be it from nearby or far afield, to come to this grand council and stand before our Khan!

If the future of our land and the unity of our people is important to you, let us put aside any petty claims and disputes, criticism or reproach, and speak honestly here, directly and substantially, without overlooking any pertinent advice. Our most honoured Khan is prepared to hear what everyone has to say and we will be attentive to every word!

Everyone fell silent after Azhibai's opening address and silence reigned for some time. Suddenly, the tall and well-built Barky-Biy turned his round face with its heavy chin sharply in Azhibai's direction.

'Please allow me, Azhibai-aga!' he folded his meadowsweet whip in half and placed it on his lap as a gesture of his desire to speak.

'Respected guests, let us hear Baryk-Biy, batyr of the Amak clan!'

Azhibai raised a hand, gesturing to the murmuring crowd for silence.

'Azhibai-aga, I listened carefully to your words about giving advice. I am not particularly skilled at giving intelligent and fine-sounding speeches in the presence of the Khan, but you have unwittingly induced me to do so. It seems that there is a gaping hole where our glorious Bokenbai once stood, who bequeathed to us either to be a united people or to become nothing more than the land trampled by our enemies. How much longer must we continue to display indecision and bow our heads to our blue-eyed neighbours to the north-west?! The noble elders and worthy representatives of their clans, all gathered here, who certainly have something to say at this council, only yesterday under the leadership of Abeke, the Khan by right and the people's will, were the same batyrs of all three zhuzes who broke the back of the Oirats. Where is the Khan's greatness? Where is our honour and our pride, which is able properly to rebuff any enemy that threatens our peace and the well-being of our people? Why should we continue to put up with those who will not consider the interests of the Khan's seat? What does our ruler have to say about that?'

'Barky speaks the truth!' Otey-Batyr, always impetuous, blurted out fervently. 'The goal of the Russian Tsars is not to unite the three zhuzes and strengthen the Kazakh people into a single state, but to tear us apart! They need the Khan's seat to agree to submit to their will without resistance! Building fortresses, allegedly to protect us from Dzungar raids, making us dependent by tying our hands with an amanat pledge and aggressive actions — these are all cunning tactics they deploy for their benefit as they appropriate our lands from west to east. It is time we came to our senses! Brothers, we cannot save our people and the integrity of our land unless we give a firm rebuff to them and their Kalmyk villains whom they set upon us!' Abulkhair could barely conceal his rage and chomped his teeth.

Only Bopai guessed his inner struggle and saw that he was keeping himself in check as best he could. Was it right that he wanted to let them speak and reveal everything that was on their minds?

'If the only way to safeguard our land and protect our people, exhausted as they are by many years of war with the Dzungars, is to launch once more into battle with our northern enemy, then let's march on with our battle cry!' Myrzatai's angry voice was loud and harsh. 'Who will take command? Surely, it should be Abulkhair-Khan, right? Or should it one of our brothers, who lusts after the Khan's power — someone sitting among us now? Or perhaps it should be the instigator of strife who sows discord between the clans and causes confusion among the people for the sake of his struggle for power?'

'That's enough, Myrzatai, calm down!' Abulkhair said, interrupting him as tactfully as possible. 'However we look at it, I think Barky and Otei's words are motivated by their worries for their people. Who else would like something to say? Please speak; first, we will listen to everyone calmly and without haste.'

Barky-Biy liked the way that Abulkhair had told Myrzatai to calm down and thus showed restraint himself. *Say what you like, but nobility and a good upbringing are in his blood. It is his way of saying that he has decided first to listen to everyone, hear the opinions of the people and analyse everything,* Barky remarked to himself.

The biys, elders and chiefs of the clans came to the centre of the ring, one after the other, and spoke. Some supported Barky and Otei and others spoke about their own particular problems and strife with other clans. Finally, having heard everyone, Abulkhair himself took the floor.

'Brothers, I sincerely appreciate you all coming to this council today. I understand that many of you when you spoke about preserving our unity, were expressing what is in your hearts and what preys on your minds. Know this: while I have the strength and the opportunity, I, too, am fighting for precisely these values. For the things that you have all spoken about. To safeguard and protect our land and our people, we do not always have to rush into battle and wage bloody wars. Therefore, when I seek compromise or enter negotiations with others, even if they are our enemy, I am not doing this because I care about my place as Khan or my prosperity; rather, I am thinking about finding a peaceful solution to the problem. Both my leadership in battles with the enemy and my ruling of the people are all part of my following a single purpose and I will not deviate from my principles. I am hiding nothing and I have put all this before you so you may judge, and I want you to approach the matter thoughtfully and with due understanding. And if, at this difficult time, when enemy forces are advancing from all sides, someone has envious eyes on my status and position as Khan, whose burden, I remind you, is to preserve the integrity of the people and protect our land, if there is anyone who greedily craves my power, then it shall be on your conscience!'

Bopai Khanum did not expect Abulkhair to say anything else. Those who sat in the seats of honour under the Khan's awning and those seated around them all suddenly fell silent.

In the silence that reigned, everyone quietly agreed with

Abulkhair's short but concise speech.

* * *

In early July, just before Abulkhair left for the city of Or[23] at Neplyuev's invitation, Bopai had a bad dream. The Khan's dark-bay five-year-old stallion was galloping across the steppe with an empty saddle, which had slipped to one side, the reins and silver bridle caught in its mane while stomping and roaring. The horse was returning home alone without its master, its chest perspiring heavily, nostrils flared and large tears dripping from its reddened eyes. Bopai herself was running from the house, stumbling as she went, and her desperate cry was echoing around the neighbourhood.

Bopai awoke in the early hours of the morning from that cry and she anxiously sat up in her bed.

'Oh, bismillah, bismillah!' and read herself a short prayer.

If I dream of something frightening, I will probably find joy in real life, Bopai said to console herself, but she could not get back to sleep and tossed and turned until morning.

Abulkhair was preparing to leave and Bopai did not want to show her vague anxiety or distress.

'Abeke, may the spirit of the holy Kydyr-Ata, who watches over all travellers, watch over you too. May your journey be a success. I entrust you to Allah alone!'

Abulkhair bade a brief farewell to Bopai and his other confidantes, who usually saw him off on his long travels, and headed for a light wagon covered in white canvas that stood before his yurt.

And this meeting with the general did not go as Abulkhair had planned either. Heavily armed and firmly settled in the town of Or, the Russian authorities made it clear that they would not stop pursuing a policy of

---

[23] Now Orsk in The Russian Orenburg Oblast

domination in the territory of the Khan's seat. Not only that, but the Khan once again was clear in his understanding that they would not hinder the constant raids of the Kalmyks from the opposite bank of the Edil or the Russian Cossacks in the lower reaches of the Zhaiyk.

'Mister Abulkhair, there are many willing to live in harmony with us by accepting their subjugation to Tsarist authority. They include those who do not approve of your one-sided policy and, besides, they are very influential people who carry much weight among their people. All the while, you persist in demonstrating a blatant rejection of our patronage. We also fail to see much benefit in using your Khan's seat to ensure our security on caravan routes where we are establishing trade relations with Central Asia.'

Abulkhair was angry, but he listened to the interpreter who was translating every word of the general's speech, so full of malicious ridicule and arrogance. For a moment, the general seemed frightened by Abulkhair's frowning, direct stare and, also, there was a note of confusion in his voice; he made considerable effort not to show it. However, when he reached into the drawer of his inconceivably long desk for his matches, his slightly trembling fingers still gave him away.

Barely able to restrain his seething anger, Abulkhair finally decided to say what was gnawing at his insides and rising in a lump to his throat. He chose a moment when the general had suddenly hesitated and when he spoke, his voice was cold and hard.

'Most honoured general, sir, you are aware that the Khan's seat is always happy to welcome amicable intentions and the due care of the Russian royal authorities. This was stated in the charter that was signed in Mantobe and all recent agreements. I am sure that the Orenburg generalship, of which you are the head, remembers this well. According to the agreement, the entire point of the Tsarist patronage was to preserve the integrity of the land where the Kazakh people reside and also to put a stop to the raids by our neighbours, the Bashkirs. And when this matter appeared to have been resolved, you suddenly decided to see unilateral hostility on our part when we repelled attacks by Esil and Zhaiyk Kalmyks and Cossacks! If we are talking about being just and fair, then why is it that the Or Fortress, built to protect our lands from outside attacks, in line with our mutual agreement and based on our treaty of alliance, remains beyond the authority of our Khan's seat?! I am compelled to remind you once more that we will not turn away from our intentions to maintain peaceful relations with the imperial authorities of Saint-Petersburg and, at the same time, to establish the integrity of the nation by securing a charter from you. And if the incursions and other aggression on the part of your loyal subjects, the Kalmyks and Russian Cossacks, will not stop, then the Khan and his people will not stop repulsing these attackers in the strongest possible manner!'

Neplyuev found he was boiling over inside from such uncompromising and resolute directness on Abulkhair's part. The fact that the Khan had shown his worth and, without yielding in the slightest, had shown no humility or submission, even in words, aroused not simply indignation in Neplyuev but utter rage, from which it took him some time to gather his thoughts.

As long as these hypocritical nomads have this khan at their head, it will be simply impossible to tame them and force them into subjugation to the Empire! He is like a wild horse that won't be saddled, and if this untamed and stubborn savage carries on like this, then he will drink plenty more of our blood. So, what am I to do with him?

All of Neplyuev's thoughts came down to this — what to do with him — and his entire consciousness was seized with this problem and how to find a way out of the impasse. Under no circumstances could he miss the opportunity to get his hands on the key to the gates to Asia and fulfil the mission that Tsar Peter had bequeathed; otherwise, his entire mission in Orenburg would not be worth a dime, and the general knew this all too well. That same night, he sent a messenger with an urgent note to Barak-Sultan, who was staying in Karnak on the slopes of Karatau. Barak had long since harboured the desire to get his hands on the title of Khan. Abulkhair must die! If Barak-Sultan wished to take the Khan's throne, then he must do something urgently — this was the secret order that Barak received from the bloodthirsty Neplyuev. Abulkhair, meanwhile, was not particularly disappointed that his negotiations with the general had yielded nothing positive. In fact, he had assumed that that was what would happen. From the very beginning, it had been as clear as day that Neplyuev did not view the Khan's seat with anything remotely close to benevolence. After all, the general was following the aggressive policy of the Russian authorities to the letter. The Orenburg governor was irritated by the Khan's uncompromising nature and his stubbornness and although he had tried to conceal the fact, he feared such a hard stance from the steppe ruler, believing that in the end, the situation would only become more aggravated. However, the general could not simply agree, as he thought it might damage his authority. Abulkhair-Khan had unmistakably recognised Neplyuev's arrogance and hubris from the start and was now sure that he could not hope for any goodwill on the governor-general's part. From now on, he needed to be prepared not for negotiations but, most likely, for more attacks. The governor would come to learn how decisively the Khan's seat could respond to anyone who dared to encroach upon its land or send its henchmen in!

 The Khan set off from Orenburg back to his seat in Mantobe on the banks of the Irgiz in a state of irritation. He bade farewell to the biys and sultans of the Adai, Tama, Tabyn and Argyn people, who had travelled with him for the sake of gravitas at a distance of half a day's journey from Or. Taking with him his faithful comrade-in-arms Bektore and five or six warriors from his guard, the Khan headed east.

The Khan and his companions never dropped the pace on their journey back to the summer camp, only stopping to allow their horses time to rest. When he was feeling fatigued, the Khan would doze in the saddle according to his long-standing habit, but he never slowed down despite the exhausting heat that was unusual, even for mid-August. Bektore was well aware of Abulkhair's qualities of endurance and tolerated the long journey without complaint. He rode briskly, either just behind or alongside the Khan and habitually kept a close eye on everything going on around them.

On this occasion, however, at the point where the Kabyrga and the Ulkeyek rivers converged on Abulkhair's route, Barak-Sultan's faithful associate Syrymbet-Batyr and his warriors were waiting for the Khan.

In the early morning of the final day of their long journey, Abulkhair and his fellow travellers had just taken to their horses when the Khan felt a sudden wave of cold anxiety run over him, making him shudder. When they approached the banks of the Kabyrga, his dark-day stallion suddenly began to snort and jerk, continually shaking its head from side to side. Usually calm and able to cover long distances quickly and without complaint, his steed suddenly displayed a temper. His master, who was unsettled as it was, saw this as inappropriate stubbornness and he whipped the stallion's right flank with his sixteen-knot lash.

This time, the Khan, who did not usually show his emotions, was clearly agitated for some reason, which did not escape the attention of Bektore, who suddenly brought his own horse to a stop. At a distance, visible to the naked eye, a group of horsemen appeared on the road up ahead, like a storm cloud might appear in the sky.

'Abeke, my Khan, that is Barak's right-hand man and his henchman Syrymbet! They do not look like a welcoming committee, so I wonder what those scoundrels have in mind!'

Drawing nearer so that they could be heard, Syrymbet, raising himself a little in the saddle and pushing up with his feet in the stirrups, spoke in a harsh tone,

'We have been waiting for you! We are the warriors of our Barak-Sultan!'

'Ah, it's you, Barak's sidekick Syrymbet! Are you waiting out on the road to rob people or something? Be on your way! I see your Barak is frightened to meet me face to face, so he hides underground in his hole like a marmot. So, you had better head off to join him, there's a good chap. Hey! Don't stand in my way! Be gone!'

However, Syrymbet did not budge at Abulkhair's barked order. His broad face barely twitched and he looked self-assuredly right at the Khan, remaining seated arrogantly in the saddle, and replied with a sneer,

'We do not take orders from you, Khan! We have our own ruler if you want to know! All the aides and servants from the Khan's seat will soon do his bidding, so you might as well say your prayers here and now!' Abulkhair felt a rush of blood to his head at such insolence and impertinence and he quivered inside at indignation. He clenched his teeth and his eyes flashed with rage.

'So, your ruler is Barak, who lurks behind in Karnak and has sent his hound to kill me?! The same Barak who sucks up to the Russians with head bowed low and dreams of seizing the Khan's throne?!'

Syrymbet did not react to these words either, continuing to stare at the Khan without a trace of shame on his face.

'We have no intention of soiling our hands on these frightened guards of yours. If you are really so brave and fearless, Khan, then come out to fight yourself!'

Realising that things were taking a bad turn, Bektore hurried forward to block Abulkhair's way and stop him, but to no avail.

'Get out of the way, Bektore! Don't stand in my way! They think I'll be afraid of Barak's weasel-like hired thugs! Give me a spear! Let him try his luck in a one-on-one! Hey, Syrymbet, if you are a real warrior, come into the centre if you're so keen and you really want it!'

Syrymbet had heard about Abulkhair's mastery of the spear and hesitated, appearing suddenly confused, but while he was taking out his spear, the big young batyr Sygai, who could hardly contain his ardour and seething energy, jumped into the centre.

'Allow me, my batyr! I want to fight in a duel! He used my father's name and called all of us weasels and thugs! That struck a nerve and I won't let that go! I'll show this turbulent Khan what is what! If you are from the noble Tore clan, then I am from the Naymans who never back down; I am the son of a Batyr-Nayman!'

When Abulkhair saw not Syrymbet but Barak-Sultan's son, the young Sygai, twirling his spear above his head, he raised his faithful spear with its multi-faceted tip and spurred his war horse forward, which chomped on the bit in anticipation of the battle.

'Ah, would you look at that! He's decided to turn tail from the fight, the son of a jackal! Wait your turn, then! And this one is about to say his farewells to the world! I'll nail this pup to the ground and stamp his face in the earth! If you die, then Syrymbet, who cowardly backed out of the fight with me, will pay the price before your father like the jackal he is! Come on then, you damned jackal pup!'

The next moment, they rushed towards each other and their spears clanged together. Having measured up to one another and assessed their capabilities, they separated and then launched at one another again. When they came together for the third time, the young batyr could not handle the Khan's powerful blow and dropped his spear, only to return to the battle, pulling his curved sabre from his sheath. Abulkhair threw down his spear and took his sabre, too. Unable to withstand the onslaught of the Khan, who wielded his sabre deftly and assuredly from left to right, the young warrior had no time to dodge and received a powerful blow to the shoulder, from which, covered in blood, he literally slid from his horse and with a groan, dropped to the dusty earth.

Seeing the badly wounded Syrgai and the enraged Abulkhair, Syrymbet realised that if he failed to strike an unexpected blow there and then knock the Khan from his saddle, there would be no stopping him. Without waiting for the proper duel to commence, he jumped up and pierced the dark-bay stallion in the flank. The horse roared wildly and toppled over, throwing Abulkhair to the ground, although the Khan was immediately on his feet with sabre in hand. Syrymbet rushed at him again with bloodshot eyes. It was not easy for Abulkhair to repel the spear attacks and strike back at the same time, but he fought with all his strength and did not give up. Syrymbet did not dare to dismount and fight Abulkhair with his sabre, so he continued to swing his spear and strike the Khan from above, circling him on his horse.

In the end, bleeding from stab wounds to the chest from the spear, Abulkhair fell on his side but never let go of his sabre.

Puffing loudly, the battle-weary Syrymbet was unable to strike the final blow and fled the scene.

The dark-bay stallion lay where it had fallen in that merciless battle, with large tears rolling from its eyes, twitched its ears and jerked its legs for the last time.

Bektore and the other warriors, who were unable to save their Khan in this dishonourable fight to the death, brought Abulkhair to his Khan's seat, seriously wounded and having lost a lot of blood.

That day, sitting in the central yurt by the side of the barely alive Abulkhair, Bopai listened to his last words, which he spoke with his lips barely moving,

'My... last... my testament... listen to me and... and stop your crying... hear me out...'

'Yes, my love, my Khan, I am listening!'

Bopai wiped her tears with the corner of her handkerchief and looked in pain at his pale, gaunt face.

'This is the end of my journey... If I knew that this is how I would end my days... Oh, how bitter it is that I did not know... It was for the sake of my people, my own... I fought the best I could with my foes and enemies... and I never yielded in the cruellest of battles... And this is how it turned out... The final blow came not from a stranger but from one of my own... A sudden blow and filthy claws wounded not only my body but, first and foremost, my heart... So much hope... So many aspirations... Ah! All I wanted was unity for my people so they never had to bow their heads to outsiders and to do that without bloodshed... Now, I am leaving without achieving this. Tell our first-born son, our flesh and blood Nuraly, that I bequeath this mission to him. Be his support; I know you will help him with your faithful counsel and wise words, as you have helped me these forty years... All these years by my side... You can do this... I know it... I believe...'

Pronouncing the word *believe*, Abulkhair breathed his last, making Bopai's aching heart shudder in the terrible realisation of the grief that had befallen her.

'My Khan, you loved your people and you burned brightly for them. You were my light and my support! You have gone and my heart has been orphaned without you!'

Bopai's wails of sorrow, her voice so full of inexpressible grief, echoed from the Khan's home far across Mantobe.

That July, the Khan's seat was overcome with great

sorrow and covered with an invisible blanket of mourning and grief. The Kazakh Khan, famed across the vast great steppe, had been laid to rest at the ancient cemetery at the confluence of the Ulkeyek and Kabyrga rivers. Endless streams of people came to the Khan's seat from all parts of the steppe. In line with the ancient Kipchak tradition, under which the glorious warriors and real men of the people were laid to rest, the Khan was buried alongside his faithful companions and witnesses of his honourable battles and achievements in the name of his people — his sabre, spear, armour and belt.

CHAPTER 7

News of Abulkhair-Khan's death reached Barak in Karnak, where the Naymans' thousand-strong herds were grazing on the fertile plains, but the sultan was not best pleased. He listened to Syrymbet, boasting of inflicting the mortal wound, with a deep frown and his face reflected nothing but anger. The realisation that he was involved in Abulkhair's death and he had the blood of the murdered Khan on his hands turned Barak's soul upside down. How could he possibly wash away this sin and justify himself? Could he really have expected such an outcome after so many years of antagonism with the Khan's seat? Removing Abulkhair had proved to be the only way to gain the confidence of the Russian authorities. Lord, what is this braggard talking about?! He is strutting about as if he has achieved something truly great. Fighting to overcome his troubled thoughts, the proud sultan feared taking a single step from his home from that day on. Based on the rumours that reached his ears, the heads of the clans, the biys and elders of all three zhuzes, who included the revered biy Kazybek of the Karakesek clan, who carried weight in the Middle Zhuz, and the noblest and most influential young sultan Abylai, all condemned this act in the harshest terms and planned to make him pay his *kun* for the Khan's murder under the decision of the court of biys.

Very soon, it became clear to Barak-Sultan that the Khan's seat was to declare a blood feud. One night, Abulkhair's middle son Eraly took a detachment and stormed Syrymbet's aul, literally drowning it in blood and cutting Syrymbet's head from his shoulders. He was to be next. His only hope of remaining alive would be to surround himself with large numbers of guards at the fortress in Karnak. It seemed there was no other way. But what if he were to go to the first wife of the Khan's seat, to Bopai-Khanum and beg for her forgiveness? Would she forgive him? Would she stop her sons Nuraly and Eraly, who were determined to take their revenge in blood?

However, Barak could not let go of his arrogance and he saw it as beneath his dignity to admit his guilt and bow his head before the family of Abulkhair-Khan. In the end, he decided he could afford the kun for the Khan's death, whatever the judges levied against him.

Bopai, meanwhile, had received no answer from the Orenburg authorities to her letter asking for consent to avenge Abulkhair's death in accordance with steppe law, so she sent a messenger to the Adai clan, to the reliable old friend of the family Shotan. Not only Shotan but the other batyrs, who had fought in the same ranks with Abulkhair in their time, needed only to receive her request for vengeance.

Shotan hurriedly arrived at the Khan's seat on the banks of the Irgiz with the batyrs Aibas from the Tabyn clan, Konai from the Zhemenei and Argynbai from the Shomekei.

After the traditional welcome dinner, Bopai announced her sentence on Barak-Sultan and asked that it be fulfilled to the letter.

'If you find Barak in Karnak, ruling over the Konyrats and Naymans, be sure to execute the sentence so his family can see; if it is somewhere outside or in the steppe, do it so all his people can see. Lower him to his knees, remove his sultan's crown and tell him that means we have removed his head! Then, as a sign that you have broken his back, remove his leather belt.

Take away his staff, all his weapons and his ring as a sign that his sultan's title and his special status have been taken from him and that he has been excluded from his noble family. It will tell everyone that he is of no use to his people. After that, pierce his earlobes, like they do to wear earrings, to ensure he will now appear no different from any ordinary old maid! Shave off his moustache and beard and use a dagger to shave part of his head, leaving clumps of hair, which will mean that his stupid head is now as useless as a bucket with holes. If that is not enough, cut the plaits of his old woman and trim the mane and tail of his horse! And remember, my dear friends, that such an arrogant and proud man as Barak is not afraid of death and simply executing this treacherous enemy would be too simple a retribution for the death of our Abulkhair! The scoundrel Barak must be left alive but dishonoured in such a way that his disgraced soul will live on, never to forget!'

After hearing all this, Shotan turned sharply to Bopai and looked right at her with a sharp look in his burning eyes:

'Oh, Bopai, this is a terrible punishment that no living person could ever wish for! None of us would ever think of punishing a guilty man in this way! The Barak that I know will not want to live any longer after all that!'

The next morning, Shotan and his companions left the Khan's seat and headed for the slopes of Karatau. When they arrived there a week later, they caught Barak in his home in Karnak. The sultan's guards were no match for the four batyrs who had suddenly appeared before them. As for Barak, taken by surprise, he was forced to endure everything that the avengers did to him precisely and in the order that Bopai had instructed.

After the sentence, handed down in absentia, had been executed, Barak fell to the floor in front of his wife and, sobbing and moaning, called out to the batyrs as they were leaving, 'Oh, such treachery! It would be better to cut off my head with my grin fixed on it and take that to Bopai than to humiliate me like this! Let Abulkhair's woman see that, even in death, I would still grin at her and be no inferior to their clan! Kill me!'

He did not know how long he remained prostrate in that state. He no longer felt anything. Humiliated by the Adai, with his humanity and his manhood violated, he was now simply unable to show his face to anyone. This terrible punishment had broken his spirit and his pride irrevocably. The blood from the cut wounds on his shaved head mingled with the tears that flowed from his dead-looking eyes. He was still breathing, but he was already dead inside. He could hear his wife sobbing, scratching at her face in grief; her howls made his head feel even heavier and he felt wholly desolate. A film now covered his eyes like a dark veil, a fog, a meaningless mirage. This was no longer life, but it was not death either, and the emptiness and barely visible reality around him flickered in vague images before him.

Having endured this unthinkable humiliation, the devastated Barak suffered badly, resigned from life and, it seemed, himself. He could not move, for his arms and legs would not do his bidding, merely trembling constantly. Barak lay, bent double, for days on end and grew so tired that he stopped counting the days and soon grew confused about time and space. He would not accept sympathy or treatment by healers and servants; he gave no answers and said nothing. It was as if Barak had resigned himself to the cruel sentence that had been handed down according to the strict tenets of the ancient steppe laws.

Summer turned to autumn, winter to spring and he saw and felt nothing. Having lost all his strength after that terrible punishment that Bopai had ordered for him, Barak-Sultan never recovered and passed from this life a couple of years later.

Two years after Abulkhair's death, on a spring day, Nuraly and his mother, Bopai-Khanum, came to the Khan's mausoleum on the banks of the Ulkeyek to plant young aspen saplings around it.

Once this had been done, Almukhambet, fulfilling the functions of mullah in addition to his clerical duties at the Khan's seat, read out the traditional prayer.

'Abeke, even if not all but just some of these saplings take root and flourish, the tall trees will form a sure sign of your eternal resting place for travellers wishing to offer their respects and pay tribute to your memory,' Bopai said, running her face over her face in prayer.

* * *

The biys, sultans and elders of the Junior Zhuz and the Argyn and Kipchak clans of the Middle Zhuz all knew about the last will of Abulkhair Khan and, having gathered at the Khan's seat on the Irgiz, proclaimed Nuraly, Abulkhair's heir, the new Khan. During the grand council at the Khan's seat, Azhibai-Biy, Zhanibek-Tarkhan and all the nobles spoke about how important it was to preserve the unity of the people, and they shared their thoughts.

'Nuraly, my dear, you are now the leader of your people and its military commander. You successfully avenged the death of your father, our Khan, who was true to the oath sworn before the people, who strove throughout his life to unite us all and prevent greedy outsiders from encroaching even an inch onto our land, but who fell victim to the greed of his own brethren. Barak, who for so long lusted after power, ended up staining his honour and name in blood and is now long gone from this world. We can only wish that such enmity will never again appear among us and that such history will never repeat itself! We hope that you will remain true to the decree of your father, Abulkhair, and will heed the wise advice of your mother, Bopai!

Know that this is the wish of the entire Alim clan that resides on the western slopes on both banks of the rivers Oyl, Sagiz and Zhem!'

The learned Azhibai, with the blessing of Aiteke-Biy, spoke sincerely and from the heart, which greatly pleased Eset-Batyr, the tarkhan of the Tama clan, who spoke next:

'Azhibai has conveyed most eloquently all the innermost thoughts that are held by the Tama clan, Nuraly! May Allah support you on your path! Be a worthy and respected khan of your people!'

'The elder brother of all Alshyns and the respected Alim

judge Azhibai-aga spoke not only for his clan but for all of us!' Zhanibek-Batyr began in an unhurried, even voice. 'At the time, not all of our brothers understood or accepted Abeke's wise policy, which he pursued with our complicated neighbour to the northwest — he signed an agreement in an attempt to save our lands and to preserve peace, despite their obvious desire to subjugate us. Back in those famous years, overcoming all tribulations, hard battle after hard battle, he proved able to resist the Dzungars, who were in danger of overrunning us. He defeated the enemy and saved his homeland. The only thing was that his homeland didn't save its lion with his heart of gold! Given my right as an elder and a father, I would like to say to our Khan Nuraly that it is important now for all of us to maintain unity in our common cause! May Almighty Allah help him continue the noble path of his father, the esteemed Abulkhair! Let it be so!'

The others present said nothing, for everything had been said. They merely nodded to express their approval.

Nuraly-Sultan stepped onto the white felt mat, touched the holy Qur'an and read the traditional oath of the Khan. Wearing a snow-white *karkara* headdress and an ivory necklace encrusted with pearls and emeralds, the magnificent royal Bopai-Khanum presented her son with the silver sword in its golden scabbard that usually hung above Abulkhair's throne.

'Son, as you inherit the high title of Khan, at this special moment, you accept the sword of pure silver, the evidence of your father's forty-year reign. Kneel now before the purity of this khan's symbol and touch the noble blade with your forehead. Remember the last will of the Khan, who devoted his entire life to ensure his people remained independent and be a just and merciful ruler, not sprinkling this sword with blood, but making it a symbol of the will and loyalty of the people!'

Nuraly accepted the heartfelt words of his mother, which

she had spoken serenely and with great dignity. He bowed his head and carefully took the sword in his hands, slowly removed it from its scabbard, knelt and touched the blade with his lips before pressing it to his forehead.

The nobles present at the ceremony all responded with their wishes of good luck.

'May the spirit of our Khan Abeke watch over Nuraly-Khan!'

'Amen!'

And so, in early November, when the dark-grey autumn blew its first frosty breath, Nuraly took the yoke of power from his father, having sworn his oath before the biys and elders at the Khan's seat.

* * *

Bopai had a clear understanding that, in this troubled time, when the authorities in Orenburg exercised an ambiguous and changeable view of the policy being implemented at the Khan's seat, preserving the title of the main Kazakh Khan was critical and so, she did everything in her power to achieve this objective.

After the proclamation of Nuraly as head of the Khan's horde, Bopai urgently prepared a letter with her seal to Empress Elizaveta Petrovna with a request to recognise the status of Nuraly as the chief Khan of the Kazakhs, having inherited the throne from his father, Abulkhair. She openly wrote that the support of the great Empress herself was important to her for further relations with the Russian authorities, as it had been in Abulkhair's time.

Bopai sent another two letters with the same content to the Orenburg Governor Ivan Neplyuev and the Ambassador in Saint-Petersburg Kutlu-Muhammed Tevkelev. Bopai knew that the Empress would seek the counsel of these two men when making her decision.

The experienced politician Neplyuev instantly realised that, despite Nuraly's legal right to inherit the title of Khan,

Bopai-Khanum's main goal was to hold power in the hands of her clan and continue to rule the Kazakh people single-handedly. He replied to the message immediately, making assurances in his response that he fully supported the idea and that Her Imperial Majesty would also approve of the decision. However, the letter he sent to the College of Foreign Affairs in Saint-Petersburg was of an altogether different content. It read as follows: *Although we recognise Abulkhair's heir as Khan, to preserve the authority of the Khan's seat, the spread of this authority should be prevented so he may not have the influence of Abulkhair.* The Orenburg governor-general sincerely hoped that once Abulkhair had been destroyed, the united Kazakh Khanate could be divided up into smaller, disparate khanates, after which a new stage of colonisation could then begin. Neplyuev was determined to bring this matter to an end and to obtain an official order to this effect from the Empress. He brought his insidious plans to the attention of Tevkelev, who, although belonging to the higher echelons of power in Saint-Petersburg, held a subordinate position.

In late February 1749, a delegation headed from the Khan's seat to Saint-Petersburg via Orenburg. It was headed by the young and energetic sultan Zhanibek, Nuraly's son-in-law, and its purpose was to deliver an official letter from Bopai and official consent from the Orenburg governor to recognise the Khanate. After a month-long, arduous journey, the envoys finally arrived at the royal palace in the remote northern city on the banks of the Neva. Entering through the grand entrance to the enormous palace, the envoys found themselves in the reception all, where the Empress Elizaveta herself and the Chancellor of the College of Foreign Affairs, Alexei Petrovich Bestuzhev-Ryumin, were waiting for them.

Zhanibek-Sultan bowed and placed his right hand on his chest in homage to the charming, fair-faced Empress. Elizaveta's head was crowned with a small bifurcated crown, encrusted with precious stones and pearls, with a sparkling diamond through the centre with a woven pattern. The Tsarina wore a luxurious dress of expensive purple fabric embroidered with gold and silver thread, with a slightly open neckline and a long hem to the floor; over that was a light cape of golden silk. Zhanibek similarly greeted the chancellor, who was dressed in a red uniform jacket with the Order of St Andrew the Apostle pinned to his left breast.

Arslan Bekmet, a fast-talking Bashkir who had come with them to act as interpreter, had already managed to relay the sultan's address word for word.

'Your Majesty, Empress Elizabeth, we extend to you our deepest respects and hasten to assure you of our most sincere intentions in your regard.'

The Empress gave a faint smile in appreciation and acceptance of the sultan's words.

'Allow me to present to Your Majesty this letter written by Abulkhair's wife, Bopai-Khanum, to you, translated by the Russian interpreter Yakub Gulaip, as well as an official address from the governor's office in Orenburg to His Excellency, Head of the Chancellery of Foreign Affairs.'

Zhanibek-Sultan deftly presented the letters to the Empress, sealed in envelopes and bearing seals, and she, handing them to her secretary, who was standing at a distance, spoke with a French accent:

'Dear Monsieur Sultan Zhanibek, I accept with sincere appreciation the message from the most-honoured Bopai-Khanum, as delivered by the minister of the Khan's seat, and I will personally see that a reply is sent in good time. Count Bestuzhev will make it known to you as soon as possible.'

'I am most grateful, Your Majesty!'

Zhanibek Sultan bowed his head again, and the Tsarina's courteous smile in return signalled that the audience was over.

The very next day, Count Bestuzhev handed the sultan the Tsarina's decree that declared that Nuraly was recognised as the Kaisak Khan. The special royal charter, delivered in early July from Saint-Petersburg by Zhanibek-Sultan upon his return to the Khan's seat on the Irgiz, brought Bopai no comfort. The northern neighbours were displaying their customary authoritarianism and did not attempt to conceal that they did not recognise Nuraly as the principal Khan of all the Kazakh people. Taking the position adopted by Governor Neplyuev as their basis, the Russian Empire was clearly showing that it had no interest in the principal Khan strengthening his authority, as had been the case under Abulkhair. Of course, Bopai understood that this decision was dictated by the intention of the Russian authorities to govern the Kazakhs. She could not help thinking that serious trials and tribulations would await Abulkhair's descendants as they tried to protect the interests of their people and safeguard vast territories, but she did her best not to reveal such worries.

* * *

Learning that Eset-Tarkhan and Azhibai-Biy, accompanied by the heads of the Alim, Adai and Tabyn clans and noble batyrs, had set off to visit Bopai-Khanum at the Khan's seat on the banks of the Irgiz to celebrate the proclamation of Nuraly as the new Khan, the Edil Kalmyks, who had settled in the lower reaches of the Zhaiyk, remembered their old enmity and decided to take revenge on the Tama clan for past wrongs. Eight years before, during a battle on the eastern side of the Ustyurt Plateau in the sands of Sam, Botagoz, the brave daughter of Eset-Batyr, had defeated their batyr Kondy by lassoing his neck and dragging him along the ground. Naturally, they had not forgotten this. Taking full advantage of the absence of anyone who could put up worthy resistance, the Torgauts decided to lay waste to Azhibai's aul, where Botagoz was living as his daughter-in-law, and destroy his entire clan. The peaceful lives of the Ak-Kete clan, residing in the valley of the rivers Oyl and Kenzhaly, were shattered by a sudden attack by bloodthirsty Kalmyks. No sooner did she hear of the enemy attack than Botagoz, the young daughter-in-law of Azhibai's family, whose home was located a short distance away on the slopes of Kelbatyr Hill, swiftly gathered the few remaining warriors, as well as shepherds and other labourers from the neighbouring auls, into a reasonable detachment. The Torgauts had already destroyed the aul, sparing neither the elderly, the women or the children and now, driving the rustled livestock, they were heading for Kelbatyr Hill, where Botagoz was waiting for them with her heavily armed men. Intoxicated with their easy victory, the Kalmyk khuntaiji immediately recognised the slight batyr at the head of the detachment in well-fitting battle armour.

'Hold on a moment! If I don't cut off your locks of hair and lay you over my saddle, girl, like a hunter's prey, then I am no khuntaiji!' the Torgaut leader roared. 'First, I have to take that maid alive — the one leading all these men. I'll challenge her to a duel. Without hurting her too much or riling her up, I'll measure up, pretend I've lost, wriggle out and steer my horse in this direction. The moment I draw near, four or five of you move quickly forward and be ready to take her prisoner! There's no other way of catching this treacherous old bird!'

Neither Botagoz nor her warriors knew what the huddled Torgauts were planning and could only see them pulling on their reins and occasionally looking over in her direction. What was clear, however, was that the enemy was not afraid of attacking their small detachment.

'We'll challenge their khuntaiji to a duel!' Botagoz said, raising her spear above her head and twirling it in the air. 'I'll go out. The rest you, stay where you are!'

One of the more experienced and younger warriors

wanted to object to her decisive action:

'How come, Botagoz, my dear, when we are all lined up in ranks, you plan to be the first to rush into the attack?! Those jackals look awfully suspicious; you can see for yourself...'

'Oh, I can see it, all right! And that is why I am going in to fight first! They've come here to avenge their Kondy-Batyr. If I keep my head down, the honour of my father, Eset-Batyr, will be stained, so I have to risk it. I challenge you, one on one!' she cried out.

Hearing that Botagoz was calling him to a duel first while he was still explaining his cunning plan to his men, the khuntaiji was nettled.

He spurred his brown stallion and with his broad face contorted with anger and red from exertion, he rushed at full speed into battle. Botagoz sprang forward on her roan horse with its white forelock, deftly playing with her lightweight spear, fearlessly stood before her adversary and engaged in a fierce battle.

In spite of his bull-like strength, the fierce khuntaiji seemed to be over-cautious and deliberately feeble with his spear; he did not wish to push forward or repel attacks too firmly. By first entering the fight confidently, the Kalmyk then behaved differently, and this was his way of putting his opponent's guard down, although it might have been seen as negligence. Botagoz's instincts, however, did not let her down. After another clash, the khuntaiji suddenly turned his horse around and rushed away, but Botagoz held her steed back, refusing to give chase. The lousy plan had failed and the Kalmyks' tricks to lure Botagoz over and capture her had come to nothing. Instead, it looked as if the khuntaiji had got cold feet and ran away.

'Hey, puppy-dog, why step forward if you don't have the nerve to fight?'

However, the Torgaut leader whipped his horse and rushed back into the attack, intent on finishing the job once and for all. He was sure he would defeat the woman at the first attempt. He prepared his spear and approached so close that their stirrups came together. However, Botagoz adroitly dodged the blow of the Torgaut with bulging eyes, whose chest was protected by chainmail, and she struck with lightning speed with her spear, striking the enemy on the unprotected back of the head. In an instant, the large khuntaiji seemed to collapse. He dropped his spear and rolled off his horse with a roar. Both sides then charged at each other and a savage fight began, leading to a chaotic melee.

The steppe was drowned in deafening sounds — the clang and ringing of metal on metal, the roar and moans of the wounded and the dying, and all the noise and confusion of a bloody battle. In a matter of half a day, the Kalmyk army had been finally crushed. They had lost their commander-in-chief, the khuntaiji, and some had died on the battlefield. Others were taken prisoner while those with more agile horses had fled in all directions. The girls and women that the Kalmyks had taken captive were released and the Tama livestock was safely returned to their pastures.

News of the victory over the Torgauts, won by Botagoz, daughter-in-law of the elder Azhibai and brave daughter of Eset-Batyr, together with the detachment she assembled, spread to all corners of the vast steppe, passed by word of mouth among the people.

Alas, after that battle, perhaps from an evil eye or unwanted words or glances in her direction, this beautiful warrior, gentle as a reed on the water, intelligent and wise, with quite awe-inspiring courage and determination, fell incurably ill and, after a short while, she died in the arms of her husband, Barysai-Batyr.

Bopai understood the grief of Azhibai and Eset and felt the acute pain of their loss.

Bopai and Nuraly went to Kenzhaly, to the slopes of Kelbatyr Hill where the Ak-Kete roamed, to express their condolences and support Azhibai, who seemed to have aged even more in this time, holding an unquenchable sadness in his eyes.

'My dear, respected Azhibai-aga, so unexpectedly has this bright star of your family and our entire nation been extinguished and your grief brings untold sadness to all of us. Indeed, no one can fight their destiny; what can be done? Oh, such grief!' Bopai said in a faltering voice and sighed bitterly.

'Oh my! And what now? We have no other choice but to obey the will of Allah! She was born a gentle maiden, but she had valour and courage in her blood. She protected her people from the enemy numerous times, but her life was so short. It was her fate to be born in such a difficult time and to live such a short life, enduring all the hardships together with her people. She could not remain indifferent as she looked at our enemies tormenting our lands, and she burned with a fire of vengeance for the spilt blood and tears of the people. But I cannot bring myself to say she was a heartless warrior in battles with our enemies. Why, oh why, did such a precious, darling girl, born to be a mother, need to take on such a heavy burden and find herself in a situation where she had to sacrifice her young life?!'

From Azhibai's words, so full of grief and pain, the home fell into a dark silence.

'Do not lose heart, Azhibai-aga! All of Abulkhair's clan and his descendants, the entire Khan's seat, all mourn the passing of Botagoz together with you. But such is Allah's will! Pull yourself together first, and then you can calm us and all the people.' Nuraly spoke in a hushed but resolute voice, and he looked directly at Azhibai.

'Ah, Nuraly, I hear what you say! Indeed, you are right — in such a sad hour, I need to offer comfort to and support you! This is what my people expect of me. How could I not have thought of this; how could I not have seen? May your words that have reminded me of this be of comfort to me at another time, too.'

* * *

A fair amount of time had passed since Nuraly had occupied his father's throne and yet the distressing news continued pouring in. The Russian Cossacks continued their armed raids on the eastern banks of the Zhaiyk, Edil and Zhem. The Torgauts did not stop either, still tormenting the Kazakh auls with the barbaric raids. As if this were not enough, the Turkmens could not calm down either and continued their battles with the Adai people for the lands in the Mangystau lowlands. Naturally, all of this caused considerable concern.

Saint-Petersburg might have officially secured Nuraly's status as Khan by charter, but Governor-General Neplyuev, who represented the Tsarist authorities in Orenburg, took the position of nothing more than an observer in these circumstances. Nuraly knew that the Russian Empire was behind all this, for it was ultimately interested in weakening the Khan's seat. Knowing this, he ruthlessly repulsed the attacks of the Zhaiyk Cossacks, preventing them from invading the land where Kazakhs had lived since time immemorial. Just as during the reign of Abulkhair, the Kazakh Khanate was ready to put up strong resistance and this presented a major obstacle in achieving the key Tsarist objective — to establish an unimpeded route through Kazakh land to the gates of Asia.

Bopai, of course, understood the worries that plagued her son, who held power in the Khan's seat and who was responsible for the destiny of his people. However, at the same time, she was becoming more and more convinced that her son's efforts to reach an agreement with the Tsarist authorities through peaceful means would come to nothing. This was particularly evident after repeated appeals were sent with envoys to Saint-Petersburg, addressed to Empress Elizaveta, stating that the Orenburg administration was doing nothing to stop the continuous Cossack and Edil Kalmyk raids. None of these appeals was answered and no outcome was achieved. Bopai finally came to realise that the only solution was to fight.

One day, not long before they departed for the wintering grounds on the banks of the Syr Darya, a messenger arrived at the Khan's seat with an urgent note from the Mangystau Adai. Shotan-Batyr informed Nuraly that clashes with Turkmens had become particularly frequent in recent times. He also reported that this could lead to an irreconcilable bloody war between the Adai and the Turkmens, where the latter enjoyed the support of the Khanate of Khiva. In spite of how tired he was, the tanned messenger entered the Khan's home right from the road and, kneeling, he delivered Shotan's message word for word to Nuraly Khan with Bopai by his side.

Giving a brief instruction to his guard, Nuraly sent the messenger to rest after his journey and looked over at Bopai, who was deep in thought. Expecting her to hint at something to start the conversation, her son looked as if to ask, *What do you say to this news?* Bopai, as was her custom, spoke calmly, weighing every word,

'Shotan is a glorious batyr who fought in the same ranks as your father when they crushed the Dzungars in the Battle of Bulantin. He was among those who avenged your father's death on Barak. There is good reason for his concern. Your great uncle, the head of a large Adai clan, wants to say that the time has come to give a just response to the Turkmens, who threaten not just a single clan from the south but our entire people! The time has come, my dear son, to resolve this problem once and for all. You must have realised this for yourself, of course.'

'Yes, mother, you are right! If this were simply a conflict between neighbours, Shotan would not have sent a special messenger. We must prepare to march out tomorrow!'

Bopai nodded approvingly, supporting her son's

decision.

During the night before the long and arduous journey, Nuraly could not sleep because of the persistent thoughts that jumped from one thing to the next. In the succession of recollections and images that appeared before him, a story of Shotan surfaced, which he had once heard from his father and Bokenbai during a winter hunt over fresh snow. That day, Nuraly's hunting dog, a ginger tazy with ragged ears, had managed to take three foxes at once, two of which Abulkhair gave as a gift to Bokenbai. In high spirits after such a successful hunt, the elders began talking on the way back to the camp about Shotan-Batyr's hunting prowess and his courage during military campaigns.

'I remember the first time we saw Shotan with a spear in hand. What a brave, courageous batyr he proved himself to be back then! And that was in the year when we fought a hundred thousand Dzungars under Tsewang Rabdan, in that same spring when the Kalmyks came to the slopes of Karatau,' Bokenbai said, spurring his stallion on a little faster. 'If I am not mistaken, it was at the Sugyndyk Pass.'

'Yes, that's exactly right! I remember he had separated from the Adai warriors and single-handedly put paid to a host of Kalmyks. Shotan was very young back then, the son of Nazar-Batyr, famous throughout the Zhary clan, and he displayed such exceptional bravery! Oh, and you must not forget, Bokenbai, that time when Shotan saved you in that battle when an enemy warrior tried to jump you in an ambush.'

'Of course I remember, Abeke! And then, three years later, at Bulantin, in the valley to the southwest of the River Sarysu, Shokan surprised the *sardar*, the commander-in-chief of the Senior Zhuz Sanyryk-Batyr!'

'Yes, that's right! A Kalmyk shouted out to the sardar, "Hey, Sanyryk! Come out and fight in a duel if you're not afraid that I will scatter your ageing bones or send out a reliable batyr!" I remember Sanyryk intended to enter the fight himself, but barely had he managed to tighten the saddle girth on his stallion when our hero jumped out before him.' Abulkhair said, unable to conceal his admiration. 'I was probably the only one who could recognise him, for he had covered his face with a white silk handkerchief he wore under his helmet. All the astonished Sanyryk could do was look at me as if to ask who on earth that was and then at the warrior, who paid no one any attention, had already rushed at that puffed-up Kalmyk. He charged in, throwing his spear from one hand to the other as he went before stabbing his opponent in the shoulder, knocking him from the saddle and grabbing his sabre with lightning-quick speed in his right hand. Sanyryk-Batyr, who was standing next to me, had time only to exclaim, "My God, is that a man or a demon, moving with the speed of a whirlwind?! Just look, the poor fellow didn't know what had hit him and he had been turned over and had his throat cut!" and, at that moment, Shotan had already placed the Kalmyk's head, heavy as cast iron, onto his spear, rushed back to us like the wind and threw the head at Sanyryk's feet. Well, Bokenbai, you saw for yourself at the Battle of Bulantin that the best warriors from each clan and each tribe were fighting to the death and so defeated our blood enemies. And Shotan was the best of the best among the twelve tribes of the Junior Zhuz, and that is no exaggeration!'

'You are so right, Abeke! Our Sanyryk, that glorified batyr famed throughout the Senior Zhuz, could not hide his pride and appreciation after that Battle of Bulantin, and he blessed each one of the warriors who served in the same ranks under your leadership. And when he presented Shotan with a dark-bay horse with a silver harness and a sword with a blade of mace and a golden hilt, our pride and joy knew no limit!'

It turned out that Nuraly remembered every word from that conversation between his father and Bokenbai after the hunt when they were generous in their praise for Shotan, whom he was to help the following day.

On that cool autumn morning, when the pale dawn had barely appeared in the sky, Nuraly-Khan's sizeable troops moved out in silence and without unnecessary publicity from the Khan's seat to the southwest. Making only short stopovers at deep freshwater wells and never deviating from the planned route, they advanced deeper and deeper to the south until they finally stopped at Shotan's well, about a kilometre from the hollow at Otes.

Next to the deep well, lined with flat, rough, black stones of the kind found in the Ustyurt Plateau, stood a hut where the guard lived. This grown man, who kept watch over the well alone, was startled to see an army approaching through a veil of dust.

'It's all right, don't get in a spin,' Nuraly said to him, slowly dismounting and, with his whip bent in his hand, he walked over to the well. 'I think this stone vessel has sufficient water, does it not? Our horses are simply parched from thirst.'

'But of course! If you have a couple of strong lads to pump the water, we'll fill the well bowl in no time. There is as much water in this bottomless well as in a river without banks, my Khan!'

'We don't need you to tell us that Shotan's well is full of water! Come on and pull!'

That year, not a drop of rain had fallen from the very beginning of June, and the Adai people and their livestock had suffered badly. That was when Shotan, the head of the camp, had dug this well on his own without outside help. His dedication and strength were legendary among the people and Nuraly had heard about this many times before. How Shotan had found water in that dry, grey earth and how he had managed to pinpoint the source of that vital resource under the multiple layers of strata remained a mystery. Some said that Shotan climbed down from his horse and literally crawled along the ground, cupping his ear and listening closely until he finally stopped in that place and took up his metal shovel. With sleeves rolled up and, despite the risk of error, he began to dig all alone, never stopping to rest until he had dug a hole ten fathoms deep, throwing the dry earth out. After that, he began to dig gently down, one or two inches at a time. Twenty days later, moisture began to seep through the yellow soil and he realised that his hearing had not failed him and that there was not much further to go until he reached considerable reserves of water beneath the seemingly lifeless earth in the middle of the wild steppe. With every movement of his shovel, the soil became wetter and wetter and the pail of soil he had to raise to the surface was getting heavier and heavier. In the end, a month later, at a depth of twenty-five fathoms, water began to flow, at first in thin streams and then in gushing torrents. Ten of the strongest lads raised Shotan to the surface, bound to a heavy harness and immediately, the sound of gushing water could be heard, which instantly filled the pit that the batyr had dug. Shotan's well brought life to the region and watered the parched earth and all who lived on it.

Having watered his horses with the fresh water from Shotan's well, Nuraly moved on with greater vigour and even quickened the pace.

Leaving the banks of the Kabyrga River one sunny October day that coloured the surrounding area in gold, Nuraly-Khan's five-thousand-strong army crossed the Ustyurt Plateau in ten days at pace and reached the Mangystau lowlands, where numerous Adai auls were settled.

Shotan knew of Nuraly's pending arrival and, receiving news that he was already close, began preparing a grand welcome for the Khan. Together with the nobles of the neighbouring clans on the Karaoi plain, who included

Esbolai-Biy of the Berish clan, Atakozy of the Adai clan and batyrs headed by Akpan, Shotan himself moved out to meet the Khan and waited for him not far from the aul. The greeting party also included a young batyr named Beket from the Adai Koskulak clan.

Shotan dismounted and passed the reins of his mottled chestnut stallion to one of the warriors beside him and headed towards Nuraly, who was approaching with a cordial smile.

'Assalamu alaikum, my dear Shotan!'

'Wa-alaikum Assalam! How was your journey? All well, I hope? Welcome to the home of your mother's kin, Nuraly, my nephew, our Khan!'

Esbolai, Atakozi and Akpan, though older than Nuraly, greeted the Khan with the appropriate courtesy. The Khan himself showed his reciprocal respect by extending both arms to them.

'May your visit to your relatives, your great uncles be blessed, my Khan!' Atakozy said, gratefully accepting the due respect that Nuraly had extended.

'Please accept our esteem for such a worthy descendant of Abeke, whose spirit watches over and supports us all, like a lion, his pride.' Esbolai-Biy said, quite overcome with emotion.

'You know that we, the Berish clan, are one of the twelve clans of the inseparable Adai people,' Akpan-Batyr followed and bowed before the Khan.

Beket, who was standing alongside, smiled brightly and said,

'Assalamu alaikum, Khan-aga!'

'Wa-alaikum as-salam, my dear!' Nuraly replied and looked closely at the young warrior's cordial-looking face.

Shotan noticed that the Khan could not recognise the young batyr and hurried to introduce him,

'This is Beket, your younger cousin on your mother's side, son of Myrzakul from the Munal-Adai. He completed his studies at the madrasah of Shergazy-Khan at Khiva and he is now a hafiz with extensive religious knowledge. Despite his young age, he knows a great deal. Beket teaches his students at the mosque that he built himself on the banks of the River Zhem. Not only that, but he is an excellent warrior, prepared to defend our lands from the dishonourable Turkmens. He has joined us today especially to meet and welcome you!'

'Splendid, well done!'

Nuraly looked respectfully at the young man's strong-willed and intelligent face. *He is indeed a real hafiz! His behaviour, his appearance — it all speaks of a remarkable mind and true spirituality!* the Khan thought and his favourable disposition was reflected in his warm look. Beket instantly sensed the benevolent inner message of the Khan.

After the official welcome, Shotan and his men accompanied the arrivals to the aul.

The next day, as if he had simply been waiting for Nuraly-Khan to arrive, a messenger rode in from the Turkmens who lived nearby, on the opposite bank of the Amu Darya. The messenger announced that the Turkmen sardars Ogylsha and Seitkutylyk, taking advantage of the support of the Khiva Khan Nader Shah, were pressuring them and forcing them to pay tribute to the Khivans. The reason why the Turkmens, fighting with the Adai people over Mangystau lands, had turned to the Kazakhs for help was because Shotan had once saved the Turkmens. The Torgauts had once attacked the aul of the Turkmen Annasaid, plundered and took prisoners — and that is when Shotan had taken a detachment, caught up with the Kalmyks, crushed them head-on and thus saved the Turkmen people. Since that time, they had come to realise that, at the critical moment, they would do best to rely specifically on Shotan-Batyr.

'Indeed, my Khan, the main threat to us now comes from Khiva!' Shotan said, relaying the Turkmen messenger's words to the Khan. 'They want to oust us from the peninsula once and for all with the help of other Turkmens, who rely on their protection. And it is the Turkmen people who will end up suffering, for their innocent civilians find themselves caught between two fires. Therefore, they are not getting involved directly, but those Khiva associates, just like the sardars I mentioned, need to be calmed down, if you will allow it. Besides, we must not forget the evil intentions of our blue-eyed enemies in the north, who are ready to gather at the right moment and charge towards us across the Edil and the Zhaiyk. If your ten-thousand-strong army could help us and protect the peninsula and the borders of the Karaoi Plain, then I think we will swiftly manage to deal with the sardars ourselves.'

Nuraly listened attentively to the elaborate plans of Shotan, who was prepared to march against Ogylsha and Seitkutylyk, and he wished him every success.

'But you need to be careful with them, Shotan. The Turkmens will not attack their own brothers with you when the decisive moment comes. Make sure that, by wanting to help the weak and become a shield for them, you don't fall into a trap.' Shotan nodded to indicate that he understood Nuraly's concerns and would heed his advice.

Without waiting for the onset of those cold November days that mark the beginning of winter, Nuraly took a small detachment and set off the next day back to his Khan's seat. He sent the bulk of his army to the north of the peninsula and another third, despite Shotan's objections, joined with the Adai warriors who were preparing to march out against the Turkmens.

Shotan's detachments bypassed the Ustyurt Plateau and emerged on the wide-open valley in the lower reaches of the right bank of the Amu Darya, near the northern border where the Turkmen people had settled. Ogylsha and Seitkutylyk's warriors were waiting for them here, confident that they would not give the Kazakhs an opportunity to advance, crush them and achieve a swift victory. Nader Shah, back on his Khiva throne in his luxurious Urgench palace, drowning in beautiful, flowering gardens, had placed great hope in these two Turkmen sardars, who seethed in their rage and hatred for the Adai people. Winter came late in those parts and the weather there was still clear and warm. On one such day, when the sun was at its zenith, the Turkmen forces attacked the Adai troops from two sides and held them in a vice-like grip, counting on their sudden, devastating blow being decisive. However, they met with strong resistance from both flanks, which held their positions well. Unable to overcome Shotan's army in one attack, they were forced to retreat that evening.

The two sides, equal in strength and rage, could have faced off against one another for a considerable time, but the Adai warriors had not rested after their long journey to the battlefield and their horses were extremely tired. Therefore, the following morning, as soon as the dawn had illuminated the sky with its pale light, Shotan took a small group of warriors and rode to the centre of the field. Without dismounting, he climbed to the top of a small hill. The Turkmens became agitated and started to move.

'Hey, Ogylsha-Sardar, listen to me! If you want to avoid excessive bloodshed on both your side and ours, fight with me alone! Whoever loses will remain defeated and our troops will not need to enter battle! If you are brave enough, come out to the centre of the battlefield — I am the Kazakh Shotan who brought the Adai her; perhaps you have heard of me?! If you are afraid, then send out one of your most worthy warriors.' It took quite a long time for the Turkmens to respond to Shotan's call for a duel.

'Looks like he's too afraid!'

'Whatever kind of batyr he might be, a sardar fears for his life too!'

'Who is this Turkmen Ogylsha if he is not afraid of our Shotan?!' the warriors accompanying Shotan talked among themselves.

'Quiet, let us wait a little longer. And if it doesn't work, we'll go into battle, come what may! Ensure the lads are ready to enter battle!'

Shotan raised his spear, decorated with owl feathers, pulled the reins to control his stallion, which was shifting impatiently from foot to foot, and turned to look over his detachment, well-armed and ready to advance.

At that moment, Ogylsha, with a red scarf around his head, advanced to the centre from the opposite side. He was riding a dark-bay stallion with a long neck that curved in an arc beneath him.

'Hey, Shotan-Kazakh! Come closer, come on over here!' Ogylsha bellowed, nervously twirling his spear in his hands. At about a hundred paces from Shotan, he stopped his horse, calculating the distance to the attack.

Shotan turned his stallion sharply and rushed forward, his spear at the ready.

In three approaches, sparks flew from the clashes of spears, but no one yielded. The excited stallions roared and chomped at the bit, sometimes bouncing off one another's flanks and the two warriors charged one another. Having no opportunity to free themselves from the reins held tight in their masters' strong hands, the horses separated, span around in excitement and then came together again as their riders engaged in battle once more.

On the fourth occasion, the chestnut horse sprang sharply towards the dark bay, from which the latter veered to the left. In the blink of an eye, Ogylsha's spear slipped from his hand and fell to the ground. Shotan, however, was an honourable warrior and he did not allow himself to take advantage of his opponent's vulnerability, so he too threw his spear to the ground, drawing instead his damask-steel sabre with its golden hilt, presented to him by Sanyryk-

Batyr after the Battle of Bulantin.

Seething with rage and with bloodshot eyes, Ogylsha repulsed the blow of Shotan's sabre with his own curved blade. Fighting with sabres is not the same as fighting with spears, for one requires lightning-quick reactions to deflect blows as well as agility and dexterity to dodge the brilliantly shining blade in time. Because of his clumsiness and the loss of his spear, Ogylsha had lost his composure and was uptight, which meant that, although he was swinging his blade frantically, he could no longer strike with precision to knock his opponent's weapon from his hand. Suddenly, Shotan's sabre slashed him on the shoulder; blood gushed in torrents and, the next moment, the Turkmen warlord's head rolled to the ground. The batyr's pied chestnut horse tensed, twitched and jumped away.

'Ha! Ha! There is the moment of truth! Victory is ours!' roared Shotan's warriors and their voices merged into a single loud boom. 'Shotan is the victor! The son of Nazar!'

All this time, Seitkutylyk, who had observed the duel, was now hurt not only by the swift death of his comrade-in-arms at the hands of his hated enemy but also by the fact that the Kazakhs now threatened Nader Shah and himself. He was hot with anger and wild rage and he would not forgive Shotan for this! Seitkutylyk decided that Shotan had to be exhausted after the fight, which meant it would be easier to knock that devil from his saddle. Intent on personally avenging the Kazakhs for this defeat, he raised his spear and charged forward.

'Shotan, seeing you are indeed a batyr, I challenge you to a second duel! Show your courage; come out and fight! The time has come for your head to roll! And I will stick your rotten head in a goatskin bottle and send it to your Khan Nuraly. Let's go!'

Shotan, who had managed to take a couple of sips of cool koumis, spurred his stallion into a gallop and reached the battle site in no time. The vicious insults that the Turkmen was spitting like a camel ignited the batyr's fury, from which Shotan gathered himself in an instant, forgetting his fatigue and repulsing Seitkutylyk's powerful attack in lightning-quick speed. The Turkmen thrashed the air with his spear and attempted to turn his long-legged horse around, but at that moment, Shotan's spear hit him under the arm, tearing the skin on his ribs. In the heat of the battle, the Turkmen sardar felt no pain and bleeding heavily, he attacked again, pointing his weapon directly at Shotan.

As he had done many times before to save his master in close combat, the chestnut stallion bounced aside in time to prevent the enemy from even getting close to his rider. In the next approach, Shotan drove the end of his spear under Seitkutylyk's other arm, causing him to shriek in pain and collapse on his horse's neck.

Shotan had achieved a fair victory in two battles, which elevated him even higher in the eyes of those around him. In no hurry to return from his victorious campaign, he travelled around the auls of the simply Turkmen folk, telling everyone he met that he would not allow any further attempts by Nader Shah to gain benefit from the Turkmen people through the dishonourable conduct of henchmen. He also made it clear to everyone that should anyone yield to incitement from Khiva and try to disturb the peace of Mangystau or the Khan's seat, they would suffer the same fate as the two dead sardars.

After the first thin coating of December snow had fallen on the steppe, young messengers arrived at Nuraly-Khan's winter seat near the banks of the Syr Darya with news from Shotan, and they were received first at the central yurt by Bopai herself.

'Praise and gratitude to our Shotan! And I thank you, too, my dears, for bringing this good news to me so swiftly. I will pass everything on to Nuraly, word for word. He left for Orenburg to meet with their general just before your arrival, for it is hardly likely that those on that side, who have been eyeing our land and barely concealing their hostility, will ever leave us alone.'

Knowing that Bopai-Khanum was the head of the central home at the Khan's seat and confident that she would convey everything they said to the Khan, the messengers rested for two days before heading back to Karaoi, the ancestral lands of the Adai people, without further delay.

CHAPTER 8

Bopai's large home, as it had been when Abulkhair was alive, was the central yurt at the Khan's seat and it was there that the most respected and esteemed guests were received, as well as messengers bringing important news from all corners of the steppe. However, since Nuraly-Khan had assumed power, her home was visited less and less and the life that once boiled and bubbled here had now gradually quietened down. With the exception of a number of clan heads, biys and elders, who came on urgent business and not for long, on the instructions of Nuraly-Khan, the yurt was almost always empty.

On one of the first days of spring, when it already felt warm by the Syr Darya, Myrzatai arrived at the Khan's seat at noon together with Esbolat-Batyr from the Altyn clan and Tekei-Batyr from the Karakeseks. The unexpected arrival of such well-known and glorious batyrs, who had been Abulkhair's faithful companions in the troubled times of enemy raids, did not alarm Bopai but surprised her and made her think.

The visitors were escorted to the seats of honour in the luxurious yurt, in line with all the traditions of hospitality. Nuraly greeted them, saying, 'Welcome, most venerable guests! We are delighted to see you at the Khan's home,' before proceeding to the main seat, situated a little higher than Bopai, who was already seated.

'I hope our brethren are all alive and well, dear guests,' Bopai said, looking over at the tanned faces of all three. 'How was your journey? Are you not tired from the road?'

Each of the guests responded in kind to Bopai's courteous words while they were served aromatic koumis, flavoured with smoked kazy and raisins, in painted wooden bowls. Enjoying the fine drink and resting a little, the guests were in no hurry to talk about the main reason for coming, discussing only the day-to-day matters and imparting that the current winter in the Kyzyl-Kum valley was mild, that the livestock was doing well on the pastures on both sides of the river and that the wolves were not particularly bothering the horses as they grazed.

It seemed that all three were waiting for Nuraly to talk about the affairs at the Khan's seat. Bopai sensed this and looked at her son, who was silently listening to the guests talking about nothing in particular. Although Nuraly noticed his mother looking at him, he continued his meal in silence.

After a while, when the tea was served, Myrzatai decided to delay matters no longer and turned to the key matter at hand.

'Nuraly, I see that you would like to know what is on the mind of the elders who have come to see you. What worries us is this: for how long will we be looking over our shoulders at Orenburg? How long will those subordinate to the Russian authorities continue to hound us with their provocations? I am talking about the Cossacks, who have swarmed all over our land like locusts. Perhaps it is time to think about how we can repel them once and for all. And if the Torgauts cross over from the other bank of the Edil again, what are we to do then? You know the situation in the south for yourself, where the Zhaumite-Turkmens, backed by Khiva, are beginning to stir things up on the banks of the Amu Darya. Your subjects have every faith in their Khan and hope that you will protect them.'

'Myrzatai has said everything as it is — we have nothing to add,' Esbolat said, straightening his broad shoulders a little and nodding as he went on. 'We can tolerate the invasive policy of Tsarist Russia not a moment longer. Over all these years, their shady dealings have been designed to deprive us of our land.

You know this yourself, Nuraly! Your Uncle Myrzatai speaks the truth: without looking over our shoulders at the authorities in Orenburg and without feeling the need to give the nod to Saint-Petersburg, we must change something fundamentally and decisively!'

Nuraly turned to Tekei-Batyr with a questioning glance as if to ask what he had to say on the matter, but Tekei was never one for words and cut the Khan short:

'The floor is yours!'

After a short pause, Nuraly spoke at first leisurely, pondering every word, but soon his speech flowed without stopping.

'Since the moment the Khan's power was passed to me, the raids and the plundering of the Zhaiyk Cossacks might not have increased, but they haven't reduced by any stretch of the imagination. The lives of our people are now worse than before and I know this very well. All twelve tribes of the Baiuly, the Alim and the Tabyn, and the seven clans under the Tama all suffer from this and this is known not only to you, Myrzatai, as head of the eight tribes of the Adai clan, but you, too, Esbolat and Tekei, as leaders of your clans. You once fought with your warriors together, under the command of my father Abulkhair, repelling the invasion of Kalmyk troops, but, as you recall, all the people were united. Now, too, we need the unity of the people. Only, why don't the people realise that the enemy can deal with us easily if each clan gathers only in its own interests and voices only its own needs?! Some of our brothers from the north, the central steppes and Semirechye don't want to help us at all! Brothers, dear friends, alas, the might of the Khan's seat is no longer what it was when the Kazakhs were a united force against the Dzungars, and the time of Abulkhair is now in the past. There is now but one way to strengthen the authority of the Khan's seat — the decision of the Khan must be implemented without discussion by a council of biys and elders, were you to approve it.'

Bopai had been listening silently all this time, pondering every word, and her clear eyes reflected a deep thought, but at that moment, she broke the silence:

'Never forget that it was the biys and the elders who proclaimed you Khan, raising you u on the white mat!' With that, she turned slightly to Nuraly. 'And they represent the entire nation, who sees you as its protection and ruler. If you wish to unite all the people under your rule, then rely on the support of these people, not on the power of the Russians, who have long been prowling with greedy eyes on your land. Understand that your father, the Khan Abeke, never deviated from this truth. And it is this that the esteemed senior comrades of yours are talking about here!'

His mother's direct, commanding tone hurt Nuraly, but he did not allow his affront to affect him and nor did he stop there in his reasoning.

'Then these people should be supporting me!' Nuraly snapped. 'They should support me and know that I do not look over my shoulder at the Russian authorities when it comes to matters that affect my people! In the year when the Cossacks began to threaten us from the fortress that they built at Uishik, did I ever turn my attention to the Russian authorities or not arrange a bloody massacre for them? Well, tell me! Everyone here was a witness! My father fought until his dying day with anyone who invaded us at the instigation of our neighbours to the north. He feared no one — the Empress who supposedly supported peace treaties and our alliance or her generals, representing her authority in Orenburg — he knew their cunning tricks and insidious intentions. You know, it is for this that he paid the price, becoming a victim of their evil policy. And my response is this: while I am alive, the Khan's Horde, left to me by Abulkhair-Khan, our nation, will never submit to anyone!'

'May it be as you say, Khan!'

'I hope to Allah this is right!'

'Well, then, let that be our agreement!'

The decisive, uncompromising words spoken by the angry Nuraly met with the approval of the three batyrs and Bopai rejoiced inside.

Oh, Almighty Allah, show Nuraly the true path and help him! Be his support and his protection so that he might continue the work of his father for the good of his people. Grant him strength and patience on this difficult journey!

* * *

The caravan of time moved rapidly onwards, leaving behind the years and the irretrievable past.

Nuraly's daughters and sons from his elder wife Rys-Khanum all grew up under their native shanyrak, but his daughter Taykara was brought up in a special way. To begin with, her father arranged for her to attend school in Orenburg so that she might obtain a Russian education. Later, she graduated from a high school in Saint-Petersburg, where she lived for five or six years. Taykara mastered the subtleties of European etiquette, revolving in the circle of Russian officials and aristocrats. With exquisite beauty, a fair countenance and radiant eyes, she literally mesmerised the Russian nobility around her. One of those who admired her beauty was General Osip Igelstrom. Having secured the support of the Tsarina and taking up the post of Governor of Orenburg, after a while he arranged for the girl to move to Orenburg. Knowing that Taykara was the Khan's daughter, he was, of course, pursuing his own cunning interests. A dyed-in-the-wool courtier, Igelstrom thought that this would be a good way of keeping someone from the nomadic Khan's seat close by.

Taykara, however, did not object to the overly partial attention from this general, who was no longer a young man, and she enjoyed the luxury and carefree Saint-Petersburg life. Despite the life in society to which she had grown accustomed, she was always glad to be able to return home. She missed her grandmother, in particular, her eldest mother, Bopai, who had raised her from a young age.

Bopai joyfully embraced her grown-up, well-educated

granddaughter, who had grown into a slender beauty and the delight of the central yurt of the Khan's seat.

'My darling, how I have missed you!'

'How can a person who misses her relatives and grandmother remain for so many years in distant Saint-Petersburg only to learn Russian, eh?' Rys said with an affectedly kindly smile; she could not hide her maternal envy as her daughter rushed first not to her but to the arms of Bopai.

'Mother, I missed the entire family, of course — you and father too. But I missed my grandmother especially and so, so much! Granny, if you want to know, all of Saint-Petersburg society knows as the granddaughter of Abulkhair and the daughter of Nuraly-Khan. In the Russian capital, I was like the envoy for the seat of the Kazakh Khan.'

'You clever thing!'

Bopai felt so proud of her granddaughter when she heard the phrase *envoy of the Khan's seat* and embraced her again, and breathed in her familiar scent.

'May the spirit of your grandfather always be with you and watch over you, my dear.'

Taykara's arrival at the Khan's seat and her father's home turned into quite the festive occasion. The last days of August on the banks of the Elek were remarkably warm and bright. The lads and lasses played on the swings, sang songs and, into the night, they played the traditional *aksuyek* team game of chasing the cow bones under the bright moonlight. The young men competed in horse races on yearlings.

Taykara spent about ten days at home and, having cured her homesickness, began to beg Bopai to travel with her to Orenburg. In the end, she succeeded in persuading her grandmother and the two of them set off one cool early morning in a comfortable, spacious wagon. Nuraly took the precaution of providing them with a security escort of one hundred reliable and well-armed warriors.

They travelled across the broad steppe at a steady pace, never driving the horses harnessed to the wagon too much. During the long journey, Bopai never tore her eyes away from the vast native expanses with their yellowed feathergrass. Sometimes, she recalled her distant past and all the things she had been through, conjuring up the images of those special moments that remained so close to her heart.

Over the thirty-or-so years she had lived with Abulkhair, she had seen so much, both at the Khan's seat and in the steppe in general. Whatever had happened, she had always been by Abulkhair's side. She tried her best always to be a support for him when he felt sorrow for the loss of a friend or rage at the conduct of an enemy. When he sought ways of maintaining the unity of his people, not through bloody and relentless battles, but through compromise and establishing peaceful relations, she shared his thoughts and always defended his honour. There was probably not a single corner left in the vast great steppe that he had not visited and where the people had experienced so many trials and tribulations. It seemed only yesterday that when he was Khan, his bright spirit was indeed the head of his people in the south and the north, the east and the west, and genuine protection from outsiders. Orenburg never could break his proud spirit or frighten him away. How many times had Abulkhair repulsed the Zhaiyk Cossacks and the Edil Kalmyks? He stopped those henchmen of the Russian authorities in countless battles across the wild steppe and would never yield to their attempts at subjugation; the Russians persisted in inciting their subjects and never once offered reconciliation. Decisive and brave, he never ceded an inch of his native land to those lackeys of Tsarist Russian authority, always resisting and always fighting. *Still, it is as if he still stands before me*, Bopai thought. *For so many years, we lived under a single shanyrak, had children and raised our children together, and, in all this time, I never once saw my Abeke display an ounce of weakness or lose a bit of hope. Even our dangerous foe to the north did not want to but was forced to acknowledge his proud nature and decisiveness. And it is not for nothing that Saint-Petersburg accepted Taykara as Abulkhair-Khan's granddaughter!*

Bopai also had memories associated with Saint-Petersburg. One day, envoys came to the Khan's seat with all manner of peculiar things from an exhibition and a special message for Bopai from the Tsarina. They said that this exhibition had been founded and building purpose-built for it by Tsar Peter himself. The Tsarina official letter asked Bopai personally to gather items from everyday life and culture, be they national costumes, jewellery, furniture and other items that might paint a picture of the life and specific features of the Kaisak people. Her Majesty was particularly interested in the clothes that Bopai herself had worn, her jewellery and things that she had used herself at home. Judging by what the envoys said, all these things would be presented at an exhibition, where people from across the world would come to view them. And everyone would learn that there were people called Kaisaks and they would leave with a lasting impression of these amazing, rare items that belonged personally to the first Khanum. Not only that, but the envoys said they would pay for these things, in essential items for the nomadic way of life — tea, sweets and other things, and all this, they assured her, would also be specified in the letter written by the Tsarina and bearing her personal seal. During those years, the policy of the Russian authorities changed with successive tsars and tsarinas, but their principal objective remained the same: the subjugation of the Khan's seat. However, in order to maintain the existing relations with the supreme powers that be in Russia, Bopai did not leave the Empress's request unanswered.

Be it for good or bad, this request presented an opportunity, by using everyday objects, to familiarise foreigners with the Kazakh people and show them the particular features of their way of life. For an entire month, under the personal supervision of Bopai, skilful seamstresses and embroiderers, weavers and blacksmiths all gathered at the Khan's seat and made incredibly beautiful furniture, clothes and jewellery. *Clothing and jewellery were sent personally to the Tsarina directly from the Khan's seat, constituting an entire dowry: a purple sleeveless camisole with a silk lining, with embroidered patterns and a silver breast piece; a short-sleeved, green-velvet camisole, trimmed with beaver fur; camisoles and knee-length coats with gilded and beaded clasps and silver belts; cast-silver hair decorations, pendants for hair braids, gold and silver bracelets with pearls... Can you believe how many years have passed since that time?!* An entire, well-laden caravan set off for Saint-Petersburg and I entrusted the security personally to Nuraly. Taykara lives in Sain-Petersburg and she could not have failed to see this famous exhibition, so admired by the Russian nobility! Bopai thought suddenly but decided not to ask her granddaughter when they were tired and on the road, but after they had arrived in Orenburg.

Taykara did not bother her grandmother with small talk. Bopai sat leaning back on a seat covered with several layers of blankets and, covering her eyes, pondered her thoughts while Taykara appeared to be dozing, exhausted by the long journey.

Thoughts are like a boundless ocean. Every turn in the road of Abulkhair's life encountered struggle, but he never despaired or complained about his fate. One autumn, when the Edil Torgauts had been crushed after their latest attempted raid, before embarking on the difficult campaign to defend Turkestan from the Dzungars, he came to the Khan's seat to rest for a few days.

Yes, that was when it was. We were alone in the central yurt and my dear Abeke started a frank conversation, sharing his innermost thoughts about the things that tormented him so much.

'Oh, Bopai, if only you knew how tired I am of this life

with its endless military campaigns and battles, spending all my time in the open steppe and on horseback. But there is no other way, you know that. It would be impossible otherwise. I am sad that our sons, so close in years, cannot spend their time, carefree and happy, in my company, that they don't receive my affection and care. I so miss the peaceful days with my children. Just look, our firstborn, Nuraly, is already grown up and has reached the age of fourteen. The time will come when he will inherit the reins of the Khan's power. He won't inherit my fate, too, will he?! And if he is indeed destined to repeat my journey, how will he manage with such a burden? Will he have the strength, the will and the fortitude to carry this weight? Will he be able to stand up to his enemies and find the right way to fight against his foe's cunning? Will he be able to show all the qualities that you and I are nurturing in him, and will he be able to protect his people's interests? You see, all this causes me great anxiety.'

When he spoke about his heir, our Nuraly, his words reflected a sadness for his people, too. Such a hard life, where he was destined the bear the burden of ensuring the unity of his people and endure all the vicissitudes of fate!

From your expression alone, my darling, I could see then how much you needed my support.

'Abeke, my Khan! There is no need to worry about Nuraly: he is growing up before our eyes, absorbing everything that is good. All forty clans of our nation have their hopes vested in you now.

Allah willing, a great campaign awaits you, in which you will liberate our sacred capital, Turkestan and save the Kazakhs from the Dzungar yoke. And may your name be glorified!'

I will never forget the look on his face, so full of warm appreciation for my words.

Abulkhair defended Turkestan and crushed the enemy army led by a famous military commander, son of Tsewang-

Rabdan. By his side in that important battle were Eset from the Tama clan and Shotan-Batyr, whom Bokenbai took into his ranks. Everyone knew that Bokenbai was a true comrade of the Khan. The enraged Oirats, who had been forced to retreat, reformed into detachments, having barely regained their senses, and continued to sack and attack the city for another seven months. Abulkhair threw everything he had into defending Turkestan, but his army had been thinned considerably and could not hold back the enemy's onslaught. Even now, Bopai could remember the profound regret that Abulkhair had felt. And yet the Oirats, who took Turkestan for a second time, were eventually defeated by a powerful repulse by the Khan's detachments and, later, the defeat of the Dzungar troops in the decisive battles of Bulantin and Anyraqai was a real achievement by the Kazakh warriors under Abulkhair-Khan, whose heroism will undoubtedly remain in popular memory.

Recalling the turning points in her life, Bopai returned to forgotten worries as she continued her journey to Orenburg.

My dear Abeke, in forty years of married life, there was never a moment when we quarrelled and how grateful I am to you and fate for this! In difficult moments, when you were worrying about pressure from the Russian authorities, you looked to me in the first instance for words of support and understanding. How can I ever forget that you saw me as your advisor, your friend and your support?! Like that year, just before you met with the Orenburg authorities, when you gathered all the biys, elders and clan heads at the Khan's seat on the bank of the Irgiz and tried to bring them to reason — you took a risk and I was a witness. I remember how you searched for arguments to back up your statements. You called the people to unify and warned about discord when the people were noisily pulling one another in different directions.

* * *

They travelled at a steady pace and stopped every day before nightfall in large auls to rest and give their horses a chance to recover their strength. A week later, Orenburg loomed before them.

A considerable time had passed since Taykara had taken her grandmother — the eldest mother from Nuraly-Khan's summer base in the floodplain of the Elek River — to her home in Orenburg. Bopai, accustomed to the expanses of her native steppe, would occasionally take one of Taykara's servants and visit the bazaar. The main reason she went there was to observe the people, those selling and those buying. She also hoped to meet people she knew there, to catch up on the news and impart her own. However, no matter how many times she went to the bazaar, which hummed like a beehive, she did not see anyone from home. However, she did see that the Tatar merchants brought with them wealthy aul residents, while the Russian merchants were known for being notorious swindlers and deceitful in their dealings. The caravan drivers were always preoccupied with their business, unloading or arranging the goods brought in carts or broken ox-drawn wagons or on camels, which they usually left tethered somewhere on the edge of the market square. Bopai had never been involved in trading and had never seen such things, so all of this was strange and surprising. *What a peculiar, bustling life this is,* she marvelled to herself. *How curious the people who live to trade and how fascinating the processes of buying and selling are! Some are shrewd and cunning, while others tirelessly prowl about. Others are busy counting money, nimbly rustling through their banknotes. This truly is the world of the bazaar, an inexhaustible source of profit!* Walking through the market, she kept her distance from other people thronging this way and that and chattering incessantly. She did not like the fortified stone dwellings arranged in their rows. In the end, she found herself hurrying to leave the bazaar and return to Taykara's house on the outskirts of the city.

Her grandson-in-law Nurmukhanbet, who was an assistant to the court judge, a superficial and frivolous kind of man, and Taykara, who had been educated in Saint-Petersburg and had learned all the manners of Russian aristocrats, meanwhile revelled in the life of the city. Taykara had been bestowed the title of *princess* and that meant she enjoyed the special privilege, only available to the wives of princes, of riding in a carriage drawn by three pairs of horses. By order of the Empress Catherine, Taykara was presented with a luxurious house, twelve to thirteen kilometres from the city on the banks of the Zhaiyk, with a decent plot of land suitable for farming. Enjoying the particular favour of Orenburg's Governor, General Osip Igelstrom, the slender and attractive Taykara, displaying all the sophistication of the highest European society, shone like a diamond at every high-society event in the city. Bopai saw for herself many times that Taykara, who had captivated the ageing general, was indeed held in high esteem, and many noble officials greatly admired her.

At Igelstrom's request, Taykara brought Bopai with her to a festive event to present her to the governor-general.

The old general, with his back-combed grey hair and neatly trimmed beard, bowed his head and, placing his right hand on his chest, greeted Bopai with particular courtesy and deference.

'Bopai-Khanum, I am extremely glad to have the honour to meet you and get to know you personally thanks to the beauty of our city, your most beautiful granddaughter Taykara! Allow me to assure you that I have heard that the Empress, Her Majesty Elizaveta Ivanovna, highly appreciated your contribution in mediating peaceful relations and holds you in the highest regard. I also know that you fulfilled the request of our great Empress by sending extremely valuable items for the Saint-Petersburg exhibition, which I have seen for myself when I personally viewed these quite remarkable specimens. Indeed, all the things that you have sent are genuine ethnographic exhibits, which give a clear understanding of who the Kaisaks are! I extend my personal gratitude to you, Khanum! Today, you are the honoured guest of our celebration! I hope you have a splendid time and thoroughly enjoy yourself.'

Igelstrom spoke gallantly and courteously, smiling at Bopai as he did so. Taykara interpreted his words and added, slightly lowering her voice,

'Granny, in turn, you show courtesy and smile back. You see, these are their rules, so to speak, so ensure you extend a fitting response to the gracious baron! I was at that exhibition with him and, as you have heard, he spared no words in telling you that he liked it very much.'

'But we have different rules, my dear Taykara! I cannot simply laugh out loud, just like that, for heaven's sake!' Bopai replied, seemingly angry at her granddaughter's words. 'Well, relay my words to your Russian gentleman then!'

While they were talking among themselves like that, the governor-general looked from one to the other in bewilderment.

Bopai turned to him and said,

'And you, too, accept our greetings and high esteem, Mister Igelstrom! You were not sparing in your praise for last year diligently endeavouring to fulfil the special request of the Tsarina, sent from Saint-Petersburg, may Allah be pleased with you! As the mother of Nuraly-Khan, the ruler of the Kazakh people, I, too, have the greatest respect for you. May nothing disrupt our mutual friendship, about which we have been talking for so long. I ask Allah only this!'

The general maintained his gallant and courteous expression throughout and nodded once again as a show of respect for Bopai. The celebration continued and a pleasant waltz could be heard from the grand ballroom. That day, the general never left Taykara's side, displaying his special favour in his words and his enchanted gaze. There was one thing that Bopai could not understand: why, seeing the way the general was behaving, did her Nurmukhanbet pretend not to notice anything? *Is this his way of showing his respect for his superiors? Or is he afraid of the general's elevated status? Where is his male pride?! It is so hard to understand what the higher echelons in this city think.*

No sooner was Nurmukhanbet free of his insignificant, unprestigious and easy job at the court, he would spend his time at meaningless parties, playing cards and drinking with his peers. It appeared that he was content with this carefree life, passing by nonchalantly in the shadow of his young wife, Taykara. Having grown accustomed to the life of Russian aristocrats and having imbibed the lifestyle of high-ranking officials, he brought up his sons Tleumukhanbet and Serikakhmet in Russian. Bopai did not approve of Nurmukhanbet's approach to raising his children, while he sincerely believed that knowledge and noble behaviour were peculiar only to Russians. Bopai believed that such an upbringing would alienate her descendants from their roots. Taykara listened to her grandmother's words of dissatisfaction but did not pay them much heed. 'Granny, but they are descendants of a hodja. They will not break with their roots, don't worry,' she said, trying to reassure her grandmother. Taykara spoke about the hodja lineage because the father of her sons, Nurmukhanbet, was the son of Abuzhalel, a hodja from a Khorasan family. *Oh, I don't know! Who would ever say that this man, who has picked up the habits of these foreigners, is a descendant of the Khorasan hodjas, who piously honour their religion?* Bopai thought in disappointment, but she did not share this thought with her granddaughter.

CHAPTER 9

Bopai had come a long way in her life and was nearing ninety years old. Taykara promised to fulfil the wish of her elder mother and would take her home and as summer arrived, they left Orenburg for the banks of the Elek in a spacious phaeton drawn by four horses.

On their journey, they stopped overnight in the auls of the Adai and Berish, Tabyn and Alim clans, where they were welcomed in rich homes and honoured in every possible way.

Having spent more than ten days on the road, they finally reached the summer seat of Nuraly-Khan.

After such a long and, it would seem, arduous journey, Bopai did not feel overly tired and wished to visit the chalky white-topped mountain the next morning, which stood nearby amidst the blossoming summer pasture in the valley of the vibrant Elek and Kargaly rivers. However, she did not tell her son or her granddaughter about the reason for this journey.

The comfortable wagon swayed gently on the steppe road without bumps or potholes, making the ride fast and easy. By sunrise, it reached the ridge on the bank of the Elek that Bopai had indicated to the driver. Climbing down from the wagon, Bopai walked a few paces, bent down and plucked up a small sprig of young blue wormwood and, reverently holding the herb in her hand, she breathed in its bitter fragrance with pleasure. The clear air of this corner of the world where she had passed her childhood and youth seemed to surge into her lungs.

Nuraly and Taykara slowly followed Bopai, who was walking ahead, her back held upright.

From the highest point on that white hilltop, the valley opened up as if on the palm, winding away to the horizon. Bopai gazed out slowly, looking long and hard into the distance. Her eyes stopped on a high ridge in the northwest, shrouded in a light haze.

Noticing where Bopai was looking, Nuraly said,

'Up there, where you are looking, is the site of Eset-Batyr's mausoleum.'

'Ah, yes, it turns out that hill is visible from here! Eset was a fine batyr, and his memory will live on not only among the people of the Tama clan but among all the Kazakhs! Azhibai-Biy, on his mother's side, was no simple man either, for he was a descendant of Alim-Ata!' Bopai said, not taking her thoughtful gaze from the outline of the hill. 'Back in the day, Eset was a reliable support for your father Abeke in battles with the Dzungars and Edil Kalmyks. *Bury me with my feet pointing west and, even after death, I will be an obstacle to the enemy and not let him pass*, he said before he died. Even after his passing, he wanted to defend his native land with his brave spirit!'

Bopai's gaze lingered over the surroundings, near and far, and then she finally dropped to her knees and explained her reason for coming to this hill to her son and granddaughter.

'I think that this hill with the white top should be the site of a new city, which will be a fortress for our khanate and our clan. When the Russians erected their Or Fortress in the north, they promised your father that it would defend our people, but in fact this never did happen. Placing their general in the fortress, they did everything they could to penetrate our lands, inciting their henchmen — Russian subjects — to launch attacks. They tried everything to intimidate our Khan, to subdue him. Nuraly, if you seriously care about the future and are thinking about strengthening your authority for the good of generations to come, then this hill is the best place to locate your Khan's seat. Our Taykara is respected and trusted by the most important general in Orenburg, Mister Igelstrom, who represents the authorities in Saint-Petersburg and I think she can convey this wish to him as a personal request. That is why I brought you here with your father, my dear, so that you could see it for yourself.' Nuraly wanted to say that he had doubts about fulfilling his mother's dream, but he held back and neither disputed nor supported the matter. After his thousand-strong army had joined Pugachev's rebellion, the authorities in Saint-Petersburg had looked at him askance. Only recently, Syrym, whom he had released from Russian captivity, and several biys and elders, had treated him in with open disdain and had been hostile to his Khan's authority. Nuraly was sure that, given the opportunity, Syrym would happily destroy him without hesitation. How could he tell his mother that he could not be involved in the construction of a fortress at this anxious time when he was worried, on the one hand, by problems with the Russians and, on the other, by internal strife?! Besides, where were the guarantees that the duplicitous powers that be in Tsarist Russia would not use this to their advantage, and that the fortress, built for the Khan's seat, would not strengthen their positions?! How could she forget that, while fortifying Or and Orenburg, the Russians had promised that these towns would be a defensive solution for them and help them in trading, only to base themselves then there and implement their invasion plans?!

The fact that Nuraly did not utter a word in support of her wishes made Bopai-Khanum a little sad. She tried to conceal her annoyance that her son had not inherited his father's ability to act boldly and decisively.

Naturally, she understood Nuraly's position — he was wary of the Russian authorities because of their increasingly fraught relations in recent years and their malicious intentions. It was dangerous for a small nation to stand up to an enormous mass of warriors with firearms capable of destroying everything and everyone whilst having nothing of their own, and this he found most depressing. But where was that character of a Khan, who would rather die than yield and would never permit anyone to trample on his honour and dignity? Had his father not instilled that quality in him? *So that is how it is — the times change and the people change, too. Oh, Abeke, my Khan, what good fortune it is that you cannot see your descendants, who have become inept and weak and yet now hold the fate of their land and people in their hands.*

Noticing that her grandmother had become withdrawn and deep in thought, Taykara tried to change the subject and cheer her up, so she smiled sweetly and said,

'Grandmother, I will certainly convey your wishes to Mister Igelstrom as soon as I return to Orenburg; I'll even tell him in your presence. You know, better still, you can tell him yourself. He has the greatest respect for you! And he could not refuse you, either. He always speaks with sincere reverence about our grandfather, the main khan of the Kazakh people. Whenever you choose to come, the general will meet you with full honours!'

'Why do I need that ginger general with his sickly-sweet, pretentious smile? There have been so many just like him, sitting all high and mighty in his Orenburg! Many times, your grandfather, the Khan, fought those dogs that the Russian Tsarina planted there to track us and control the land of the Kazakhs. He spent his entire life in battle in the saddle of his war horse. Until his dying day, he gave all his strength to prevent them from invading our sacred lands and ruling over us and after many bloody battles, he finally laid his head. Your late grandfather defended his people to the last drop of his blood. And the Russians could never break his proud spirit. Whoever has been in power has looked greedily at our lands, but they have all failed to subjugate us. Taykara, my dear, I know all this all too well, for I have seen much and lived long on this long-suffering land. You see, I was by Abeke's side and never strayed from his true path, and the Tsars of Saint-Petersburg know this oh so well! My testament to my children and you, my grandchild, is not to build your lives by looking up to the Russians or trusting their notions!'

Taykara heard and understood some of what Bopai had said, but the rest simply passed her by. She simply laughed and hugged her grandmother tenderly around the neck.

'Oh, my darling granny! I'll take you to Orenburg next summer too! You're bound to miss your favourite granddaughter and spoil her rotten, right?! I'll really miss you!'

'Oh, my petal, I have lived long enough under your care in that stone city called Orenburg, and now I will remain here under the family shanyrak that your grandfather left me. I will not go anywhere and I entrust you to the Almighty! I will remind you once more that it is no easy matter ruling many people over a vast territory and being the Khan of the great steppe. Support your father, Nuraly-Khan, for, after all, you have grown closer to those Russian rulers and have gained their trust...'

* * *

That year, the River Zhosaly, which flowed into the wide Elek, broke its banks even before the middle of March. The melt water filled the hollows and ravines and then the small streams all flooded, turning the expansive plains into a boundless body of water. The first cranes and white herons to return from the south settled near the water and spent days on end searching for what little food they could find.

Bopai admired the marvellous view of nature's rejuvenation from atop her horse, looking down from a mountain ridge, and for a moment, her mind was cast back to her youth, somewhere a long, long time before.

The rich, opulent aul of Syuindyk resided here from early spring and throughout the summer, grazing its livestock on both sides of the river's floodplain. When she was a carefree girl at a tender age and still everyone's favourite, could she have known what awaited her and what fate had in store?! She was destined to become the wife of Abulkhair, the defender of her native land and all the people. She became a mother, producing heirs and successors to continue their father's life path. There was a place for good days in her life, bad days, weakness and courage that are inherent in all people.

The name of Bopai-Khanum was known to all Kazakh people across the great steppe. After Abulkhair, she strove to transfer her experience as a mediator to her Nuraly, the elected Khan and direct heir and devoted her attention to ensuring he did not stray far from his people or alter the fundamental principles of state administration. She spared no effort and generously shared her wisdom with her sons Eraly and Kozhakhmet, Aishauk and Adil so that they would be respectable and worthy descendants of their noble ancestors. Later, she gave all the affection in her heart to each new grandchild as they grew up and became adults.

I have travelled the long road of my life without ever pausing or stopping for breath. What will I leave for the future and what will I take with me? What valuable lesson will I be able to pass on to subsequent generations from my long life? In honouring the memory of the Abulkhair, the main Khan of the Kazakhs, will the people remember me, his constant companion and faithful friend? Oh, let them forget. There is no problem with that! Who am I when all is said and done? Our Khan, too, lived not to glorify his name, after all. The victories he won in fierce battles in their troubled time did glorify his name and, yes, he did not take the path of victor by his own will. The Khan never boasted of his victories and never aspired for glory. The most important thing for him was always to remain human. I did what was in my power — I was a faithful wife and I tried to be useful, not simply as a friend, but as a counsellor, backing him up whenever he needed it. I think I was worthy of his high status. I might not have exalted him, but not once did I ever dishonour him. I was destined to receive the gifts of life from Allah through Abulkhair, and that is something to be grateful for! Bopai spent days on end in such meditation once she was of an age when her strength was already failing her. Such thoughts did not tire her but nor did they bring her cheer.

Bopai never missed the five daily *namaz* prayers and on that day, she rose as ever at sunrise, performed her ritual ablutions, laid out her prayer rug and recited the first Sunnah of the morning prayer.

'I turn to face the Qibla and dedicate this morning namaz to Almighty Allah alone, fulfilling the sacred duty of all Muslims!'

After reciting the *farj*, she voiced her homage to the Almighty, fingering the ninety-nine beads of her rosary, and then left the house.

The horizon, illuminated by the morning light, was about to be drowned by the first rays of the springtime sun. Bopai felt at ease as she looked at the emerging circle of the sun and the snow-white clouds that floated leisurely in the blue sky above. Thanking God for the beginning of another day, she repeated the prayer of consolation with particular feeling and, with the words, 'In sha Allah! *As Allah wills it!*' she slowly ran her hands over her face. The clear, cool morning air from the vast meadows filled her soul and, for a few moments, gave a sense of freshness to her weary and anxious heart.

It was nearing the middle of May and the days were clear and warm in the steppe, but Bopai found herself resigned more and more to sad recollections of a youth never to return, of a longed-for time now left far behind. It seemed like only yesterday that she was a rosy-cheeked little girl whose laughter rang out across a world so full of joy, over which she soared on the wings of dreams. How fleeting that time of her youth had been, when the moonlit nights on the flowering meadow near the aul were spent at play, on the swings, singing songs and enjoying festivities. *Oh, my springtime years, why did you have to be so short?! At the end of my days, when my journey is about to reach its end, the past is like a mirage, a chance vision that fades into the reality of the everyday.*

In those final days of spring, every living thing on the banks of the Zhosaly was rejuvenated and triumphant, but Bopai, even though she was not ailing, had been seized by apathy and was in the habit of lying at length in her bed, decorated with silver and glazed ornaments, deep in thought. She often imagined scenes from the past, recalling all the good things she had experienced with Abulkhair and her entire life, which seemed to have passed by in a flash.

One evening, Bopai summoned Nuraly and expressed her last will: if, by Allah's will, she was to follow her ancestors, she wanted to be buried in her native land, on the land by the banks of the Elek, instead of being taken to Abulkhair on the distant shores of Ulkeyek. Having expressed her wish, which she had long wanted to impart to her son but somehow had hitherto never managed, Bopai suddenly felt a lightness as if she had rid herself of a heavy burden.

Soon after this conversation, Bopai-Khanum thanked the Almighty for her life, filled with significant and vibrant moments, and, at peace, she closed her eyes forever. The wise mother of the Khan's clan, having met with eternity, came to rest in her native land just as she had wished.

And so, Bopai-Khanum found peace after devoting her long life to the rulers of the Khan's seat — father and son — sharing her wisdom in her endeavour to preserve the unity of the people and her native land, as witnessed by the Sun and the Moon, unchanging in their eternal movement across the firmament. It was the last day of May 1780.

BOPAI-KHANSHA[24]
EPILOGUE

Aikumis went into labour precisely when expected and, one early morning, when dawn was barely breaking over the horizon, she gave birth.

The midwife who delivered the baby and tied off the umbilical cord then cried out happily,

'Bismillah! A daughter has been born, a daughter for the Sultan! A girl has appeared under this shanyrak! And she already has quite the character on her! Just listen to that booming voice from her first day!'

'Well, just like the girl's father, Ablai Khan's blood runs through her, so of course she has a character!' a distant sister-in-law said, wiping and wrapping the crying baby in a white sheet. 'Look at this little one — she is so small, but she clenches her fist and just won't let go! She'll most likely be braver than any son could be.'

Aikumis, who had just given birth, looked affectionately at her healthy newborn child while her sister-in-law, the midwife, smiled as she placed the little girl next to her, arms and legs twisting every which way, and said,

'May she enjoy a long life, my dear Aikumis!'

Only three days before, Kasym-Sultan, whose base was at the foot of Mount Zhekebatyr, received all his close and distant relatives who had rushed to congratulate him on the birth of his daughter.

Kenesary, who was barely three years old and had already learned to speak, was particularly happy that day. The older children, delighted by the babbling and fidgeting of the little heir, spoke to him importantly like grown-ups: 'You're a big man now — an older brother!'

'Be gentle with your little sister!'

Kasym-Sultan had been thinking about what to call the

---
[24] Khansha means 'wife of the khan'

baby girl and, right before the shildekhana, the occasion to mark the birth of children, he announced,

'I have chosen a name — Bopai! The noble daughter-in-law of the Tore clan, the support and faithful companion of the most esteemed Abulkhair Khan, Bopai-Khanum, was famous for her wisdom and courage, so let my daughter inherit these same qualities!' With these words, he handed the little girl to the Imam to perform the naming ceremony by reciting a special prayer.

'Amen, esteemed Sultan! 'May it be as you wish!'

And the little girl, named in honour of Bopai-Khanum, glorified the family of Kasym-Sultan, by striding the path of independence for her people. Alongside her brother Kenesary, she led an army and went down in history as the legendary warrior Bopai-Khansha.

Made in the USA
Monee, IL
16 March 2024